K1

D1178952

'*Bonjour*, Gabriel.'

Emmaline.

She looked even more beautiful than the image of her that inhabited his dreams at night. Her lace-lined bonnet of natural straw perfectly framed her flawless face. The dark blue of her walking dress made her eyes even more vibrant.

Good God. After two years she still had the power to affect him.

'*Why* did you come to see me?'

Her lips trembled before she spoke. 'Oh, Gabriel. I need you.'

The hard earth he'd packed around his emotions began to crack.

She swallowed and went on, 'I need your help.'

He came to his senses. 'Help with what?'

She met his eyes. 'I need you to find Claude.'

'Claude.' The son who'd driven a wedge between them.

AUTHOR NOTE

Here is the final book in my Three Soldiers Series, *Valiant Soldier, Beautiful Enemy,* Gabriel Deane's story. Unlike the heroes of *Gallant Officer, Forbidden Lady* and *Chivalrous Captain, Rebel Mistress,* Gabriel Deane was a career soldier, a man who believed the army was where he belonged. Like so many other men and women, both in history and in today's world, Gabriel gave up a normal conventional life for service to his country. He went where his government sent him and valiantly did what he was ordered to do, no matter how difficult or dangerous.

While the Three Soldiers Series has focused on the effect of war on the soldier, specifically the effect of one horrific event, the theme of this book is how war affects everyone, the soldier and civilian alike. The more important message of all the books is that, in spite of war, love can still flourish and lead to happy endings.

That is my wish for all the soldiers
and their families in today's world:
Love and a happy ending.

**Look for Claude's story
AN OFFICER, NOT A GENTLEMAN?
coming soon in
Mills & Boon® Historical *Undone!* eBooks**

VALIANT SOLDIER, BEAUTIFUL ENEMY

Diane Gaston

First published in Great Britain 2011
by Mills & Boon, an imprint of Harlequin (UK) Limited.
Harlequin (UK) Limited, Eton House, 18-24 Paradise Road, Richmond, Surrey TW9 1SR

© Diane Perkins 2011

ISBN: 978 0 263 21837 4

Harlequin (UK) policy is to use papers that are natural, renewable and recyclable products and made from wood grown in sustainable forests. The logging and manufacturing process conform to the legal environmental regulations of the country of origin.

Printed and bound in Great Britain
by CPI Antony Rowe, Chippenham, Wiltshire

As a psychiatric social worker, **Diane Gaston** spent years helping others create real-life happy endings. Now Diane crafts fictional ones, writing the kind of historical romance she's always loved to read. The youngest of three daughters of a US Army Colonel, Diane moved frequently during her childhood, even living for a year in Japan. It continues to amaze her that her own son and daughter grew up in one house in Northern Virginia. Diane still lives in that house, with her husband and three very ordinary housecats. Visit Diane's website at http://dianegaston.com

Previous novels by the same author:

THE MYSTERIOUS MISS M
THE WAGERING WIDOW
A REPUTABLE RAKE
INNOCENCE AND IMPROPRIETY
A TWELFTH NIGHT TALE
   (in *A Regency Christmas* anthology)
THE VANISHING VISCOUNTESS
SCANDALISING THE TON
JUSTINE AND THE NOBLE VISCOUNT
   (in *Regency Summer Scandals*)
*GALLANT OFFICER, FORBIDDEN LADY
**CHIVALROUS CAPTAIN, REBEL MISTRESS

*_Three Soldiers_ mini-series

And in Mills & Boon® Historical *Undone!* eBooks:

THE UNLACING OF MISS LEIGH

Look for Claude's story
AN OFFICER, NOT A GENTLEMAN?
coming soon in
Mills & Boon® Historical *Undone!* eBooks

Did you know that some of these novels
are also available as eBooks?
Visit www.millsandboon.co.uk

Dedication

In memory of my cousin, Lt. Commander
James H. Getman, who lost his life at age 31
while on active duty with the U.S. Coast Guard.
And to all who lost their lives while
serving their country. We are grateful.

Prologue

Badajoz, Spain—1812

A woman's scream pierced the night.

Countless screams had reached Captain Gabriel Deane's ears this night, amidst shattering glass, roaring flames and shouts of soldiers run amok. The siege of Badajoz had ended and the pillaging had begun.

The marauding soldiers were not the French, not the enemy known to live off the bounty of the vanquished. These were British soldiers, Gabe's compatriots, prowling through the city like savage beasts, plundering, killing, raping. A false rumour saying Wellington would permit the plundering had sparked the violence.

Gabe and his lieutenant, Allan Landon, had been ordered into this cauldron, but not to stop the rioting. Their task was to find one man.

Edwin Tranville.

Edwin's father, General Tranville, had ordered them to find his son, who'd foolishly joined the marauders. Once inside the city Gabe and Landon had enough to do to save their own skins from drunken men in the throes of a bloodlust that refused to be slaked.

The scream sounded again, not distant like the other helpless cries of innocent women and children—this woman's cry was near.

They ran in the direction of the sound. A shot rang out and two soldiers dashed from an alley, almost colliding with them. Gabe and Landon turned into the alley and emerged in a courtyard illuminated by flames shooting from a burning building nearby.

A woman stood over a cowering figure wearing the uniform of a British Officer. She raised a knife and prepared to plunge its blade into the British officer's back.

Gabe seized her from behind and wrenched the knife from her grasp. "Oh, no, you don't, *señora*." She was not in need of rescue after all.

"She tried to kill me!" The British officer, covering his face with bloody hands, attempted to stand, but collapsed in a heap on the cobblestones.

At that moment another man stepped into the light. Lieutenant Landon swung around, pistol ready to fire.

"Wait." The man raised his hands. "I am Ensign Vernon of the East Essex." He gestured to the unconscious officer. "He was trying to kill the boy. And he attempted to rape the woman. I saw the whole thing. He and two others. The others ran."

The two men who passed them? If so, it was too late to pursue them.

"The boy?" Gabe glanced around. What boy? He saw only the woman and the red-coated officer she was about to kill. And nearby the body of a French soldier, pooled in blood.

Gabe kept a grip on the woman and used his foot to roll over her intended victim. The man's face was gashed from temple to chin, but Gabe immediately recognised him.

He glanced up. "Good God, Landon, do you see who this is?"

Ensign Vernon answered instead. "Edwin Tranville." His voice filled with disgust. "General Tranville's son."

"Edwin Tranville," Gabriel agreed. They'd found him after all.

"The bloody bastard," Landon spat.

Vernon nodded in agreement. "He is drunk."

When was Edwin not drunk? Gabe thought.

Another figure suddenly sprang from the shadows and Landon almost fired his pistol at him.

The ensign stopped him. "Do not shoot. It is the boy."

A boy, not more than twelve years of age, flung himself atop the body of the French soldier.

"Papa!" the boy cried.

"Non, non, non, Claude." The woman strained against Gabe's grip. He released her and she ran to her son.

"Good God, they are French." Not Spanish citizens of Badajoz. A French family trying to escape. What the devil had the Frenchman been thinking, putting his family in such danger? Gabe had no patience for men who took wives and children to war.

He knelt next to the body and placed his fingers on the man's throat. "He's dead."

The woman looked up at him. *"Mon mari."* Her husband.

Gabe drew in a sharp breath.

She was lovely. Even filled with great anguish, she was lovely. Hair as dark as a Spaniard's, but with skin as fair as the very finest linen. Her eyes, their colour obscured in the dim light, were large and wide with emotion.

Gabe's insides twisted in an anger that radiated clear to his fingertips. Had Edwin killed this man in front of his family? Had he tried to kill the boy and rape the woman, as the ensign said? What had the two other men done to her before it had been Edwin's turn?

The boy cried, *"Papa! Papa! Réveillez!"*

"Il est mort, Claude." Her tone, so low and soft, evoked a memory of Gabe's own mother soothing one of his brothers or sisters.

Fists clenched, Gabe rose and strode back to Edwin, ready to kick him into a bloody pulp. He stopped himself.

Edwin rolled over again and curled into a ball, whimpering.

Gabe turned his gaze to Ensign Vernon and his voice trembled with anger. "Did Edwin kill him?" He pointed to the dead French soldier.

The ensign shook his head. "I did not see."

"What will happen to her now?" Gabe spoke more to himself than to the others.

The woman pressed her son against her bosom, trying to comfort him, while shouts sounded nearby.

Gabe straightened. "We must get them out of here." He gestured to his lieutenant. "Landon, take Tranville back to camp. Ensign, I'll need your help."

"You will not turn her in?" Landon looked aghast.

"Of course not," he snapped. "I'm going to find her a safe place to stay. Maybe a church. Or somewhere." He peered at Landon and at Ensign Vernon. "We say nothing of this. Agreed?"

Landon glared at him and pointed to Edwin. "He ought to hang for this."

Gabe could not agree more, but over fifteen years in the army had taught him to be practical. He doubted any of the soldiers would face a hanging. Wellington needed them too much. General Tranville would certainly take no chances with his son's life and reputation. Gabe and Landon needed to protect themselves lest Tranville retaliate.

More importantly, Gabe needed to protect this woman.

"He is the general's son." His tone brooked no argument. "If we report his crime, the general will have our necks, not Edwin's." He tilted his head towards the woman. "He may even come after her and the boy." The captain looked down at the now-insensible man who had caused all this grief. "This bastard is so drunk he may not even know what he did. He won't tell."

"Drink is no excuse—" Landon began. He broke off and, after several seconds, nodded. "Very well. We say nothing."

The captain turned to Vernon. "Do I have your word, Ensign?"

"You do, sir," the ensign readily agreed.

Glass shattered nearby and the roof of the burning building collapsed, sending sparks high into the air.

"We must hurry." Gabe paused only long enough to extend a handshake to the ensign. "I am Captain Deane. That is Lieutenant Landon." He turned to the woman and her son. "Is there a church nearby?" His hand flew to his forehead. "Deuce. What is the French word for church?" He tapped his brow. "*Église?* Is that the word? *Église?*"

"*Non.* No church, *capitaine,*" the woman replied. "My…my *maison*—my house. Come."

"You speak English, *madame?*"

"*Oui, un peu*—a little."

Landon threw Edwin over his shoulder.

"Take care," Gabe said to him.

Landon gave a curt nod before trudging off in the direction they had come.

Gabe turned to the ensign. "I want you to come with me." He looked over at the Frenchman's body. "We will have to leave him here."

"Yes, sir."

The woman gazed at her husband, her posture taut as if she felt pulled back to his side. Gabe's heart bled for her. She put an arm around her son, who protested against leaving his father, and Gabe felt their struggle as if it were his own.

"Come," she finally said, gesturing for them to follow her.

They made their way through the alley again and down a narrow street.

"*Ma maison,*" she whispered, pointing to a wooden door that stood ajar.

Gabe signalled them to remain where they were. He entered the house.

Light from nearby fires illuminated the inside enough for him to see the contents of a home broken and strewn across the floor: legs from a chair, shards of crockery, scattered papers, items that had once formed the essence of everyday life. He searched the large room to be certain no one hid there. He continued into a small kitchen and a bedroom, both thoroughly ransacked.

He walked back to the front door. "No one is here."

The ensign escorted the mother and son through the doorway. The woman's hand flew to cover her mouth as her eyes darted over the shambles of what had once been her life. Her son buried his face into her side. She held him close as she picked her way through the rubble towards the kitchen.

Determined to make her as comfortable as possible, Gabe strode into the bedroom and pulled the remains of the mattress into the large room, clearing a space for it in the corner. He found a blanket, half-shredded, and carried it to the mattress.

The woman emerged from the kitchen and handed him water in a chipped cup. The boy gripped her skirt, like a younger, frightened child.

He smiled his thanks. As he took the cup, his fingertips grazed her hand and his senses flared at the contact. He gulped down the water and handed her back the cup. "The—the *Anglais,* did they hurt you?" What was the French word? *"Violate? Moleste?"*

Her long graceful fingers gripped the cup. *"Non. Ils m'ont pas molester."*

He nodded, understanding her meaning. She had not been raped. Thank God.

"Can you keep watch?" he asked Ensign Vernon. "I'll sleep for an hour or so and relieve you." He'd not slept since the siege began, over twenty-four hours before.

"Yes, sir," the ensign replied.

They blocked the door with a barricade of broken furniture. The ensign found the remnants of a wooden chair with the seat and legs intact. He placed it at the window to keep watch.

The mother and child curled up together on the mattress. Gabe slid to the floor, his back against the wall. He glanced over at her and her gaze met his for one long moment as intense as an embrace.

Gabe was shaken by her effect on him. It did him no credit to be so attracted to her, not with the terror she'd just been through.

Perhaps he was merely moved by her devotion to her child, how she held him, how she gazed upon him. Gabe had often watched his own mother tend as lovingly to his little sisters.

Or maybe her devotion to her son touched some deep yearning within him. The girls had come one after the other after Gabe was born, and he had often been left in the company of his older brothers, struggling to keep up.

What the devil was he musing about? He never needed to be the fussed over like his sisters. Much better to be toughened by the rough-housing of boys.

Gabe forced himself to close his eyes. He needed sleep. After sleeping an hour or two, he'd be thinking like a soldier again.

The sounds of looting and pillaging continued, but it was the woman's voice, softly murmuring comfort to her son, that finally lulled Gabe to sleep.

The carnage lasted two more days. Gabe, Ensign Vernon and the mother and son remained in the relative safety of her ransacked home, even though the forced inactivity strained Gabe's nerves. He'd have preferred fighting his way through the town to this idleness.

His needs were inconsequential, however. The woman and child must be safeguarded.

What little food they could salvage went to the boy, who was hungry all the time. Ensign Vernon occupied the time by drawing. Some sketches he kept private. Some fanciful pictures of animals and such he gave to the boy in an attempt to amuse him. The boy merely stared at them blankly, spending most of his time at his mother's side, watching Gabe and Vernon with eyes both angry and wary.

None of them spoke much. Gabe could count on his fingers how many words he and the woman spoke to each other. Still, she remained at the centre of his existence. There was no sound she made, no gesture or expression he did not notice, and the empty hours of waiting did not diminish his resolve to make certain she and her son reached safety.

On the third day it was clear order had been restored. Gabe led them out, and the woman only looked back once at what had been her home. Outside, the air smelled of smoke and burnt wood, but the only sound of soldiers was the rhythm of a disciplined march.

They walked to the city's centre where Gabe supposed the army's headquarters would be found. There Gabe was told to what building other French civilians had been taken. They found the correct building, but Gabe hesitated before taking the mother and son inside. It was difficult to leave her fate to strangers. In an odd way he did not understand, she had become more important to him than anything else. Still, what choice did he have?

"We should go in," he told her.

Ensign Vernon said, "I will remain here, sir, if that is agreeable to you."

"As you wish," Gabe replied.

"Goodbye, *madame*." The ensign stepped away.

Looking frightened but resigned, she merely nodded.

Gabe escorted her and her son through the door to the end of a hallway where two soldiers stood guard. The room they guarded was bare of furniture except one table and a chair, on which a

British officer sat. In the room were about twenty people, older men, once French officials perhaps, and other women and children whose families had been destroyed.

Gabe spoke to the British officer, explaining the woman's circumstance to him.

"What happens to them?" he asked the man.

The officer's answer was curt. "The women and children will be sent back to France, if they have money for the passage."

Gabe stepped away and fished in an inside pocket of his uniform, pulling out a purse full of coin, nearly all he possessed. Glancing around to make certain no one noticed, he pressed the purse into the woman's hands. "You will need this."

Her eyes widened as her fingers closed around the small leather bag. *"Capitaine—"*

He pressed her hand. "No argument. No—" he pronounced it the French way "—*argument.*"

She closed her other hand around his and the power of her gaze tugged at something deep inside him. It was inexplicable, but saying goodbye felt like losing a part of himself.

He did not even know her name.

He pulled his hand from hers and pointed to himself. "Gabriel Deane." If she needed him, she would at least know his name.

"Gabriel," she whispered, speaking his name with the beauty of her French accent. *"Merci. Que Dieu vous bénisse."*

His brows knit in confusion. He'd forgotten most of the French he'd learned in school.

She struggled for words. *"Dieu*…God…" She crossed herself. *"Bénisse."*

"Bless?" he guessed.

She nodded.

He forced himself to take a step back. *"Au revoir, madame."*

Clenching his teeth, Gabe turned and started for the door before he did something foolish. Like kiss her. Or leave with her.

She was a stranger, nothing more, important only in his fantasies. Not in reality.

"Gabriel!"

He halted.

She ran to him.

She placed both hands on his cheeks and pulled his head down to kiss him on the lips. With her face still inches from his, she whispered, "My name is Emmaline Mableau."

He was afraid to speak for fear of betraying the swirling emotions inside him. An intense surge of longing enveloped him.

He desired her as a man desires a woman. It was foolish beyond everything. Dishonourable, as well, since she'd just lost her husband to hands not unlike his own.

He met her gaze and held it a moment before fleeing out the door.

But his thoughts repeated, over and over—*Emmaline Mableau.*

Chapter One

Brussels, Belgium—May 1815

Emmaline Mableau!

Gabe's heart pounded when he caught a glimpse of the woman from whom he'd parted three years before. Carrying a package, she walked briskly through the narrow Brussels streets. It was Emmaline Mableau, he was convinced.

Or very nearly convinced.

He'd always imagined her back in France, living in some small village, with parents…or a new husband.

But here she was, in Belgium.

Brussels had many French people, so it was certainly possible for her to reside here. Twenty years of French rule had only ended the year before when Napoleon was defeated.

Defeated for the first time, Gabe meant. *L'Empereur* had escaped from his exile on Elba. He'd raised an army and was now on the march to regain his empire. Gabe's regiment, the Royal Scots, was part of Wellington's Allied Army and would soon cross swords with Napoleon's forces again.

Many of the English aristocracy had poured into Brussels after the treaty, fleeing the high prices in England, looking for elegant living at little cost. Even so, Brussels remained primed for French rule, as if the inhabitants expected Napoleon to walk its streets any day. Nearly everyone in the city spoke French. Shop signs were in French. The hotel where Gabe was billeted had a French name. *Hôtel de Flandre.*

Gabe had risen early to stretch his legs in the brisk morning air. He had few official duties at present, so spent his days exploring the city beyond the Parc de Brussels and the cathedral. Perhaps there was more of the cloth merchant's son in him than he'd realised, because he liked best to walk the narrow streets lined with shops.

He'd spied Emmaline Mableau as he descended the hill to reach that part of Brussels. She'd been rushing past shopkeepers who were just raising their shutters and opening their doors. Gabe bolted down the hill to follow her, getting only quick glimpses of her as he tried to catch up to her.

He might be mistaken about her being Emmaline Mableau. It might have been a mere trick of the eye and the fact that he often thought of her that made him believe the Belgian woman was she.

But he was determined to know for certain.

She turned a corner and he picked up his pace, fearing he'd lose sight of her. Near the end of the row of shops he glimpsed a flutter of skirts, a woman entering a doorway. His heart beat faster. That had to have been her. No one left on the street looked like her.

He slowed his pace as he approached where she had disappeared, carefully determining which store she'd entered. The sign above the door read *Magasin de Lacet.* The shutters were open and pieces of lace draped over tables could be seen though the windows.

A lace shop.

He opened the door and crossed the threshold, removing his shako as he entered the shop.

He was surrounded by white. White lace ribbons of various widths and patterns draped over lines strung across the length of the shop. Tables stacked with white lace cloth, lace-edged handkerchiefs and lace caps. White lace curtains covering the walls. The distinct scent of lavender mixed with the scent of linen, a scent that took him back in time to hefting huge bolts of cloth in his father's warehouse.

Through the gently fluttering lace ribbons, he spied the woman emerging from a room at the back of the shop, her face still obscured. With her back to him, she folded squares of intricate lace that must have taken some woman countless hours to tat.

Taking a deep breath, he walked slowly towards her. "Madame Mableau?"

Still holding the lace in her fingers and startled at the sound of a man's voice, Emmaline turned. And gasped.

"Mon Dieu!"

She recognised him instantly, the *capitaine* whose presence in Badajoz had kept her sane when all seemed lost. She'd tried to forget those desolate days in the Spanish city, although she'd never entirely banished the memory of Gabriel Deane. His brown eyes, watchful then, were now reticent, but his jaw remained as strong, his lips expressive, his hair as dark and unruly.

"Madame." He bowed. "Do you remember me? I saw you from afar. I was not certain it was you."

She could only stare. He seemed to fill the space, his scarlet coat a splash of vibrancy in the white lace-filled room. It seemed as if no mere shop could be large enough to contain his presence. He'd likewise commanded space in Badajoz, just as he commanded everything else. Tall and powerfully built, he had filled those terrible, despairing days, keeping them safe. Giving them hope.

"Pardon," he said. "I forgot. You speak only a little English. *Un peu Anglais.*"

She smiled. She'd spoken those words to him in Badajoz.

She held up a hand. "I do remember you, *naturellement*." She had never dreamed she would see him again, however. "I—I speak a little more English now. It is necessary. So many English people in Brussels." She snapped her mouth closed. She'd been babbling.

"You are well, I hope?" His thick, dark brows knit and his gaze swept over her.

"I am very well." Except she could not breathe at the moment and her legs seemed too weak to hold her upright, but that was his effect on her, not malaise.

His features relaxed. "And your son?"

She lowered her eyes. "Claude was well last I saw him."

He fell silent, as if he realised her answer hid something she did not wish to disclose. Finally he spoke again. "I thought you would be in France."

She shrugged. "My aunt lives here. This is her shop. She needed help and we needed a home. *Vraiment,* Belgium is a better place to—how do you say?—to rear Claude."

She'd believed living in Belgium would insulate Claude from the patriotic fervour Napoleon had generated, especially in her own family.

She'd been wrong.

Gabriel gazed into her eyes. "I see." A concerned look came over his face. "I hope your journey from Spain was not too difficult."

It was all so long ago and fraught with fear at every step, but there had been no more attacks on her person, no need for Claude to risk his life for her.

She shivered. "We were taken to Lisbon. From there we gained passage on a ship to San Sebastian and then another to France."

She'd had money stitched into her clothing, but without the *capitaine's* purse she would not have had enough for both the passage and the bribes required to secure the passage. What would have been their fate without his money?

The money.

Emmaline suddenly understood why the captain had come to her shop. "I will pay you back the money. If you return tomorrow, I will give it to you." It would take all her savings, but she owed him more than that.

"The money means nothing to me." His eyes flashed with pain.

She'd offended him. Her cheeks burned. "I beg your pardon, Gabriel."

He almost smiled. "You remembered my name."

She could not help but smile back at him. "You remembered mine."

"I could not forget you, Emmaline Mableau." His voice turned low and seemed to reach inside her and wrap itself around her heart.

Everything blurred except him. His visage was so clear to her she fancied she could see every whisker on his face, although he must have shaved that morning. Her mind flashed back to those three days in Badajoz, his unshaven skin giving him the appearance of a rogue, a pirate, a libertine. Even in her despair she'd wondered how his beard would feel against her fingertips. Against her cheek.

But in those few days she'd welcomed any thought that strayed from the horror of seeing her husband killed and hearing her son's anguished cry as his father fell on to the hard stones of the cobbled street.

He blinked and averted his gaze. "Perhaps I should not have come here."

Impulsively she touched his arm. "*Non, non,* Gabriel. I am happy to see you. It is a surprise, no?"

The shop door opened and two ladies entered. One loudly declared in English, "Oh, what a lovely shop. I've never seen so much lace!"

These were precisely the sort of customers for whom Emmaline had improved her English. The numbers of English ladies coming to Brussels to spend their money kept increasing since the war had ended.

If it had ended.

The English soldiers were in Brussels because it was said there would be a big battle with Napoleon. No doubt Gabriel had come to fight in it.

The English ladies cast curious glances towards the tall, handsome officer who must have been an incongruous sight amidst all the delicate lace.

"I should leave," he murmured to Emmaline.

His voice made her knees weaken again. She did not wish to lose him again so soon.

He nodded curtly. "I am pleased to know you are well." He stepped back.

He was going to leave!

"*Un moment*, Gabriel," she said hurriedly. "I—I would ask you to eat dinner with me, but I have nothing to serve you. Only bread and cheese."

His eyes captured hers and her chest ached as if all the breath was squeezed out of her. "I am fond of bread and cheese."

She felt almost giddy. "I will close the shop at seven. Will you come back and eat bread and cheese with me?"

Her aunt would have the *apoplexie* if she knew Emmaline intended to entertain a British officer. But with any luck Tante Voletta would never know.

"Will you come, Gabriel?" she breathed.

His expression remained solemn. "I will return at seven." He bowed and quickly strode out of the shop, the English ladies following him with their eyes.

When the door closed behind him, both ladies turned to stare at Emmaline.

She forced herself to smile at them and behave as though nothing of great importance had happened.

"Good morning, *mesdames.*" She curtsied. "Please tell me if I may offer assistance."

They nodded, still gaping, before they turned their backs and whispered to each other while they pretended to examine the lace caps on a nearby table.

Emmaline returned to folding the square of lace she'd held since Gabriel first spoke to her.

It was absurd to experience a *frisson* of excitement at merely speaking to a man. It certainly had not happened with any other. In fact, since her husband's death she'd made it a point to avoid such attention.

She buried her face in the piece of lace and remembered that terrible night. The shouts and screams and roar of buildings afire sounded in her ears again. Her body trembled as once again she smelled the blood and smoke and the sweat of men.

She lifted her head from that dark place to the bright, clean white of the shop. She ought to have forgiven her husband for taking her and their son to Spain, but such generosity of spirit eluded her. Remy's selfishness had led them into the trauma and horror that was Badajoz.

Emmaline shook her head. No, it was not Remy she could not forgive, but herself. She should have defied him. She should have refused when he insisted, *I will not be separated from my son.*

She should have taken his yelling, raging and threatening. She should have risked the back of his hand and defied him. If she had refused to accompany him, Remy might still be alive and Claude would have no reason to be consumed with hatred.

How would Claude feel about his mother inviting a British officer to sup with her? To even speak to Gabriel Deane would be a betrayal in Claude's eyes. Claude's hatred encompassed every-thing *Anglais,* and would even include the man who'd protected them and brought them to safety.

But neither her aunt nor Claude would know of her sharing dinner with Gabriel Deane, so she was determined not to worry over it.

She was merely paying him back for his kindness to them, Emmaline told herself. That was the reason she'd invited him to dinner.

The only reason.

The evening was fine, warm and clear as befitted late May. Gabe breathed in the fresh air and walked at a pace as rapid as when he'd followed Emmaline that morning. He was too excited, too full of an anticipation he had no right to feel.

He'd had his share of women, as a soldier might, short-lived trysts, pleasant, but meaning very little to him. For any of those women, he could not remember feeling this acute sense of expec-tancy.

He forced himself to slow down, to calm himself and become more reasonable. It was curiosity about how she'd fared since Badajoz that had led him to accept her invitation. The time they'd shared made him feel attached to her and to her son. He merely wanted to ensure that Emmaline was happy.

Gabriel groaned. He ought not think of her as Emmaline. It conveyed an intimacy he had no right to assume.

Except she had called him by his given name, he remembered. To hear her say *Gabriel* was like listening to music.

He increased his pace again.

As he approached the shop door, he halted, damping down his emotions one more time. When his head was as steady as his hand he turned the knob and opened the shop door.

Emmaline stood with a customer where the ribbons of lace hung on a line. She glanced over at him when he entered.

The customer was another English lady, like the two who had come to the shop that morning. This lady, very prosperously dressed, loudly haggled over the price of a piece of lace. The difference between Emmaline's price and what the woman wanted to pay was a mere pittance.

Give her the full price, Gabe wanted to say to the customer. He suspected Emmaline needed the money more than the lady did.

"Très bien, madame," Emmaline said with a resigned air. She accepted the lower price.

Gabe moved to a corner to wait while Emmaline wrapped the lace in paper and tied it with string. As the lady bustled out she gave him a quick assessing glance, pursing her lips at him.

Had that been a look of disapproval? She knew nothing of his reasons for being in the shop. Could a soldier not be in a woman's shop without censure? This lady's London notions had no place here.

Gabe stepped forwards.

Emmaline smiled, but averted her gaze. "I will be ready in a *minute.* I need to close up the shop."

"Tell me what to do and I'll assist you." Better for him to be occupied than merely watching her every move.

"Close the shutters on the windows, if you please?" She straightened the items on the tables.

When Gabe secured the shutters, the light in the shop turned dim, lit only by a small lamp in the back of the store. The white lace, so bright in the morning sun, now took on soft shades of lavender and grey. He watched Emmaline glide from table to table, refolding the items, and felt as if they were in a dream.

She worked her way to the shop door, taking a key from her pocket and turning it in the lock. *"C'est fait!"* she said. "I am finished. Come with me."

She led him to the back of the shop, picking up her cash box and tucking it under her arm. She lit a candle from the lamp before extinguishing it. "We go out the back door."

Gabe took the cash box from her. "I will carry it for you."

He followed her through the curtain to an area just as neat and orderly as the front of the shop.

Lifting the candle higher, she showed him a stairway. "*Ma tante*—my aunt—lives above the shop, but she is visiting. Some of the women who make the lace live in the country; my aunt visits them sometimes to buy the lace."

Gabe hoped her aunt would not become caught in the army's march into France. Any day now he expected the Allied Army to be given the order to march against Napoleon.

"Where is your son?" Gabe asked her. "Is he at school?" The boy could not be more than fifteen, if Gabe was recalling correctly, the proper age to still be away at school.

She bowed her head. "*Non.*"

Whenever he mentioned her son her expression turned bleak.

Behind the shop was a small yard shared by the other shops and, within a few yards, another stone building, two storeys, with window boxes full of colourful flowers.

She unlocked the door. "*Ma maison.*"

The contrast between this place and her home in Badajoz could not have been more extreme. The home in Badajoz had been marred by chaos and destruction. This home was pleasant and orderly and welcoming. As in Badajoz, Gabe stepped into one open room, but this one was neatly organised into an area for sitting and one for dining, with what appeared to be a small galley kitchen through a door at the far end.

Emmaline lit one lamp, then another, and the room seemed to come to life. A colourful carpet covered a polished wooden floor. A red upholstered sofa, flanked by two small tables and two adjacent chairs, faced a fireplace with a mantel painted white. All the tables were covered with white lace tablecloths and held vases of brightly hued flowers.

"Come in, Gabriel," she said. "I will open the windows."

Gabe closed the door behind him and took a few steps into the room.

It was even smaller than the tiny cottage his uncle lived in, but had the same warm, inviting feel. Uncle Will managed a hill farm in Lancashire and some of Gabe's happiest moments had been spent working beside his uncle, the least prosperous of the Deane family. Gabe was overcome with nostalgia for those days. And guilt. He'd not written to his uncle in years.

Emmaline turned away from the window to see him still glancing around the room. "It is small, but we did not need more."

It seemed…safe. After Badajoz, she deserved a safe place. "It is pleasant."

She lifted her shoulder as if taking his words as disapproval.

He wanted to explain that he liked the place too much, but that would be even more difficult to put into words.

She took the cash box from his hands and put it in a locking cabinet. "I regret so much that I do not have a meal sufficient for you. I do not cook much. It is only for me."

Meaning her son was not with her, he imagined. "No pardon necessary, *madame*." Besides, he had not accepted her invitation because of what food would be served.

"Then please sit and I will make it ready."

Gabe sat at the table, facing the kitchen so he could watch her.

She placed some glasses and a wine bottle on the table. "It is French wine. I hope you do not mind."

He glanced up at her. "The British pay smugglers a great deal for French wine. I dare say it is a luxury."

Her eyes widened. "*C'est vrai?* I did not know that. I think my wine may not be so fine."

She poured wine into the two glasses and went back to the

kitchen to bring two plates, lace-edged linen napkins and cutlery. A moment later she brought a variety of cheeses on a wooden cutting board, a bowl of strawberries and another board with a loaf of bread.

"We may each cut our own, no?" She gestured for him to select his cheese while she cut herself a piece of bread.

For such simple fare, it tasted better than any meal he'd eaten in months. He asked her about her travel from Badajoz and was pleased that the trip seemed free of the terrible trauma she and her son had previously endured. She asked him about the battles he'd fought since Badajoz and what he'd done in the very brief peace.

The conversation flowed easily, adding to the comfortable feel of the surroundings. Gabe kept their wine glasses filled and soon felt as relaxed as if he'd always sat across the table from her for his evening meal.

When they'd eaten their fill, she took their plates to the kitchen area. Gabe rose to carry the other dishes, reaching around her to place them in the sink.

She turned and brushed against his arm. "Thank you, Gabriel."

Her accidental touch fired his senses. The scent of her hair filled his nostrils, the same lavender scent as in her shop. Her head tilted back to look into his face. She drew in a breath and her cheeks tinged pink.

Had she experienced the same awareness? That they were a man and a woman alone together?

Blood throbbed through his veins and he wanted to bend lower, closer, to taste those slightly parted lips.

She turned back to the sink and worked the pump to fill a kettle with water. "I will make coffee," she said in a determined tone, then immediately apologised. "I am sorry I do not have tea."

"Coffee will do nicely." Gabe stepped away, still pulsating with arousal. He watched her light a fire in a tiny stove and fill a coffee pot with water and coffee. She placed the pot on top of the stove.

"Shall we sit?" She gestured to the red sofa.

Would she sit with him on the sofa? He might not be able to resist taking her in his arms if she did.

The coffee eventually boiled. She poured it into cups and carried the tray to a table placed in front of the sofa. Instead of sitting beside him, she chose a small adjacent chair and asked him how he liked his coffee.

He could barely remember. "Milk and a little sugar."

While she stirred his coffee, he absently rubbed his finger on the lace cloth atop the table next to him. His fingers touched a miniature lying face down on the table. He turned it over. It was a portrait of a youth with her dark hair and blue eyes.

"Is this your son?" If so, he'd turned into a fine-looking young fellow, strong and defiant.

She handed him his cup. "Yes. It is Claude." Her eyes glistened and she blinked rapidly.

He felt her distress and lowered his voice to almost a whisper. "What happened to him, Emmaline? Where is he?"

She looked away and wiped her eyes with her fingers. "Nothing happened, you see, but everything…" Her voice trailed off.

He merely watched her.

She finally faced him again with a wan smile. "Claude was so young. He did not—does not—understand war, how men do bad things merely because it is war. Soldiers die in war, but Claude did not comprehend that his father died because he was a soldier—"

Gabe interrupted her. "Your husband died because our men were lost to all decency."

She held up a hand. "Because of the battle, no? It was a hard siege for the British, my husband said. Remy was killed because of the siege, because of the war."

He leaned forwards. "I must ask you. The man who tried to molest you—did he kill your husband?"

She lowered her head. "*Non.* The others killed my husband. That one stood aside, but his companions told him to violate me."

His gut twisted. "I am sorry, Emmaline. I am so sorry." He wanted even more than before to take her in his arms, this time to comfort her.

He reached out and touched her hand, but quickly withdrew.

"You rescued us, Gabriel," she said. "You gave us money. You must not be sorry. I do not think of it very much any more. And the dreams do not come as often."

He shook his head.

She picked up the miniature portrait of her son and gazed at it. "I told Claude it happened because of war and to try to forget it, but he will not. He blames the *Anglais,* the British. He hates the British. All of them. If he knew you were here, he would want to kill you."

Gabe could not blame Claude. He'd feel the same if he'd watched his family violently destroyed.

"Where is Claude?" he asked again.

A tear slid down her cheek. "He ran away. To join Napoleon. He is not yet sixteen." She looked Gabe directly in the face. "There is to be a big battle, is there not? You will fight in it." Her expression turned anguished. "You will be fighting my son."

Chapter Two

Emmaline's fingers clutched Claude's miniature as she fought tears.

"I did not mean to say that to you." The pain about her son was too sharp, too personal.

"Emmaline." Gabriel's voice turned caring.

She tried to ward off his concern. "I am merely afraid for him. It is a mother's place to worry, no?" She placed the small portrait on the table and picked up her cup. "Please, drink your coffee."

He lifted his cup, but she was aware of him watching her. She hoped she could fool him into thinking she was not distressed, that she would be able to pretend she was not shaken.

He put down his cup. "Most soldiers survive a battle," he told her in a reassuring voice. "And many are not even called to fight. In Badajoz your son showed himself to be an intelligent and brave boy. There is a good chance he will avoid harm."

She flinched with the memory. "In Badajoz he was foolish. He should have hidden himself. Instead, he was almost killed." Her anguish rose. "The soldiers will place him in the front ranks. When my husband was alive the men used to talk of it. They put the young ones, the ones with no experience, in the front."

He cast his eyes down. "Then I do not know what to say to comfort you."

That he even wished to comfort her brought back her tears. She blinked them away. "There is no comfort. I wait and worry and pray."

He rubbed his face and stood. "It is late and I should leave."

"Do not leave yet," she cried, then covered her mouth, shocked at herself for blurting this out.

He walked to the door. "I may be facing your son in battle, Emmaline. How can you bear my company?"

She rose and hurried to block his way. "I am sorry I spoke about Claude. I did not have the—the *intention* to tell you. Please do not leave me."

He gazed down at her. "Why do you wish me to stay?"

She covered her face with her hands, ashamed, but unable to stop. "I do not want to be alone!"

Strong arms engulfed her and she was pressed against him, enveloped in his warmth, comforted by the beating of his heart. Her tears flowed.

Claude had run off months ago and, as Brussels filled with British soldiers, the reality of his possible fate had eaten away at her. Her aunt and their small circle of friends cheered Claude's patriotism, but Emmaline knew it was revenge, not patriotism, that drove Claude. She'd kept her fears hidden until this moment.

How foolish it was to burden Gabriel with her woes. But his arms were so comforting. He demanded nothing, merely held her close while she wept for this terrible twist of fate.

Finally the tears slowed and she mustered the strength to pull away. He handed her a clean handkerchief from his pocket, warmed by his body.

She wiped her eyes. "I will launder this for you."

"It does not matter," he murmured.

She dared to glance up into his kind eyes and saw only concern shining in them.

"I am recovered," she assured him. New tears formed and she wiped them with his handkerchief. "Do not worry over me."

He stood very still and solid, as if she indeed could lean on him.

"I will stay if you wish me to," he said.

She took in a breath.

She ought to say no. She ought to brush him away and tell him she needed no one to be with her.

Instead, she whispered, "Please stay, Gabriel."

Something softened in his face and he reached out his hand to her. "I will help you with the dishes."

Her tension eased. He offered what she needed most at the moment: ordinary companionship.

They gathered the cups and coffee pot and carried them to the little sink. She filled the kettle with water and put it on the stove again. While it heated he took the tablecloth to the door to shake out. She dampened a cloth and wiped the table and the kitchen. When the water was hot, Gabriel removed his coat and pushed up his shirt sleeves. He washed and rinsed. She dried and put the dishes away.

What man had ever helped her do dishes? Not her husband, for certain. She'd not even required it of Claude. But it somehow seemed fitting that Gabriel should help her.

When they finished, he wiped his hands on the towel and reached for his coat.

Her anxieties returned. "You will stay longer?"

He gazed at her. "Longer? Are you certain?"

Suddenly she knew precisely what she was asking of him and it was not merely to keep her from being alone. "I am certain."

She picked up a candle and took his hand in hers, leading him towards the stairway. There were two small rooms above stairs. She kept the door to Claude's bedroom closed so she would not feel its emptiness. She led Gabriel into the other room, her bedroom, her excitement building. She kicked off her shoes and climbed atop the bed.

He held back, gazing at her.

How much more permission did she need to give?

She'd vowed to have no more of men since her husband's death. Claude could be her only concern. He needed to release the past and see that he had his whole life ahead of him.

If Napoleon did not get him killed in the battle, that is.

Until Claude returned to her, she could do nothing, but if God saw fit to spare him in the battle, Emmaline had vowed to devote her life to restoring her son's happiness.

But Claude was not here now and Gabriel would not remain in Brussels for long. The British army would march away to face Napoleon; both Claude and Gabriel would be gone. What harm could there be in enjoying this man's company? In making love with him? Many widows had affairs. Why not enjoy the passion Gabriel's heated looks promised?

"Come, Gabriel," she whispered.

He walked to the edge of the bed and she met him on her knees, her face nearly level with his. He stroked her face with a gentle hand, his touch so tender it made her want to weep again.

"I did not expect this," he murmured.

"I did not, as well," she added. "But it—it feels *inévitable,* no?"

"Inevitable." His fingers moved to the sensitive skin of her neck, still as gentle as if she were as delicate as the finest lace.

She undid the buttons on his waistcoat and flattened her palms against his chest, sliding them up to his neck.

She pressed her fingers against his smooth cheek. "You shaved for dinner, *n'est-ce pas?*" Her hands moved to the back of his neck where his hair curled against her fingers.

He leaned closer to her and touched his lips to hers.

Her husband's kisses had been demanding and possessive.

Gabriel offered his lips like a gift for her to open or refuse, as she wished.

She parted her lips and tasted him with her tongue.

He responded, giving her all that she could wish. She felt giddy with delight and pressed herself against him, feeling the bulge of his manhood through his trousers.

"Mon Dieu," she sighed when his lips left hers.

He stepped away. "Do you wish me to stop?"

"No!" she cried. "I wish you to commence."

He smiled. *"Très bien, madame."*

She peered at him. "You speak French now?"

"Un peu," he replied.

She laughed and it felt good. It had been so long since she had laughed. "We shall make love together, Gabriel."

He grinned. *"Très bien."*

She unhooked the bodice of her dress and pulled the garment over her head. While Gabriel removed his boots and stockings, she made quick work of removing her corset, easily done because it fastened in the front. She tossed it aside. Now wearing only her chemise, she started removing the pins from her hair. As it tumbled down her back, she looked up.

He stood before her naked and aroused. His was a soldier's body, muscles hardened by campaign, skin scarred from battle.

Still kneeling on the bed, she reached out and touched a scar across his abdomen, caused by the slash of a sword, perhaps.

He held her hand against his skin. "It looks worse than it was."

"You have so many." Some were faint, others distinct.

He shrugged. "I have been in the army for over eighteen years."

Her husband would have been in longer, had he lived. He'd been rising steadily in rank; perhaps he would have been one of Napoleon's generals, preparing for this battle, had he lived.

She gave herself a mental shake for thinking of Remy, even

though he'd been the only man with whom she'd ever shared her bed.

Until now.

A flush swept over her, as unexpected as it was intense. "Come to me, Gabriel," she rasped.

He joined her on the bed, kneeling in front of her and wrapping his arms around her, holding her close. His lips found hers once more.

He swept his hand through her hair. "So lovely." She felt the warmth of his breath against her lips.

His hand moved down, caressing her neck, her shoulders. Her breasts. She writhed with the pleasure of it and was impatient to be rid of her chemise. She pulled it up to her waist, but he took the fabric from her and lifted it the rest of the way over her head. With her chemise still bunched in his hands he stared at her, his gaze so intense that she sensed it as tangibly as his touch.

"You are beautiful," he said finally.

She smiled, pleased at his words, and lay against the pillows, eager for what would come next.

But if she expected him to take his pleasure quickly, she was mistaken. He knelt over her, looking as if he were memorising every part of her. His hands, still gentle and reverent, caressed her skin. When his palms grazed her nipples, the sensation shot straight to her most feminine place.

Slowly his hand travelled the same path, but stopped short of where her body now throbbed for him. Instead, he stroked the inside of her thighs, so teasingly near.

A sound, half-pleasure, half-frustration, escaped her lips.

Finally he touched her. His fingers explored her flesh, now moist for him. The miracle of sensation his fingers created built her need to an intensity she thought she could not bear a moment longer.

He bent down and kissed her lips again, his tongue freely tasting her now. Her legs parted, ready for him.

She braced for his thrust, a part of lovemaking always painful for her, but he did not force himself inside her. Wonder of wonders, he eased himself inside, a sweet torture of rhythmic stroking until gradually he filled her completely. The need inside her grew even stronger and she moved with him, trying to ease the torment.

More wonders, he seemed to be in complete unison with her, as if he sensed her growing need so he could meet it each step of the way. The sensation created by him was more intense than she had ever experienced. Soon nothing existed for her but her need and the man who would satisfy it.

The intensity still built, speeding her forwards, faster and faster, until suddenly she exploded with sensation inside. Pleasure washed through her, like waves on the shore. His grip on her tightened and he thrust with more force, convulsing as he spilled his seed inside her. For that intense moment, their bodies pressed together, shaking with the shared climax.

Gabe felt the pleasure ebb, making his body suddenly heavy, his mind again able to form coherent thought. He forced himself not to merely collapse on top of her and crush her with his weight. Instead, he eased himself off her to lie at her side.

As soon as he did so she flung her arms across her face. He gently lowered them.

She was weeping.

He felt panicked. "Emmaline, did I injure you?" He could not precisely recall how he might have done so, but during those last moments he'd been consumed by his own drive to completion.

She shook her head. "*Non.* I cannot speak—"

"Forgive me. I did not mean to distress you." He ought not

to have made love to her. He'd taken advantage of her grief and worry. "I did not realise…"

She swiped at her eyes and turned on her side to face him. "You did not distress me. How do I say it?" He could feel her search for words. "I never felt *le plaisir* in this way before."

His spirits darkened. "It did not please you."

Tears filled her eyes again, making them sparkle in the candle-light. She cupped her palm against his cheek. "*Tu ne comprends pas.* You do not comprehend. It pleased me more than I can say to you."

Relief washed through him. "I thought I had hurt you." He wrapped his arms around her and held her against him, resting her head against his heart.

Gabe allowed himself to enjoy the comfort of her silky skin against his, their bodies warming each other as cool night air seeped through the window jamb.

She spoke and he felt her voice through his chest as well as hearing it with his ears. "It was not so with my husband. Not so… long. So…much *plaisir.*"

The image of a body in a French uniform flashed into Gabe's mind, the body they had been forced to abandon in Badajoz. Now he'd made love to that man's wife. It seemed unconscionable. "Has there been no other man since your husband?"

"No, Gabriel. Only you."

He drew in a breath, forcing himself to be reasonable. He'd had nothing to do with the Frenchman's death. And three years had passed.

He felt her muscles tense. "Do you have a wife?"

"No." Of that he could easily assure her. He'd never even con-sidered it.

She relaxed again. "*C'est très bien.* I would not like it if you had a wife. I would feel *culpabilité.*"

He laughed inwardly. They were both concerned about feeling the *culpabilité,* the guilt.

They lay quiet again and he twirled a lock of her hair around his fingers.

"It feels agreeable to lie here with you," she said after a time.

Very agreeable, he thought, almost as if he belonged in her bed.

After a moment a thought occurred to him. "Do you need to take care of yourself?"

"Pardon?" She turned her face to him.

"To prevent a baby?" He had no wish to inflict an unwanted baby upon her.

Her expression turned pained. "I do not think I can have more babies. I was only *enceinte* one time. With Claude. Never again."

He held her closer, regretting he'd asked. "Did you wish for more children?"

She took a deep breath and lay her head against his chest again. "More babies would have been very difficult. To accompany my husband, you know."

What kind of fool had her husband been to bring his family to war? Gabe knew how rough it was for soldiers' wives to march long distances heavy with child, or to care for tiny children while a battle raged.

"Did you always follow the drum?" he asked.

She glanced at him. "The drum? I do not comprehend."

"Accompany your husband on campaign," he explained.

"Ah!" Her eyes brightened in understanding. "Not always did I go with him. Not until Claude was walking and talking. My husband did not wish to be parted from his son."

"From Claude?" Not from her?

Had her marriage not been a love match? Gabe could never see the point of marrying unless there was strong devotion between the man and woman, a devotion such as his parents possessed.

Emmaline continued. "My husband was very close to Claude. I think it is why Claude feels so hurt and angry that he died."

"Claude has a right to feel hurt and angry," Gabe insisted.

"But it does not help him, eh?" She trembled.

He held her closer. "Everyone has hardship in their lives to overcome. It will make him stronger."

She looked into his eyes. "What hardship have you had in your life?" She rubbed her hand over the scar on his abdomen. "Besides war?"

"None," he declared. "My father was prosperous, my family healthy."

She nestled against him again. "Tell me about your family."

There was not much to tell. "My father is a cloth merchant, prosperous enough to rear eight children."

"Eight? So many." She looked up at him again. "And are you the oldest? The youngest?"

"I am in the middle," he replied. "First there were four boys and then four girls. I am the last of the boys, but the only one to leave Manchester."

Her brow knitted. "I was like Claude, the only one. I do not know what it would be like to have so many brothers and sisters."

He could hardly remember. "It was noisy, actually. I used to escape whenever I could. I liked most to stay with my uncle. He managed a hill farm. I liked that better than my father's warehouse." His father had never needed him there, not with his older brothers to help out.

"A hill farm?" She looked puzzled.

"A farm with sheep and a few other animals," he explained.

She smiled at him. "You like sheep farming?"

"I did." He thought back to those days, out of doors in the fresh country air, long hours to daydream while watching the flocks graze, or, even better, days filled with hard work during shearing time or when the sheep were lambing.

"Why did you not become a farmer, then?" she asked.

At the time even the open spaces where the sheep grazed seemed too confining to him. "Nelson had just defeated Napoleon's fleet in Egypt. Lancashire seemed too tame a place compared to the likes of Egypt. I asked my father to purchase a commission for me and he did."

"And did you go to Egypt with the army?" Her head rested against his heart.

He shook his head. "No. I was sent to the West Indies."

He remembered the shock of that hellish place, where men died from fevers in great numbers, where he also had become ill and nearly did not recover. When not ill, all his regiment ever did was keep the slaves from revolting. Poor devils. All they'd wanted was to be free men.

He went on. "After that we came to Spain to fight Napoleon's army."

Her muscles tensed. "Napoleon. Bah!"

He moved so they were lying face to face. "You do not revere *L'Empereur?*"

"No." Her eyes narrowed. "He took the men and boys and too many were killed. Too many."

Her distress returned. Gabe changed the subject. "Now I have told you about my life. What of yours?"

She became very still, but held his gaze. "I grew up in the Revolution. Everyone was afraid all the time, afraid to be on the wrong side, you know? Because you would go to *la guillotine.*" She shuddered. "I saw a pretty lady go to the guillotine."

"You witnessed the guillotine?" He was aghast. "You must have been very young."

"*Oui.* My mother hated the Royals, but the pretty lady did not seem so bad to me. She cried for her children at the end."

"My God," he said.

Her gaze drifted and he knew she was seeing it all again.

Gabe felt angry on Emmaline's behalf, angry she should have to endure such a horror.

He lifted her chin with his finger. "You have seen too much."

Her lips trembled and his senses fired with arousal again. He moved closer.

Her breathing accelerated. "I am glad I am here with you."

He looked into her eyes, marvelling at the depth of emotion they conveyed, marvelling that she could remain open and loving in spite of all she'd experienced. A surge of protectiveness flashed through him. He wanted to wipe away all the pain she'd endured. He wanted her to never hurt again.

He placed his lips on hers, thinking he'd never tasted such sweetness. He ran his hand down her back, savouring the feel of her, the outline of her spine, the soft flesh of her buttocks. Parting from her kiss, he gazed upon her, drinking in her beauty with his eyes. The fullness of her breasts, the dusky pink of her nipples, the triangle of dark hair at her genitals.

He touched her neck, so long and slim, and slid his hand to her breasts. She moaned. Placing her hands on the sides of his head, she guided his lips to where his fingers had been. He took her breast into his mouth and explored her nipple with his tongue, feeling it peak and harden.

Her fingernails scraped his back as he tasted one, then the other breast. She writhed beneath him. Soon he was unable to think of anything but Emmaline and how wonderful it felt to make love to her, how he wished the time would never end. Even if he had only this one night with her, he would be grateful. It was far more than he'd expected.

The need for her intensified and he positioned himself over her. She opened her legs and arched her back to him. His chest swelled with masculine pride that she wanted him, wanted him to fill her and bring her to climax.

He entered her easily and what had before been a slow, sublime climb to pleasure this time became a frenzied rush. She rose to meet him and clung to him as if to urge him not to slow down, not to stop.

As if he could. As if he ever wanted this to end, even knowing the ecstasy promised.

The air filled with their rapturous breathing as their exhilaration grew more fevered, more consuming. Gabe heard her cry, felt her convulse around him and then he was lost in his own shattering pleasure.

Afterwards they did not speak. He slid to her side and Emmaline fell asleep in his arms as the candle burned down to a sputtering nub. While it still cast enough light, he gazed upon her as she slept.

He did not know what the morning would bring. For all he knew she might send him away in regret for this night together. Or he might be called away to the regiment. Would the regiment be ordered to march, to meet Napoleon's forces?

Would he face her son in battle and take from her what she held most dear?

Chapter Three

Emmaline woke the next morning with joy in her heart. The man in her bed rolled over and smiled at her as if he, too, shared the happy mood that made her want to laugh and sing and dance about the room.

Instead he led her into a dance of a different sort, one that left her senses humming and her body a delicious mix of satiation and energy. She felt as if she could fly.

His brown eyes, warm as a cup of chocolate, rested on her as he again lay next to her. She held her breath as she gazed back at him, his hair rumpled, his face shadowed with beard.

This time she indulged her curiosity and ran her finger along his cheek, which felt like the coarsest sackcloth. "I do not have the razor for you, Gabriel."

He rubbed his chin. "I will shave later."

From the church seven bells rang.

"It is seven of the clock. I have slept late." She slipped out of the tangled covers and his warm arms, and searched for her shift. "I will bring you some water for washing *tout de suite*."

His brows creased. "Do not delay yourself further. I will fetch the water and take care of myself."

She blinked, uncertain he meant what he said. "Then I will dress and begin breakfast."

He sat up and ran his hands roughly through his hair. She stole a glance at his muscled chest gleaming in the light from the window. He also watched her as she dressed. How different this morning felt than when she'd awoken next to her husband. Remy would have scolded her for oversleeping and told her to hurry so he could have fresh water with which to wash and shave.

As she walked out of the room, she laughed to herself. Remy would also have boasted about how more skilled at lovemaking a Frenchman was over an Englishman. Well, this Englishman's skills at lovemaking far exceeded one Frenchman's.

She paused at the top of the stairs, somewhat ashamed at disparaging her husband. Remy had been no worse than many husbands. Certainly he had loved Claude.

Early in her marriage she'd thought herself lacking as a wife, harbouring a rebellious spirit even while trying to do as her much older husband wished. She'd believed her defiance meant she had remained more child than grown woman. When Remy dictated she and Claude would accompany him to war, she'd known it would not be good for their son. She had raged against the idea.

But only silently.

Perhaps her love for Remy would not have withered like a flower deprived of sun and water, if she'd done what she knew had been right and kept Claude in France.

Emmaline shook off the thoughts and hurried down the stairs to the kitchen to begin breakfast, firing up her little stove to heat a pot of chocolate and to use the bits of cheese left over from the night before to make an omelette with the three eggs still in her larder. Gabriel came down in his shirtsleeves to fetch his fresh water and soon they were both seated at the table, eating what she'd prepared.

"You are feeding me well, Emmaline," he remarked, his words warming her.

She smiled at the compliment. "It is enjoyable to cook for some-one else."

His eyes gazed at her with concern. "You have been lonely?"

She lowered her voice. "*Oui,* since Claude left." But she did not want the sadness to return, not when she had woken to such joy. "But I am not lonely today."

It suddenly occurred to her that he could walk out and she would never see him again. Her throat grew tight with anxiety.

She reached across the table and clasped his hand. "My night with you made me happy."

His expression turned wistful. "It made me happy, too." He glanced away and back, his brow now furrowed. "I have duties with the regiment today, but if you will allow me to return, I will come back when you close the shop."

"*Oui!* Yes." She covered her mouth with her hand. "Oh, I can-not, Gabriel. I have no food to cook and I have slept too late to go to the market." She flushed, remembering why she'd risen so late.

His eyes met hers. "I will bring the food."

Her heart pounded. "And will you stay with me again?"

Only his eyes conveyed emotion, reflecting the passion they'd both shared. "I will stay."

The joy burst forth again.

Gabe returned that evening and the next and the next. Each morning he left her bed and returned in the evening, bringing her food and wine and flowers. While she worked at the shop, he performed whatever regimental duties were required of him. It felt like he was merely marking time until he could see her again.

They never spoke of the future, even though his orders to march could come at any time and they would be forced to part. They talked only of present and past, Gabe sharing more with Emma-line than with anyone he'd ever known. He was never bored with her. He could listen for ever to her musical French accent, could watch for ever her face animated by her words.

May ended and June arrived, each day bringing longer hours of sunlight and warmth. The time passed in tranquillity, an illusion all Brussels seemed to share, even though everyone knew war was imminent. The Prussians were marching to join forces with the Allied Army under Wellington's command. The Russians were marching to join the effort as well, but no one expected they could reach France in time for the first clash with Napoleon.

In Brussels, however, leisure seemed the primary activity. The Parc de Brussels teemed with red-coated gentlemen walking with elegant ladies among the statues and fountains and flowers. A never-ending round of social events preoccupied the more well-connected officers and the aristocracy in residence. Gabe's very middle-class birth kept him off the invitation lists, but he was glad. It meant he could spend his time with Emmaline.

On Sundays when she closed the shop, Gabe walked with Emmaline in the Parc, or, even better, rode with her into the country with its farms thick with planting and hills dotted with sheep.

This day several of the officers were chatting about the Duchess of Richmond's ball to be held the following night, invitations to which were much coveted. Gabe was glad not to be included. It would have meant a night away from Emmaline.

His duties over for the day, Gabe made his way through Brussels to the food market. He shopped every day for the meals he shared with Emmaline and had become quite knowledgeable about Belgian food. His favourites were the *frites* that were to be found everywhere, thick slices of potato, fried to a crisp on the outside, soft and flavourful on the inside.

He'd even become proficient in bargaining in French. He haggled with the woman selling mussels, a food Emmaline especially liked. Mussels for dinner tonight and some of the tiny cabbages that were a Brussels staple. And, of course, the *frites.* He wandered through the market, filling his basket with other items that would please Emmaline: bread, eggs, cheese, cream, a bouquet of flowers. Before leaving the market, he quenched his thirst with a large mug of beer, another Belgian specialty.

Next stop was the wine shop, because Emmaline, true to her French birth, preferred wine over beer. After leaving there, he paused by a jewellery shop, its door open to the cooling breezes. Inside he glimpsed a red-coated officer holding up a glittering bracelet. "This is a perfect betrothal gift," the man said. He recognised the fellow, one of the Royal Scots. Buying a betrothal gift?

Gabe walked on, but the words repeated in his brain.

Betrothal gift.

Who was the man planning to marry? One of the English ladies in Brussels? A sweetheart back home? It made no sense to make such plans on the eve of a battle. No one knew what would happen. Even if the man survived, the regiment might battle Napoleon for ten more years. What kind of life would that be for a wife?

No, if this fellow wanted to marry, he ought to sell his commission and leave the army. If he had any intelligence at all he'd have taken some plunder at Vittoria, like most of the soldiers had done. Then he'd have enough money to live well.

Gabe halted as if striking a stone wall.

He might be talking about himself.

He could sell his commission. *He* had enough money.

He could marry.

He started walking again with the idea forming in his mind and taking over all other thought. He could marry Emmaline. His time with her need not end. He might share all his evenings with her. All his nights.

If she wished to stay in Brussels, that would be no hardship for him. He liked Brussels. He liked the countryside outside the city even better. Perhaps he could buy a farm, a hill farm like Stapleton Farm where his uncle worked. When Gabe had been a boy all he'd thought of was the excitement of being a soldier. Suddenly life on a hill farm beckoned like a paradise. Hard work. Loving nights. Peace.

With Emmaline.

He turned around and strode back to the jewellery shop.

The shop was now empty of customers. A tiny, white-haired man behind the counter greeted him with expectation, *"Monsieur?"*

"A betrothal gift," Gabe told him. "For a lady."

The man's pale blue eyes lit up. *"Les fiançailles?"* He held up two fingers. *"Vous êtes le deuxième homme d'aujourd'hui."* Gabe understood. He was the second man that day purchasing a betrothal gift.

The jeweller showed him a bracelet, sparkling with diamonds, similar to the one his fellow officer had held. Such a piece did not suit Emmaline at all. Gabe wanted something she would wear every day.

"No bracelet," Gabe told the shopkeeper. He pointed to his finger. "A ring."

The man nodded vigorously. *"Oui! L'anneau."*

Gabe selected a wide gold band engraved with flowers. It had one gem the width of the band, a blue sapphire that matched the colour of her eyes.

He smiled and pictured her wearing it as an acknowledgement of his promise to her. He thought of the day he could place the ring on the third finger of her left hand, speaking the words, "With this ring, I thee wed, with my body I thee worship...."

Gabe paid for the ring, and the shopkeeper placed it in a black-velvet box. Gabe stashed the box safely in a pocket inside his coat, next to his heart. When he walked out of the jewellery shop he felt even more certain that what he wanted in life was Emmaline.

He laughed as he hurried to her. These plans he was formulating would never have entered his mind a few weeks ago. He felt a sudden kinship with his brothers and sisters, unlike anything he'd ever felt before. With Emmaline, Gabe would have a family, like his brothers and sisters had families. No matter she could not have children. She had Claude and Gabe would more than welcome Claude as a son.

As he turned the corner on to the street where her lace shop was located, he slowed his pace.

He still had a battle to fight, a life-and-death affair for both their countries. For Gabe and for Claude, as well. He could not be so dishonourable as to sell out when the battle was imminent, when Wellington needed every experienced soldier he could get.

If, God forbid, he should die in the battle, his widow would inherit his modest fortune.

No, he would not think of dying. If Emmaline would marry him before the battle, he would have the best reason to survive it.

With his future set in his mind, he opened the lace-shop door. Immediately he felt a tension that had not been present before. Emmaline stood at the far end of the store, conversing with an older lady who glanced over at his entrance and frowned. They continued to speak in rapid French as he crossed the shop.

"Emmaline?"

Her eyes were pained. "Gabriel, I must present you to my aunt." She turned to the woman. *"Tante Voletta, puis-je vous présenter le Capitaine Deane?"* She glanced back at Gabe and gestured towards her aunt. "Madame Laval."

Gabe bowed. *"Madame."*

Her aunt's eyes were the same shade of blue as Emmaline's, but shot daggers at him. She wore a cap over hair that had only a few streaks of grey through it. Slim but sturdy, her alert manner made Gabe suppose she missed nothing. She certainly examined him carefully before facing Emmaline again and rattling off more in French, too fast for him to catch.

Emmaline spoke back and the two women had another energetic exchange.

Emmaline turned to him. "My aunt is unhappy about our… friendship. I have tried to explain how you helped us in Badajoz. That you are a good man. But you are English, you see." She gave a very Gallic shrug.

He placed the basket on the counter and felt the impression of the velvet box in his pocket. "Would you prefer me to leave?"

"Non, non." She clasped his arm. "I want you to stay."

Her aunt huffed and crossed her arms over her chest. How was Gabe to stay when he knew his presence was so resented?

He made an attempt to engage the woman. *"Madame* arrived today?"

Emmaline translated.

The aunt flashed a dismissive hand. *"Pfft. Oui."*

"You must dine with us." He looked at Emmaline. "Do you agree? She will likely have nothing in her house for a meal."

Emmaline nodded and translated what he said.

Madame Laval gave an expression of displeasure. She responded in French.

Emmaline explained, "She says she is too tired for company."

He lifted the basket again. "Then she must select some food to eat. I purchased plenty." He showed her the contents. *"Pour vous, madame."*

Her eyes kindled with interest, even though her lips were pursed.

"Take what you like," he said.

"I will close the shop." Emmaline walked to the door.

Madame Laval found a smaller basket in the back of the store. Into it she placed a bottle of wine, the cream, some eggs, bread, cheese, four mussels and all of the *frites.*

"C'est assez," she muttered. She called to Emmaline. *"Bonne nuit, Emmaline. Demain, nous parlerons plus."*

Gabe understood that. Emmaline's aunt would have more to say to her tomorrow.

"Bonne nuit, madame." Gabe took the bouquet of flowers and handed them to her, bowing again.

"Hmmph!" She snatched the flowers from his hand and marched away with half their food and all his *frites*.

Emmaline walked over to him and leaned against him.

He put his arms around her. "I am sorry to cause you this trouble."

She sighed. "I wish her visit in the country had lasted longer."

He felt the velvet box press against his chest. "It is safer for her to be in the city."

She pulled away. "Why? Have you heard news?"

He kept an arm around her. "No, nothing more. There is to be a ball tomorrow night. There would not be a ball if Wellington was ready to march."

They walked out of the shop and across the courtyard to her little house. Once inside, Gabe removed his coat; as he did so he felt the ring box in its pocket and knew this was not the time to show it to her. Her aunt, unwittingly, had cast a pall on Gabe's excitement, his dreams for the future.

She busied herself in readying their meal. Their conversation was confined to the placement of dishes and who would carry what to the table.

When they sat at the table, she remarked, "It is a lovely meal, Gabriel. I like the mussels."

He smiled at her. "I know."

As they began to eat, she talked about her aunt. "Tante Voletta came to Brussels a long time ago. After her husband went to the guillotine—"

Gabe put down his fork. "Good God. He went to the guillotine?"

She waved a hand. "That was when they sent everyone to the guillotine. He was a tailor to some of the royals, you see. *Voilà!* That was enough. Tante Voletta came here, to be safe. She opened the shop."

"Why does she dislike me?" he asked. "The English were opposed to the Terror."

She smiled wanly. "Ah, but the English are an enemy of Napoleon. My aunt reveres Napoleon. He made France great again, you see." Her smile fled. "Of course, he killed many by making them soldiers."

What she feared for her son, he remembered.

He turned the subject back to her aunt. "I dislike causing you distress with your aunt. What can I do?"

She shrugged. "You can do nothing."

He gave her a direct look. "Would you prefer I not spend the night tonight?"

Her lips pressed together. "Stay with me. She will know we are lovers soon enough. Everyone around us knows it by now and will delight in telling her of all your coming and going."

He frowned. "Do I cause trouble for you with your neighbours, as well?"

She smiled again. "*Non,* Gabriel. Here a widow is allowed lovers. They might think I am wise to bed you. Most of my neighbours like the money the English bring. My aunt likes English money, too, but she would never say so."

They talked of inconsequentials through the rest of the meal and the cleaning up afterwards. The sky was not quite dark.

Emmaline wiped her hands on the towel. "I am tired tonight. Do you mind if we sleep early?"

"Whatever you wish, Emmaline." Gabe was not about to make anything more uncomfortable for her.

Their lovemaking that night was bittersweet, slow and filled with emotion, as if both of them realised how fragile it could be to love each other.

The words 'With my body I thee worship' repeated in Gabe's mind as his eyes drank in her beauty and his fingers memorised the feel of her. He wanted to erase the tension between them that her aunt's arrival had caused. He wanted to convince her with his body that he needed her in his life.

They reached the pinnacle of pleasure in a slow climb this night, but finally writhed together in its acute glory. No night-time sharing of confidences this time. They merely held each other in silence.

Perhaps in the morning, with the hope of dawn, he could make love to her again and bare his soul to her as they lay next to each other in tangled linens.

Gabe drifted off into disturbed dreams. He was a child again, cast out of doors, alone in a storm, no one near to hear his calls, no one to shelter him. Lightning flashed in his dream and its clap of thunder jarred him awake, his heart pounding.

The sound came again.

Emmaline sat up. The sound repeated. It was not thunder, but something hitting the window, which was open only a crack.

"Someone is out there." She scrambled out of the bed, a sheet wrapped around her.

She lifted the sash and looked out the window.

"Maman!" a voice called in a loud whisper. *"Maman!"*

"Mon Dieu," she cried. "It is Claude." She grabbed her nightdress and put it on. "My son is here."

Chapter Four

Emmaline dashed out, not even bothering to put on a robe. She ran down the stairs, threw open the front door and hugged her only child, who now stood a head taller than she.

He lifted her off her feet and crossed the threshold. *"Maman!"* He spoke in French. "I am here."

Her feet touched the floor again and she stepped back to look at him. In the unlit room she could see little more than a shadow, a shadow that looked so much like her late husband that it made her gasp.

"Let me light a candle so I can see you." She pulled him further into the room. "Why are you here? Have you come home to me?"

"No, *Maman.*" It seemed as if his voice had deepened the few months he'd been away. "You must tell no one, but the army is nearby. Close enough for me to come see you. I cannot stay long. I must return before dawn."

She lit a taper from the dying coals in the kitchen stove and moved around the room lighting candles. "Do you need food? Something to drink?"

"Whatever is quickly prepared." He sank down on her sofa.

In the light she could see his hair, as dark as her own, pulled back in a queue. His face had matured a bit, even to the point of a thin moustache above his lip. He did, indeed, look as Remy must have looked in his youth. Claude wore the blue coat of his uniform with the gray overalls that the soldiers wore to keep their white trousers clean. He would have been able to slip through the streets unseen.

"Do not light too many candles," he told her. "No one must know I am here."

She blew out the one she'd just lit. "I'll bring you some wine." There was wine left in the bottle she and Gabriel had shared. She poured it into a glass for Claude and brought it to him.

Gabriel! She had forgotten. She hoped he did not show himself.

He drank half of it quickly. "Thank you, *Maman*."

She sat opposite him and reached out to touch his face. "I'll prepare your food, but please tell me first if you are well. Tell me why you are so close by."

He took another sip. "I cannot tell you why we are close by, but I am very well. They have allowed me to join the cavalry, Maman. I am a cuirassier. That is a great privilege."

Claude had loved horses from the time he could toddle across a room. When they had travelled with his father, Claude was happiest riding with his father on his horse. Poor Coco, the mare, had been lost to them after Badajoz, another heartbreak for Claude.

Here in Brussels, Emmaline could never afford to keep a horse, but Claude had befriended Mr Engles, who ran a stables nearby. Claude performed whatever chores the man would give him, anything to be with the horses. Eventually Mr Engles began to pay him and Claude saved every franc until he could purchase a horse of his own. Named Coco. Claude rode Coco away to Napoleon's army, and most likely having Coco was why Claude was allowed to join the cuirassiers.

"I am not surprised." She smiled at her son. "You probably ride better than most of them."

Would being in the cavalry keep him safer than the infantry? She prayed it was so.

He finished the wine. "They are veterans of the war and I have learned much from them."

Learned how to fight and kill, she thought. But had they taught him how to face men wanting to kill him?

She took his glass and stood. "I will bring you more. And some food."

He rose and followed her to the kitchen, but suddenly froze. "What is this, Maman?"

She glanced over her shoulder and saw him pointing to Gabriel's red coat, hanging over the chair.

"An *English soldier's* coat?" His voice cracked. He gaped at her in disbelief. After a moment his face flushed with colour. "You have an *English soldier* here?" He looked around, as if the man would step out from behind a curtain.

"Claude, I can explain—"

"Where is he? In your bed?" His voice squeaked again.

Before she could say another word, he dashed to the stairs and leaped up them four at a time.

She ran after him. "Claude. Wait!"

"Show yourself," Claude shouted in French. "Show yourself, you dog."

From the bottom of the stairs, Emmaline glimpsed Gabriel in his shirt and trousers, standing in the doorway of her bedchamber. Claude charged him and they disappeared into the room. As she hurried up the stairs she heard something crash to the floor.

"I'll kill you!" Claude yelled.

Emmaline reached the doorway. From the light of a candle Gabriel must have lit, she could see Claude trying to strike him and Gabriel, larger and stronger, holding him off.

"I'll kill you!" Claude cried again, his arms flailing. He sounded like a wounded child.

"Stop it, Claude." She tried to pull him away from Gabriel. "Someone will hear you. They will discover you are here."

He immediately stopped, but glared at her, his chin trembling. "*He* knows I am here. *He* is the enemy."

"*Non, non,* Claude." Emmaline faced him. "Do you know who this is? Do you?"

He spat. "An Englishman in your bed. How could you do such a thing?" He took two breaths before charging Gabriel again. "Did you force her?"

Gabriel again held him off.

Emmaline jumped between them. "He did not force me, Claude. He is our rescuer. Do you not remember him?"

Claude backed away, looking puzzled.

"This is the captain who kept us safe in Badajoz." She tried to keep her voice down.

"Claude——" Gabriel started.

Claude leaned forwards, pointing his finger at him. "Do not say a word! There is nothing you can say to me, you English dog!"

Emmaline pushed him back. "Calm yourself, Claude. We will go downstairs and talk about this."

He looked as if he was about to cry. "This is traitorous, Maman."

"I cannot be a traitor to Napoleon. I am not in his army. You are." She seized his arm and yanked him towards the door. "Come downstairs." She turned to Gabriel and spoke in English, "Will you come, too?"

Gabriel nodded.

He did not follow immediately, though. Emmaline took advantage and spoke to Claude. "You must remain calm and quiet. If someone hears you yelling and fighting, you will be discovered."

"Do not be a fool, *Maman,*" he countered. "*He* will turn me in. I am already lost."

"*He* is Gabriel Deane, a good man who will do what is right."

A part of her wanted Gabriel to take her son prisoner. At least

Claude would stay alive, but she'd been a soldier's wife too long not to understand that Claude would find being a prisoner worse than death.

Claude sat down on the sofa and she sat down next to him, leaving the chair opposite the sofa for Gabriel.

He entered. "Shall I pour wine?"

"*Oui,* Gabriel. *Merci.*" She forgot to switch to English.

He brought the glasses and the wine and placed them on the table, pouring the first and handing it to Claude.

Claude kept his arms crossed over his chest.

"Take it, Claude," Emmaline said in French.

He rolled his eyes, but did as she said. Gabriel handed the next glass to Emmaline before pouring one for himself.

"Tell Claude I have no intention of hurting you in any way. That—that I have the highest esteem for you," Gabriel said.

Emmaline translated.

Claude closed his eyes as if he wished not to hear. "I cannot speak with him about you, *Maman.* Ask him what he will do with me."

She turned to Gabriel. "Claude believes you will take him prisoner, but I beg you will let him go."

His brow furrowed. "This is asking a great deal of me, Emmaline. My duty—"

Her throat tightened. "Please, Gabriel. Please allow him to leave."

He glanced away, as if thinking.

"What are you saying?" Claude asked her in French.

She gestured for him to be quiet. "Gabriel?"

He rubbed his face. "For you, Emmaline, but only if he swears he has not been gathering information for Napoleon."

She turned to Claude. "Have you come to Brussels for any other reason than to see me?"

He looked surprised. "*Non, Maman.* What other reason could there be?"

"To find out about the English?"

He gave her a withering glance. "I cannot learn anything in the dark. And I must return before light or be branded a deserter." His expression reminded her of when he'd been five years old. "I wanted to see you before—before the battle."

She grasped his hand. He averted his gaze.

She turned to Gabriel. "He only came to see me."

Gabriel nodded. "Very well. I'll do as you desire."

She squeezed Claude's hand. "Gabriel will allow you to go."

He blinked in surprise. "Then I must leave posthaste."

"I will pack you some food." She rose, shaking inside at the thought of saying goodbye to her son, not knowing if he would ever return to her.

She wrapped bread and cheese in a cloth and, with tears pricking her eyes, brought it to him.

He took the package in his hand. "We must blow out the candles."

She blew out the nearest one and started to move to the others, but Gabriel said, "I'll do it."

Claude walked towards the door.

"Claude." Emmaline's throat was tight with emotion. Her son put his arms around her and held her close. "Please be careful," she said. "Come back to me."

"I will, *Maman.*" His voice sounded raspy and very young. "Do not worry." He held her even tighter.

A moment later he was gone, fading into the night like a wisp of smoke.

She covered her face with her hands.

And felt strong arms embracing her again. She turned around and let Gabriel's embrace envelop her. "I am so afraid for him. So afraid I will lose him." She sobbed.

"I know," he murmured. "I know."

When her sobs turned to shudders, he picked her up in his arms and carried her upstairs, laying her on the bed and holding her against him.

When she quieted she said, "I fear I'll never see him again."

"I know," he murmured again.

Gabe rose with the first glimmer of dawn, but he'd hardly slept.

The ring remained hidden in his uniform pocket, along with all his hopes for the future. He'd lain awake most of the night, debating whether to ask her to marry him that morning. Was there any chance at all she'd say yes?

She'd defended him with her son, he'd realised, and with her aunt. That heartened him. He was certain he could convince Madame Laval that an Englishman could be as good for her niece as a Frenchman. And he could show Claude he was nothing like the men who'd killed his father and almost raped his mother.

If he had enough time.

But time was a commodity Gabe no longer possessed. Claude's visit meant the French were near and were not likely to be waiting for the Allied Army and the Prussians to meet them on French soil. If the French were marching into Belgium, the battle was imminent.

He pulled on his clothing and glanced at Emmaline, looking so beautiful in sleep it took his breath away.

He understood why soldiers married on the eve of battle. Merely gazing at her made him desire to pledge his fidelity for ever. For the first time, surviving a battle really meant something to him—he wanted to survive to be with her for ever. And if it was his lot to die in battle, as his wife she would receive all his worldly goods. Either way he could provide her with a secure life.

Gabe picked up his boots and carried them below stairs so his footsteps would not wake her. In the kitchen, he lit the stove and put the kettle on. He made some of the Belgian coffee that he'd become accustomed to. He brought the coffee pot to the dining table. After pouring a cup, he leaned back in the chair, against his coat that still hung there. He reached in to the inside pocket and removed the small velvet box. Opening it, he gazed at the ring, imagining it upon Emmaline's finger.

If he did not propose to her this morning, he might not get a second chance.

He closed his fingers around the velvet box and heard her step on the stairway. He stood and quickly shoved the box in his trouser pocket.

"You are awake already." She sounded weary and tense. "I will make you breakfast."

"No, sit." He pulled out her chair. "I will serve you today."

"*Non,* Gabriel, it is for a woman to do." She took his arm, as if to prevent him from entering the kitchen.

He faced her, placing his hands at her waist and leaning his forehead against hers. They stood silent that way, Gabriel savouring her scent, her heat, the softness of her skin.

"Today I will cook for you," he said again, easing her into her chair, stroking a stray lock of hair off her forehead.

He walked into the kitchen and cracked the eggs into the pan. He glanced back at her.

She sat with her elbows on the table, her face in her hands. Thinking of her son, he thought. Worrying over him. Missing him.

When Gabe had been a boy, returning from visiting his uncle on the farm, he'd sometimes wondered if his family had noticed he'd been gone. It often seemed as if they greeted him the same as they would if he'd been gone an hour.

He shook his head and attended to the eggs. This was time to think of Emmaline, not himself.

He poured her coffee and placed her eggs on a plate, adding

bread, butter and jam. She looked up as he approached, putting a smile on her face. As he sat opposite her, he felt the ring in his pocket, reminding him of his decision.

Later, he would ask her, after she finished eating.

"This is very good." She looked at him and he could tell she was trying to be cheerful.

Their conversation was forced, all the ease between them these past weeks gone. They talked mostly of the food, as if they were two strangers seated together at a dinner party. When finished, Gabe gathered the dishes and carried them back into the kitchen.

Emmaline followed him, putting her palm on his back. "I will tend to the dishes. You have done enough." She glanced out of the window that looked over a narrow alley. "It is very light outside. I will have to open the shop soon."

Gabe thrust his hand in his pocket and closed his fingers around the velvet box. He released it and drew his hand out to touch her on her shoulders. "Come away for a moment." He led her to the sofa and sat down with her, clasping her hand in his. "I have something to ask you."

She met his gaze with interest, but only as much as if he were preparing to ask her what she would like him to purchase for their dinner.

He glanced down at her hand, imagining the ring on her long, graceful fingers.

"We have had a short time together," he began.

She nodded, her expression turning wary. "You are going to say goodbye to me."

He squeezed her hand. "I am going to propose that I never say goodbye to you."

Her brows rose.

"Emmaline, I am asking you to marry me. I want you—want to be with you for ever."

She paled. "Marry me?"

"I know the timing is ill. With Napoleon's army so near, there must be a battle soon. But maybe we can marry quickly. I will find out the rules, see if it is possible—"

She pulled her hand away. "We cannot marry!"

His heart was pounding fast. "Maybe not before the battle, but afterwards, then."

She jumped to her feet. "*Non,* Gabriel. How can I marry you? You are a British soldier."

"I can sell my commission. After the battle."

Her eyes flashed. "After the battle? Do you think that will make a difference?"

His face stung as if she'd slapped him. "Have I not shown you in every possible way the sort of man I am? Have we not been happy together?"

She looked away. "It is not the sort of happiness that can last."

"Has it not been, Emmaline?" Gabe rubbed his hand against the outside of his pocket, feeling the box through the cloth. "I have experienced enjoyment that is meant to be fleeting. I know the difference. You cannot pretend this was a mere diversion for you."

She could not meet his eye. "Of course I have enjoyed being with you, but I do not want to marry you."

He leaned towards her. "Why?"

She took a breath. "My son despises you—"

"He does not know me. When the war is over, there will be time—"

She lifted her hand for him to stop. "The war will never be over for Claude. Do you not see? It will never be settled in his heart. I have tried—" Her voice cracked with emotion. She looked into his eyes. "I am all Claude has. He has lost too much. He has endured too much. I cannot abandon him."

"I do not wish you to abandon him. He is a part of you. I want you both." Gabriel's insides felt as if they'd turned to stone. He knew even as he spoke the words that he'd lost her, that, if she believed she must choose between them, she must choose her son.

She lowered her gaze and her long lashes made shadows on her cheeks. "No, Gabriel. I cannot turn away from my son. Not even for you."

He felt as if he'd had the breath knocked out of him. His very reason to exist had simply vanished like smoke into thin air.

He turned away and retrieved his coat.

Emmaline's chest constricted as she watched him put on his coat, his back to her. Never had it occurred to her that he might want to marry her. How could he have thought of this time as anything but a brief affair? Soldiers were always having liaisons in whatever place they were billeted. She'd seen it herself and, of course, Remy had threatened her with it when she had balked at going to Spain with him.

But Gabriel had said the word *marriage,* and all she could see was the hurt and anger and betrayal in Claude's eyes from the night before.

She wanted more than anything to believe their days and nights could continue as they had done, full of passion and pleasure and companionship, but she knew better. He could promise her anything, but he could not promise to heal Claude's wounds. Once, long ago, she'd chosen a husband's wishes above what she'd known was best for her son. She would not do so again.

Or Claude might be lost for ever.

Gabriel, his back still to her, buttoned his coat, his scarlet uniform coat, the coat he would wear in the battle when the Allied forces met Napoleon's army, when this man who had given her so much happiness would face her son, who knew nothing of what it was to fight in a battle.

Men died in battle.

For the thousandth time she prayed that God would spare Claude's life. She prayed for Gabriel, as well.

Even though she would never see him again.

He walked to the door without looking at her. Her legs trembled and the room seemed to close in on her.

He opened the door, but turned to her. "Goodbye, Emmaline." His voice was so soft she could hardly hear him.

A moment later he was gone.

Wanting to sink to the floor in a miserable heap, Emmaline instead forced herself to square her shoulders, to tackle the chores that needed finishing before she opened the shop. She started for the kitchen to wash the dishes, but something on the dining table caught her eye.

A small black-velvet box.

Chapter Five

Gabe made his way back to his hotel as if wearing blinders, noticing no one and nothing, not even the weather. On previous mornings, he'd savoured this same walk, enjoying all the sights and sounds, savouring the fresh morning air. This morning his mind was as mechanical as an automaton, turning it over and over that Emmaline was lost to him.

Back in his room at the Hôtel de Flandre Gabe shaved and changed. He would regain control of his emotions, he told himself. There were plenty of women in the world besides Emmaline, women with whom to share brief moments of pleasure. It would be enough. No longer would he dream of a home, a wife, a family. He would remain in the army where he belonged.

Conjuring up visions of another life had been a momentary lapse of sanity.

As a soldier he had one duty now. For Emmaline he had compromised that duty, delaying the report that the French were near, but he would delay no longer.

Gabe went straight to the Allied Army headquarters. As he entered the white-stone building, the two men he least desired to encounter walked towards him: Edwin Tranville, the man who'd tried to rape Emmaline, and his father, General Lord Tranville.

The general had managed to inherit a title since Gabe had last seen him.

"What are you doing here, Deane?" the general barked. As a greeting, it was one of Tranville's most cordial. His son, whose face bore a scar from his temple to his mouth, created by Emmaline's knife, did not even bother to acknowledge him.

"Sir." Gabe bowed to the general, a respect the man did not deserve. "I need to see Wellington or one of his aides-de-camp."

"You?" Tranville's brows rose. "What reason could you possibly have to see the Duke or his aides?"

If Tranville had not been Gabe's superior officer, he would not have replied. "The French army has crossed into Belgium."

Tranville frowned. "How can you know that? What evidence do you have?"

"I encountered a French soldier in the city last night." This was wasting Gabe's time.

Tranville's eyes narrowed. "Encountered? Where?"

Gabe glanced from the general to his son, who was now leaning against the wall, as if needing it to keep him upright. How much did Edwin remember about that night in Badajoz? Gabe wondered. Had he told his father about it?

No matter what, Gabe refused to lead them to Emmaline. "I saw him on the street."

Tranville laughed. "On the street? Not having a casual stroll through the Parc? Do not be a damned fool. If you saw anything at all, it was probably a Dutch infantryman."

"I did not mistake the uniform. The man was not desiring to be seen and why would a Dutch infantryman be trying to hide?"

Why did he even bother arguing with Tranville? Gabe did not care if Tranville believed him or not. "In any event, I feel it is my duty to report it."

Tranville's nostrils flared. "Do not mention this to Wellington. Do not waste his Grace's time."

Gabe shrugged. "To one of his aides, then."

Tranville huffed. "You will say nothing. Am I making myself clear? Your duty has been discharged by making your report to me."

Gabe persisted. "And you will pass on this information?"

The general's voice rose. "As I am your superior officer, you will not question what I will or will not do. The Duchess of Richmond is giving a ball tonight, in case you did not know, and I will not have his Grace and other *gentlemen* distracted by this foolishness." He emphasized the word *gentlemen.*

When General Tranville became Gabe's superior officer, he had made certain that Gabe did not rise in rank past captain. The general did not believe in field promotions or those based on merit. Gabe had come from the merchant class and only true gentlemen advanced the proper way, by purchasing a higher rank. It was a matter of pride to Gabe that he did not advance through purchase, although his family, and now he, could have afforded it.

Tranville waved a dismissive hand. "Go see to your men or whatever nonsense you must attend to. You can have no further business here."

A string of invectives rushed to the tip of Gabe's tongue. He clamped his teeth together.

"Yes, sir!" he responded, bowing and performing a precise about-face.

Gabe walked away, keeping a slow pace so that Tranville would not suspect he'd been roused to anger.

As he reached the door to the outside, he heard Edwin drawl, "How very tiresome."

Later that evening Gabe learned his information had been accurate and that General Tranville had not passed it on. Wellington heard about Napoleon's march towards Brussels at the Duchess of Richmond's ball, a good twelve hours after Gabriel reported it to Tranville. Wellington was said to have remarked, "Napoleon has humbugged me, by God. He has gained twenty-four hours' march on me."

Gabe would have saved Wellington half that time.

The next day Gabe's regiment, the Royal Scots, joined other Allied forces at Quatre Bras where they met the French. How quickly it all came back, the pounding of cannon, the thundering of horses, battle cries and wounded screams, a terrible, familiar world, more real to Gabe than his idyll at Brussels. The fighting was hard, but almost comforting in its familiarity.

Musket volleys assaulted Gabe and his men. Six times steel-helmeted cuirassiers charged at them with slashing swords.

As Gabe yelled to his soldiers to stand fast, he scanned the French cavalry thundering towards them. Was Emmaline's Claude among them? Would Gabe see her son struck down? Would his own sword be forced to do the deed?

The weather turned foul. Black storm clouds rolled in and soon thunder and lightning competed with the roar of cannon. Late in the battle Gabe glimpsed the cuirassiers charging upon the 69th Regiment, seizing their colours. Feeling traitorous, Gabe blew out a relieved breath. If the French cuirassiers had been vanquished, Claude would have had a greater chance of being one of the casualties. Gabe prayed Claude had survived.

For Emmaline's sake.

The battle ended in a great deal of mud, with neither side the victor, and both the Allies and the French retreated.

The following day Gabe's regiment marched to a location Wellington had chosen to next engage Napoleon, near a village called Waterloo.

That night the rain continued to fall in thick, unrelenting sheets, soaking the earth into mud. Gabe and Allan Landon, now a captain like himself, were fortunate to share a reasonably dry billet with another officer. After Badajoz, Gabe had become good friends with Landon, although their temperaments and backgrounds were often directly opposed to each other. Landon, with his rigid sense of right and wrong, came from an aristocratic family and had, God help him, political ambitions. Gabe would rather impale himself on his sword than deal with politics.

Good thing he had never told Landon about partaking of the spoils of war. At Vittoria, in Spain, Napoleon's brother, Joseph Bonaparte, had fled in panic, abandoning his riches, which were scattered across a field, tempting even the most honest of men. Gabe, like countless other soldiers, had filled his pockets. Not Landon, though. Landon had been appalled.

The shack's roof pounded with the rain. Gabe and Landon huddled near their small fire that gave them little relief from the chill.

One of the junior officers, streams of water dripping off the capes of his cloak, appeared in their doorway of their shack. "General Tranville wants to see you, Captains."

Gabe groaned. "More nonsense. I'll make a wager with you."

Landon clapped him on the back. "You know I never gamble."

They wrapped themselves in their cloaks and dashed through the downpour to the peasant's hut that Tranville had made his billet.

"Mind your boots! Mind your boots!" Tranville shouted as they entered. Edwin, a sour look on his scarred face, manned the door.

They cleaned as much of the mud off as they could, the rain sneaking down the collars of their coats. After closing the door behind them, Edwin took a swig from a flask. Some sort of spirits, Gabe reckoned.

Tranville barked orders at them, nothing more than mere posturing, however.

He fixed the men with what he must have thought was a steely glare. "I'll have no laggardly behaviour, do you hear? You tell your men they are to hop to or they'll answer to me."

"Yes, sir!" chirped a young lieutenant.

Gabe put on his most bland expression. He could endure Tranville for this brief period, but only because it was warm and dry in the hut.

"Landon," Tranville went on, "I want you to find Picton tonight. See if he has any message for me."

General Picton was the commander of the 5th Division of which the Royal Scots were a part. Landon's task was to carry messages for Picton and Tranville during the battle, but it was ridiculous to send Landon out in this weather merely on the off chance Picton might have a message.

Landon must have had the same reaction. He glanced over to the small window, its wooden shutters clattering from the wind and rain. "Yes, sir."

"And stay available to me tomorrow. I may need you during the battle."

Landon knew that already, of course. "Yes, sir."

Tranville nodded in obvious approval. His gaze drifted to Gabe and his lips pursed, but luckily his glance continued to his son, who was sitting on a stool sneaking sips from his flask.

There was a knock on the door and Tranville signalled for Edwin to open it. With a desultory expression, Edwin complied.

"Oh, Good God," Edwin drawled, stepping aside.

Jack Vernon, the ensign—now lieutenant—who'd been with them in Badajoz, stood in the doorway.

Gabe poked Landon to call his attention to Vernon. He noticed that Tranville caught his gesture and quickly erased any expression from his face.

Vernon slanted a glance at Gabe and Landon before turning back to Tranville and handing him a message.

Tranville snatched the paper from Vernon's hand and snapped at him, "You will wait for my reply."

Gabe exchanged another glance with Landon. This was not the first time Vernon and Tranville had encountered each other, obviously. Whatever had transpired between them had left them acrimonious.

Tranville stretched his arm and seemed to be writing as slowly as he could. He dragged out this interaction with Vernon, presuming it would annoy the lieutenant, no doubt. Finally Tranville said, "Leave now."

Landon spoke up, "With your permission, I'll leave now, as well."

"Go." He waved him away.

Vernon left, Landon right behind him.

"Do you have further need of me?" asked Gabe.

"Of course not," snapped Tranville. "All of you go."

Once outside Tranville's billet, Landon and Gabe pulled Vernon aside. "Do you have time for some tea?" Landon asked.

Vernon nodded gratefully.

They led him through the rain to the shack and heated a kettle on the small fire. The third officer in the billet lay snoring in a corner.

When they finally warmed their hands on the tin mugs of tea, Vernon glanced to their sleeping mate and back to them. "I need to tell you. I broke my word about keeping silent about Badajoz. I was forced to tell General Tranville."

Gabe straightened. "Tranville!"

Vernon held up his hand. "It was not something I wished to do, but I had little choice. I showed him the drawings I made of the incident. Tranville threatened my family; the only way I could silence him was by threatening to expose Edwin. You are safe," he assured them. "I did not show enough to identify you, not even your uniforms."

"Did you show the woman's face? Or her son's?" Gabe asked, his chest tightening.

Vernon shook his head.

Relieved, Gabe rubbed his face. "Damned Tranville. I hope some Frenchman puts a ball through his head."

"Watch your tongue, Gabe," Landon cautioned, gesturing to their sleeping roommate.

Vernon rose. "I had better deliver my message."

Gabe shook his hand.

Before he walked out he turned to Gabe. "What of the woman, Captain? Do you think she found a safe place for herself and her son?"

"She did," Gabe answered. "In fact, she lives in Brussels. I saw her there."

Landon sat up straight. "You did not tell me that."

Gabe shrugged. There was no more he wanted to say.

"And the boy?" Vernon asked.

Gabe looked from one to the other. "In the army." Let them think he had joined a Belgian regiment.

After Vernon left, Landon turned to Gabe. "How did you come to know the woman was in Brussels?"

"I encountered her by chance." Which was almost the truth, if you didn't add that he deliberately pursued her all the way to her shop.

"I thought she was French," Landon said.

"She came to Belgium to live with a relative, she said." He did not wish to talk about her. "I do not know a great deal more."

Except everything she'd shared as they lay in each other's arms after making love. Except how her smile seemed to make colours brighter. How the warmth of her skin made him feel as if he'd come home at last.

Landon dropped the subject and soon left to find Picton. For the rest of the night Gabe tried to ignore the water dripping from the ceiling and the wind whistling through the cracks in the walls. Mostly he tried not to think of Emmaline, how comforting it felt to sleep next to her, how wrenching it felt to lose her.

He needed sleep before facing cannonade, charging cavalry and thousands of soldiers marching towards them to the sound of the *Pas de Charge*.

The next day the rain dwindled to a light drizzle, but did not cease until mid-morning when the sun was finally visible again. Everyone prepared for what they knew would be the main battle.

Gabe conferred with his lieutenants and saw to the readiness of his company, ensuring they had dry powder and plenty of ammunition. His uniform was damp from the incessant rain, but those of his men were soaked through. As the sun heated the air, clouds of vapor rose from their coats and from the ground, lending an eerie cast to the scene.

The two armies faced each other across a gently sloping valley at a right angle to the Brussels road. One farm, La Haye Sainte, fortified by the King's German Legion, was on one side of the valley. Hougoumont, another farm, occupied by the Coldstream Guards, was on the other. Gabe's Royal Scots, along with other regiments of British, Dutch, German and Belgian troops, were strung the length between the farms with the forest of Soignes to their backs. Wellington ordered these troops to remain on the back slope of the ridge, so for most of them the battle was heard and not seen. Gabe witnessed a bit more from horseback. He watched the first attack on Hougoumont a little before noon, the first action of the day. Two hours later it was the Royal Scots' turn. The formidable French column advanced into the valley. The ground trembled under their feet. Their drums pounded in the Allies' ears as they marched up the hill.

The Royal Scots and the other regiments were ready. Hidden behind the crest, Gabe held his men back until Picton gave the order. All at once the British rose up in front of the French column and fired. Front ranks, standing shoulder to shoulder, fired on order, then dropped down to reload. Those behind them moved forwards and fired. Front ranks advanced again. Volley after nonstop volley poured into the French columns. Countless Frenchmen fell, only to be trampled on by the hoards of their comrades marching behind them.

Gabe rode along the line of his men, urging them to stand and keep firing, but, as devastating as their muskets were, there were simply too many enemy soldiers coming at them. In seconds they would be overpowered.

All was not lost. The British cavalry came in the nick of time, charging down the hill, routing the French infantry. Gabe cheered the French infantry's frantic retreat. He watched the cavalry cut a swathe through the fleeing men, slaughtering them as if scything grain.

The sight brought relief, but no pleasure, and soon turned to horror. The British cavalry were cut off by French cuirassiers. The tables were turned, and now it was the British on the run and the French cavalry on the slaughter.

Was Emmaline's Claude among them? Gabe wondered. Was he quenching his thirst for vengeance, or had he already fallen? Claude was too young and new to battle to hone the instinct for survival that became second nature to veteran soldiers, an instinct that had served Gabe well.

By four o'clock, fighting continued around Hougoumont and La Haye Sainte and Gabe prepared for another attack of infantry. Again the men were pulled back to the far side of the ridge. Gabe rode to the crest of the hill to see for himself what they would face next. Again the ground trembled, but this time with the pounding of horses' hooves. Like a huge, unstoppable wave thousands of French cavalry, line after line of them, charged directly towards them.

Wellington gave the order to form square, a battlefield formation where men stood three deep, a line presenting bayonets, a line to fire, a line to reload. Cavalry horses would not charge into the bayonets and the muskets could fire at will. The interior of the square sheltered the wounded, the artillerymen and the officers, whose job it was to make sure the men stood fast, kept shooting and closed any gap.

"Fire at the horses," Gabe shouted to his men. Without his horse, a cavalryman was helpless.

Gabe wound up in the same square as Landon, who, thank God, was unscathed. Gabe might have got his wish about General Tranville. He'd been seen falling from his horse during that first infantry charge and no one had seen him since. His son Edwin, coward that he was, had disappeared at the beginning of the battle. Gabe presumed he was hiding somewhere that cannon fire and musket balls could not reach.

"Fire at the horses," Gabe yelled again. "Stand fast."

Gabe's square held and, as far as he could tell, the other British squares held as well, even though the French charged again and again. Between charges Landon rode off to render assistance to Hougoumont, which was now on fire. Gabe stayed with his company, their numbers dwindling with each attack, the square becoming smaller and smaller.

The ground around them was littered with dead and dying horses and men, their screams melding with the boom of cannon and crack of musket fire. The air filled with smoke and it was difficult to see much further than ten to twelve feet.

Between cavalry attacks, Gabe worried that the French would train their artillery on the squares, or that more columns of infantry would join the charge. Neither happened. Just more cavalry. As the latest onslaught neared, a gap formed on one side of the square. Gabe rode to it. "Close the gap," he ordered.

A cuirassier on a dark bay horse rode directly for the opening, but Gabe's men fired on him as they closed ranks again. The rider jerked like a rag doll as several balls hit him. The horse was such a beauty, Gabe was glad his men had missed it. Its rider tumbled from the saddle as the horse ran on. The man rolled towards the square, landing about four feet from Gabe. His helmet came off and bounced into the body of a French comrade.

Facing Gabe was the youthful countenance of Claude Mableau. The boy struggled to rise. One of his men aimed his musket at him.

"Do not fire," Gabe cried, dismounting. "He's no threat." He ran out of the square and grabbed Claude by the collar, dragging him inside to where the other wounded lay.

"A Frenchie, Captain?" one of the man asked.

"Spare him," Gabe ordered, not caring if the man thought him soft on the French. "He's just a boy."

Emmaline's boy.

Chapter Six

She'd heard the guns all day, the booming of cannon fire, like the thunder of the two previous days without the rain.

Everyone said this was the big battle, not the one two days before when the cannons were also heard. It seemed to Emmaline that plenty of wounded men came into Brussels after that one. If this were the big battle, it could only get worse.

Tante Voletta had insisted they close the shop and pack up all the lace to hide in the attic.

"Those English will use our lace for bandages, I am sure of it," her aunt had said. "They are gauche."

For two days they packed away lace. It helped make the time pass, but now that the task was done, nothing was left to distract her. Emmaline's heart seized with fear at each battle sound. Did that cannon ball strike Claude? Was he anywhere near it? Would he come back to her? Or had he died already, in that first battle? Had he been placed at the front of the charge so the musket balls would hit him first?

He was a soldier's son, she forced herself to remember. Perhaps he was born with a soldier's sense of self-preservation. Besides, she would know if he died. She was certain she would feel his life leave his body as profoundly as she felt when she gave birth to him.

Tante Voletta sent her out to purchase stores of food. Many of the English had fled to Antwerp, but still what shops were open had few supplies. Perhaps other shopkeepers had hidden their stock, as well.

The streets remained busy with wagons carrying supplies, people fleeing or wounded arriving. Rumours were everywhere. On one corner it was believed that Napoleon was at the city gates; on another corner the Allies had him in retreat. Either way the rumours went made Emmaline feel sick inside. There could be no possible victory for her in this battle.

A wagon of wounded British soldiers came into view. Emmaline ran alongside it. "What news of the battle?" she asked them.

"Bloody hard going," one of the soldiers answered, which told her nothing.

Their red coats reminded her of Gabriel. Perhaps they knew how he fared. "Are you Royal Scots?"

"No, ma'am," he answered.

The wagon rolled on.

Emmaline put her fingers on her chest, feeling for the beautiful ring she wore on a chain around her neck, hidden under her clothing. Somehow she did not believe a mere war could kill Gabriel Deane. He was too clever, too strong and too good a man to be lost to battle. She only wished they could have parted with loving words, not the harsh ones that had escaped her lips when she refused his proposal.

She closed her eyes and could still see the wounded look on his face. Why had he not understood? It was impossible for her to marry Gabriel, a British soldier, when her son so vehemently hated him. Gabriel should have known that.

The sound of a hundred hooves thundered in her ears. She dropped her basket as an entire regiment of Hanoverian cavalry galloped past her. Emmaline froze, expecting to see Napoleon himself on the heels of these German horsemen.

No one came.

She bent down to retrieve her basket and was seized with a sharp anxiety, like shafts piercing her skin. No more shops—she just wanted to go home, to wait in solitude for some final word of who was winning and who was losing, who was alive and who had died. Whether Claude would return to her.

The towers of St Michael's Cathedral loomed above her. She glanced up at them and whispered a prayer that God would deliver Claude back to her.

She added a prayer for Gabriel. Not for him to return, but for him to live.

She crossed herself and hurried to the lace shop, walking around the back and entering the yard through the gate. After opening the rear door of the shop, she climbed the stairs to her aunt's rooms.

"This is all you could purchase?" Her aunt took the basket from Emmaline's hands and peered inside it.

She wrapped her arms around her still-shaking chest. "There was not much to buy."

A cannon boomed and they both turned towards the sound.

"I am weary of that!" her aunt exclaimed. She examined each item in the basket. "Did you hear any news of the battle?"

Emmaline shook her head. "No one knows the outcome."

"Pfft!" Tante Voletta waved a hand. "Napoleon will win."

Emmaline kept silent. She did not want the French to win. Claude would never leave the army if that happened. "Do you need my company? Because I would rather go to my own rooms."

"Go," her aunt said. "But come to me when you learn of the victory."

Emmaline, however, did not go out in search of news.

She spent the evening on her sofa, hugging her knees and repeating her prayers. She lay down and pressed her hand against the ring under her dress. As she felt its circle in her fingers, she watched the flame of a single candle. The cannonade stopped and as darkness fell she could hear the rumble of wagons passing through the streets. Her candle grew shorter and shorter and soon her eyes grew heavy. She fought to stay awake. How could she sleep while the fate of her son was in question?

The sounds in the street were rhythmic and lulling. Her eyes closed.

And flew open again.

A loud rapping at the door startled her awake. She sat up, heart pounding.

"Emmaline," she heard a man's voice. "Open the door."

Gabriel!

She flew to the door and pulled it open.

He was a mere shadow in the dark yard, but as he stepped inside, she could see he carried something over his shoulder.

Her eyes widened.

"I've brought your son."

"Claude!" Her hands clasped over her mouth. Was he dead? "Claude!"

"He's wounded." Without another word he carried him upstairs.

She grabbed the candle and followed. Claude's head lolled back and forth with each step Gabriel made.

Gabriel opened the door to Claude's room and placed him on the bed. Immediately he began to undress him.

Emmaline lit more candles, her hands trembling. "Where is he hurt?"

"His head." He ripped away Claude's bloody shirt. "His neck. And leg."

She stood by the bed, finally able to touch her son. She helped pull off his trousers, stained with his blood. He'd been shot in the thigh, but a quick examination showed that the musket ball had passed through. On his neck, right above his collarbone, was another wound. She placed a finger near the spot.

Claude flinched and moaned—signs of life, at least.

"Water." Gabriel's voice sounded forced. "Need to wash. See the wounds better."

She sprang to her feet. "I'll fetch some."

She returned with a stack of towels, a pitcher of water, a basin and cup. As she placed them on the bedside table, Gabriel swayed and looked as if he might collapse to the floor.

She hurried to him, helping him regain his balance. "Are you injured, Gabriel?"

He shook his head. "Tired."

"Sit in the chair." She eased him over to a wooden chair near the bed and ran to pour him a cup of the water.

He drank it greedily, but gestured for her to return to Claude.

Emmaline washed away blood and mud and bits of grass and cloth from her son's skin and from his hair. Beneath his matted hair was a long gash. A musket ball had scraped him, but had not penetrated. His thigh had a huge hole in it from which blood still oozed. His chest was riddled with round red spots, turning to bruises.

"His chest plate stopped some of the musket balls," Gabriel said. The cuirassiers wore steel chest plates, like the armour of medieval times.

The most worrisome wound was the one on his neck. The musket ball needed to come out.

She turned to Gabriel. "He needs a surgeon."

He rubbed his face. "Won't find one. There are thousands who need a surgeon. Most worse off." His gaze met hers. "Too many." A haunted expression came over his face.

Emmaline could not allow herself to think of what horrors he'd seen. She must think only of Claude, how to keep him alive.

She forced herself to remain calm. "I will remove the ball."

"Emmaline—" he began in a warning tone.

She set her jaw in resolve. "There is no other choice. I have seen it done before. I must try."

She ran from the room and gathered any items she could think of that would help her remove the ball: her knitting needles, a long embroidery hook, tweezers, scissors. The sky was turning light. At least she would be able to see better.

Back in Claude's room, she pushed the bed to the window and set her tools on the bed next to her son.

Gabriel rose from the chair. "I'll hold him still."

How he would have the strength to do so, she didn't know, but he stood on the opposite side of the bed and held Claude's shoulders. She carefully inserted the knitting needle into the wound to find the path of the musket ball. Claude's eyes opened and he cried out. Gabriel held him fast.

Swallowing against a sudden wave of nausea, Emmaline did not have to probe far. "It is not deep!"

Her tweezers were about five inches long, plenty of length to reach the ball. It took several tries to pull it out, all the while Claude writhing with the pain of it. He quickly lost consciousness and became limp. Finally she manoeuvred the ball to the opening and was able to hold it between her fingers. Gabriel released Claude and leaned against the wall.

"One more thing if you can stand it," she said to Gabriel. "I want to sew his head wound closed."

Gabriel's arms trembled as he held Claude's head while Emmaline put thread and needle through the skin, but Claude did not regain consciousness.

"Sit down now," she told Gabriel after she was done.

She bandaged the wounds and covered Claude with clean linens and a blanket. He again moaned, but it was a relief to hear him make any sound. Later, as she had done when he was ill as a child, she would spoon broth down his throat and wipe his brow with cool compresses if he became feverish. There was little else she could do.

She stepped back from his bed.

Gabriel rose. "I must leave."

She touched his arm. "Take some food first. Something to drink." She wanted to tell him not to leave her, to stay. With his steadying presence, she felt as if she could do anything to keep Claude alive. Without him, she was alone.

She walked downstairs with him and made him sit at the table where he'd sat so many happier times before.

"Just something to drink," he said.

She gave him wine and he drank it like water.

"Now I must go." He stood again and walked towards the door.

"Gabriel." She ran to him as he opened the door. "Who won the battle?"

He gave her a weary look. "The Allies."

She was relieved. When—*if*—Claude recovered, he would not return to the French army. There would be no need if the British had won. He could have a normal, peaceful life.

Gabriel put his hand on the doorknob again.

"Gabriel!" she called again.

He turned.

She swallowed against a threat of tears. "Thank you for my son."

He touched her face with a gentle hand and started to walk away.

She seized his arm. "Gabriel. How did you find him? You said there were so many…"

Again a bleak look crossed his face. "The cuirassiers attacked. I saw him fall near me."

"They let you save him?" Surely it would be difficult to protect a Frenchman when so many were in need.

His eyes turned hard. "No one could stop me." He crossed the threshold and made his way to the gate and out of her life.

Emmaline leaned against the door jamb, tears burning her eyes, a sob choking her throat. What had he risked for her?

To save her son.

Chapter Seven

London—June 1817

Two years after the battle of Waterloo, Gabe's life could not have been more altered. Waterloo had ended the war and Napoleon had been exiled to Saint Helena, far enough away in the south Atlantic to pose no further threat. For a time, Gabe's Royal Scots had been part of the Army of Occupation in France. Gabe wished they'd been sent somewhere more distant, not so close to Brussels, not so filled with reminders of what he most wanted to forget.

The orders finally came that the whole battalion would be shipped to Canterbury. Once there, however, Gabe's battalion was disbanded and he was placed on half-pay. In what seemed like an instant he had no regiment, no orders and literally nothing to do.

Now he was in London and, like other officers let loose in a non-military world, was haunting the Horse Guards hoping to discover a regiment looking for officers, or visiting the War Office to get the forms necessary to write to regimental agents for a commission to purchase. On this warm June afternoon Gabe strode into the War Office to pick up more copies of the form the office had run out of the week before. Gabe had performed this same errand the day before and the day before that, without success. He was not optimistic that this day would yield a different result.

Three other officers of his acquaintance were on their way out.

"Deane!" one of them cried, slapping him on the back. "Come for more forms, have you?" He spoke with a thick Irish accent that had earned him the nickname 'Irishman'.

"Indeed," Gabe responded without enthusiasm. "Are you going to tell me they have a new supply?"

Another man, Major Hanson, stepped up. "Not going to tell you that. Webberly even offered a bribe if the fellow would find him one copy, but apparently there are still none to be had today. Maybe tomorrow, the fellow said."

Webberly, the third of the trio, shook his head. "I was certain a bribe would work."

Gabe gave him an impassive look. "I'd be grateful for the opportunity to pay a bribe." What else was he to do with his money?

Hanson jostled him. "Do not speak so loud. The clerks will smell a profit."

The clerks already knew of Gabe's willingness to bribe them for more forms. He'd made the offer days ago.

Irishman laughed. "Now, Captain Deane, my dear fellow, are you so eager for a commission? It would mean leaving our company and the fine accommodations of the Stephen's Hotel."

They all had rooms in the Stephen's Hotel on Bond Street, a place popular with military men.

Gabe responded with sarcasm, "Not at all. I'm merely pining for the lost luxuries of army life."

"You are wasting your time today, Deane," Hanson told him. "Come with us. We plan to make great use of a tavern and deprive it of several pints of ale."

It was tempting to seek the oblivion that alcohol could bring. Most of the officers at Stephen's Hotel drank too much, but, after

Brussels, Gabe had learned that whatever you wanted to drown with drink was still with you when morning came. Along with the devil of a headache.

"Not this time."

The men bid him goodbye, and Gabe proceeded to the clerk's desk anyway.

The clerk barely glanced at him. "No forms today. Maybe tomorrow."

Gabe tapped on the man's desk with a finger. "If the forms do arrive tomorrow, will you save me some?"

The clerk raised one brow. "For the amount we agreed upon?"

Gabe gave him a level stare. "Indeed."

The clerk grinned. "We have a wager going here as to who among you officers will be the first to break down and accept a commission to the West Indies."

The 1st battalion of the Royal Scots was stationed in the West Indies. There were always commissions open there, because so many officers caught fevers and died.

Gabe had survived that dreadful place once; he had no desire to chance it again, even if it would free him from the tedium of London.

Gabe had already travelled to Manchester, the home of his youth and where his family still resided, a place he'd not seen for at least ten years. It was nearly like going to a foreign land. Factories and warehouses had sprouted everywhere. Nieces and nephews had sprouted as well, too many for him to count. His mother and father had turned shockingly old and neither they nor his brothers or sisters seemed to know what to do with him.

He'd wound up spending most of his time with a twelve-year-old nephew who asked question after question about every battle on the Peninsula and every detail of Waterloo. The boy had reminded him of Emmaline's Claude, or, more accurately, what he imagined Claude might have been like if not for Badajoz.

After a few weeks of intense discomfort on all sides, Gabe made an excuse to leave. He suspected the family was relieved he was no longer there to distract them from the routines of running what was now a very prosperous drapery warehouse. With Manchester's new mills and a canal that improved the shipping of goods, the town seemed to have turned into a Garden of Eden for cloth merchants.

After Manchester, Gabe visited his uncle on the hill farm. Even that idyll was about to be lost. Stapleton Farm was up for sale and his uncle would soon be vying with younger men by the scores who were also seeking employment. Had matters turned out differently in Brussels, Gabe might have bought the place. He'd learned his lesson, though. He belonged in the army. No sense dreaming otherwise.

He'd returned to London and the tedious days of applying for a commission. What odds were offered that he would be the one to break down and go to the West Indies? Surely he'd be a safe bet.

"I'll be back tomorrow," he said to the clerk who'd already turned his attention back to the papers on his desk.

"Undoubtedly," the man replied.

Gabe walked out of the office and back on to the street. He took a breath.

Lawd. He needed more to do. Exercising his horse in the morning and visiting the War Office or Horse Guards in the afternoon was simply not enough.

Most of his fellow officers attended society balls and other entertainments in the evenings, hoping to find a wealthy heiress to marry. Even that occupation was closed to Gabe. With the glut of younger sons in town, the son of a merchant was no matrimonial prize. Besides, marriage was not in the cards for him. He'd learned that lesson in Brussels.

Gabe walked slowly back to the hotel, ignoring the book shops, ironmongers, milliners and tea shops on Bond Street. Head down, he approached the entrance of Stephen's Hotel, hoping not to see anyone he knew. He was not in a humour for friendly discourse on the weather or any other subject. As he entered the hotel, he removed his shako and threw his gloves inside it. Holding it under his arm, he crossed the hall, making his way to the stairway.

"Captain!" The footman who attended the lobby called after him. "Captain!"

He'd almost made good his escape. Turning, he fixed his fiercest glare on the unfortunate fellow.

The man took a step back. "Ah, sir." He bowed. "You have a caller. Waiting in the front parlour." The footman gestured to the room and withdrew posthaste.

Gabe clenched his hand into a fist. Who did he know in London who would call upon him? Allan Landon, perhaps? He'd seen Allan a few weeks ago, but neither of them had shared their direction. He knew other officers, but they were all staying in this hotel. If they wished to waste his time, they would simply knock at his door.

He rubbed his forehead.

On the other hand, he had written countless letters trying to find a commission. Maybe his caller had an answer for him.

He entered the room, dropping his hat on a table inside the door.

The parlour looked empty at first, although the curtains were open and fresh flowers were in a vase on the mantel.

A sound came from the high-backed chair facing the fireplace. A swish of skirts and a peek of a bonnet.

A woman?

She stood before him. *"Bon jour, Gabriel."*

Emmaline.

She looked even more beautiful than the image of her that inhabited his dreams at night. Her lace-lined bonnet of natural straw perfectly framed her flawless face. The dark blue of her walking dress made her eyes even more vibrant.

Good God. After two years, she still had the power to affect him.

"What are you doing here?" His tone came out more sharply than he intended.

She clasped her white-gloved hands together. "I came to see you, Gabriel."

He shook his head. "I meant, why are you in London?"

She fingered the front of her dress. "To see you."

She had come to see him?

Gabe had laboured hard to bury the deep wound of losing her, but now she was here. Was it possible she'd regretted sending him away? Enough to travel this long distance to find him? Enough to search for him, to discover where he lived?

Against his better judgement, a tiny seed of hope germinated. He managed to disguise the fact. "How did you find me?"

"With luck." She smiled wanly. "A maid at my hotel said many officers stayed here."

He really did not care about how she had found him. Only one question truly burned inside him. "*Why* did you come to see me?"

Her lips trembled before she spoke. "Oh, Gabriel. I need you."

The hard earth he'd packed around his emotions began to crack.

She swallowed and went on, "I need your help."

He came to his senses. "Help with what?"

She met his eye. "I need you to find Claude."

"Claude." The son who'd driven a wedge between them.

Of course it would be for Claude that she would travel all this way, to a foreign country that had so recently been at war with her birthplace.

She stepped closer to him. "It is so terrible. He is here in England." Her gaze still managed to hold him in thrall. "Do you remember how he was so filled with hatred?"

Could he forget?

She took a breath. "He became a cuirassier to get revenge for—for what happened at Badajoz. What happened to his father. And to me. All these years Claude has not forgotten any of it. Fighting the English in the war was supposed to be the revenge, but, *alors,* you know what happened."

"Why come to England, then, if he hates it so?" Wouldn't Claude want to stay away and keep his mother away, as well?

She wrung her hands. "He remembers one name from that day—Edwin Tranville. He has come to England to kill him."

Edwin Tranville. Gabe pressed his fingers against his temple. Damned Edwin Tranville. "What has this to do with me, Emmaline?"

Her eyes pleaded. "I need you to find Claude and stop him."

What a fool he was. She'd come to England for her son, not for him.

He gave her a level look. "What makes you believe I would help you?"

She lowered her gaze so that her long dark lashes cast shadows on her cheeks. "Oh, Gabriel. Who else can help me? I cannot go to—to the *gendarmerie* and tell them my son wants to kill a man. I might as well send Claude to a guillotine. I came to you, because I do not know anyone else." Her voice cracked with emotion. "I know only you."

Her emotion shook him. He paced in front of her. "Well, I cannot help you." His response was firm. "I have my own life to attend to, Emmaline. I am waiting for a new commission. Word could come any day and, when it comes, I must be here or the position will go to someone else."

"You are not in the army any more?" Her gaze flicked over his uniform coat and her brow creased as if in confusion.

"My regiment was disbanded. I'm on half-pay."

"Half-pay? What is that?" Her eyes widened suddenly and her

voice rose. "Do you need money, Gabriel? I can pay you money to help me."

"I do not need money," he snapped. What he needed she could not give him, not without forsaking her son. "The army pays half of a salary when a soldier is idled, but do not concern yourself. I have plenty of money."

"Even so…" she fingered the front of her dress "…I will pay for your help."

Did she think he would accept money for such a thing? It galled him that she would presume they could make some sort of business arrangement after what they'd had together.

What he thought they'd had.

"How old is Claude now?" he asked.

She looked puzzled. "He is now eighteen years."

"I was in the army, taking care of myself when I turned eighteen. Claude is his own man now. He must act on his own and accept the consequences."

She seized his arm. "You do not understand. He will be caught. He will hang for murder."

Her touch radiated through him. "That is his decision."

"*Non, non,* Gabriel," she cried. "You must stop him. He cannot hang. I cannot bear it."

Gabe felt himself weaken. Claude was her whole world, more important to her than anything or anyone else. Gabe had carried Claude off the Waterloo battlefield for that reason—for *her*—even while the cries of countless other wounded men had filled his ears. He did not regret doing so, but how many times was he expected to rescue Claude for her?

He closed his hands around her arms and lifted her away from him. He must think of himself now. Not of Emmaline. "I cannot go looking for him."

She did not relent. "Then find Edwin Tranville. Warn him. Tell him to hide himself until I find Claude. I will send word to you when Claude returns to Brussels with me."

He blew out a breath. "I am not going to look for Edwin Tranville." He wanted nothing to do with Edwin Tranville. "No more discussion."

He walked to the door and opened it. If she did not leave soon, his rapidly eroding resolve might entirely wash away. "I bid you good day."

He pictured himself holding her in his arms, inhaling her essence, feeling her warm curves against his body.

She paused to face him. "I am staying at the Bristol Hotel, if you decide differently."

He closed the door behind her and immediately paced the room, angry at her for making this request, angrier at himself for hoping she'd come for *him*. He turned towards the windows and watched her step out of the building onto the pavement. She took a few steps, then stopped to look for something in her reticule. She pulled out a lace-edged handkerchief and dabbed at her eyes.

His insides twisted.

With one distraught glance toward the building she started to walk away.

But the three officers he'd run into at the War Office were approaching her, returning from the tavern, no doubt. They swayed with drink and talked so loudly he could almost hear their words. They exclaimed in pleasure when catching sight of her.

The three men circled her, doffing their hats and bowing, their greetings too exuberant, too ungentlemanly. She tried to push past them, but they blocked her path. She stiffened and tried again.

Three drunk men in red coats? It was like Badajoz.

Gabe sensed her panic as if he were inside her skin. He grabbed his shako and hurried out of the parlour, crossing the hall to the front door. As he opened it the three men were right there, about to step inside. Through them Gabe saw Emmaline rushing away.

Hanson put an arm around Gabe's shoulder. "Deane, my good friend. You just missed the most delectable creature. In fact, you might be able to catch up to her if you hurry." Contrary to his words, though, he pushed Gabe inside with them.

"She was a sight for sore eyes, that is to be sure," agreed Irishman. "A pity Webberly scared her off. Never did know how to approach a lady."

Webberly shoved him. "What *lady* would be walking out of Stephen's alone?" He laughed. "Shall we wager on whose room she was visiting?"

Gabe clenched a fist. "I saw the three of you through the window. You frightened her."

Hanson guffawed. "And you were rushing to her rescue? Great strategy, Deane! No better way to get a woman into bed than to come to her rescue."

Irishman staggered ahead. "I've a bottle in my room if you've a mind to wet your whistle before dinner is served."

"Come with us," Hanson said to Gabe.

"No, I have an errand." He drew back.

"Come to us when you are done." Irishman gestured for Hanson and Webberly to hurry. "We'll save you a drink."

"Four-to-one odds Deane is going after that fancy piece," Webberly cried.

The others laughed, but Gabe was already across the threshold. Once outside he ran out to Bond Street and managed to catch sight of Emmaline in the distance, walking alone.

He followed her, as he had that first day he'd glimpsed her in Brussels. Irishman, Hanson and Webberly were harmless enough, but that did not mean there were no other men out there who could pose a danger to her.

He stayed close enough to keep her in sight, all the while cursing himself for involving himself with her again, for even caring about her safety when she so obviously cared only for what assistance he could render her. As soon as she was safely back to her hotel, he'd wash his hands of her.

"It is none of my affair!" he said aloud, receiving a startled glance from a gentleman passing by.

Walking back to her hotel, Emmaline still trembled inside. The three officers had frightened her badly, bringing back the terror of Badajoz, but she'd collected her wits in time. Straightening to her full height, she had ordered them to leave her alone. They immediately backed off, apologising with exaggerated politeness. She was glad she'd not panicked and run away. Inside she still felt the fear, but she'd learned that, even when afraid, it was best to demand what she wanted.

She had not hidden her fears for Claude from Gabriel, however. She'd even mentioned the guillotine to him. She well knew that the British hanged men for murder, but her imagination kept showing Claude ascending steps to a guillotine. She again could hear the sound of the blade being raised, the excited rumblings of the crowd, the blade whizzing in its descent and the indescribable sound of it doing its work. It was as if she were still a girl standing in the Place de la Revolution holding her mother's hand.

She forced herself to concentrate on putting one foot in front of the other, making her way to her hotel on Cork Street. It was not a far walk from Gabriel.

Gabriel.

How she had missed him. A part of her had wanted to weep for the joy of gazing upon him again, hearing his voice, inhaling his essence. The pain of sending him away had settled into a dull, enduring ache, but now the wound had reopened and bled freely again.

He was still so angry with her.

She could not blame him. He'd offered her his name and his protection and she'd sent him away, knowing that if she chose him her son would be lost to her for ever and she would never have a chance to help Claude find a way to happiness and peace.

It would be impossible to make Gabriel understand. It was not him she had rejected so cruelly. She simply could not turn away from her son, not when it was her fault Claude was so vengeful.

She should have defied her husband all those years ago, run away with Claude so her husband could not take him away from her. She'd been cowardly.

C'est vrai, she would never have met Gabriel, then. She would never have known those brief weeks of bliss with him. She would never have hurt him so acutely, either. Now she had wounded him all over again by coming to see him and asking for his help.

Her head was reeling. How was she to find Claude on her own? No one in England would help her, not with her French accent and story of a son who planned to kill an Englishman. *Non,* she would be reported to the English *gendarmerie;* perhaps she and Claude both would climb up to the scaffold.

She needed Gabriel. Needed him. Gabriel had found Claude on a battlefield littered with thousands of dead and dying men; he would know how to find him in England. Gabriel would protect her, as well, keep her safe from Edwin Tranville, who still frightened her as much as he had the day he'd tried to rape her and kill Claude, the day he'd laughed when the other men killed her husband. Emmaline should have killed Edwin Tranville herself that day. Gabriel had stopped her.

Gabriel.

Did all her thoughts return to him? When she had risen from her chair in the parlour she thought her heart might stop at the sight of him. She'd forgotten how grand he was, how formidable, a man who could do anything, even come through a battle unscathed to return her son to her.

And here she was, asking him to do it again, to find Claude

against nearly impossible odds, to again snatch him from the jaws of death. She had no doubt that Gabriel could do it.

If he would agree.

Emmaline entered her hotel and told the hall servant to send her dinner to her room. She'd procured the most inexpensive room available, trying to conserve her funds so that she could pay Gabriel all she possessed to help her find Claude. Instead he'd been insulted by her offer of money.

Emmaline climbed three sets of stairs to her room and immediately took off her bonnet and gloves. She undid the buttons of the blue spencer she'd sewn to match her blue muslin dress. She was still French enough to take pride in her appearance.

When Claude had been recuperating, he'd wanted to learn English. She'd had plenty of time to sew while drilling him in English words and phrases.

If she'd only known why he wanted to speak the language.

She had sewn clothes for him, because he had outgrown his old ones, and next for herself, using as inspiration the gowns of the most fashionable English ladies who came into the lace shop. She'd been glad to see her clothes were not out of place in London.

Had Gabriel admired her appearance? She wished for his admiration of her ensemble as strongly as she detested the attention it had brought from the three drunken soldiers.

She lay upon the bed and stared at the ceiling, but her mind's eye saw only Gabriel: his dark unruly hair; his chocolate brown eyes; the expressive mouth that had once pressed against her own lips.

She groaned.

She ached for him. Seeing Gabriel this day made her yearn for those glorious nights when he shared her bed. She'd been happy with him. Even with Claude in the army and Napoleon on the march again, those days with Gabriel had been the happiest she had ever known and she'd missed him every day thereafter. She pulled out the ring she still wore on a chain under her dress. This reminder of him rested always against her heart and kept him near to her, even after two years' absence.

Finding Gabriel when she came to London had been far easier than she expected. One of the hotel maids here had told her to ask for him at Stephen's Hotel.

"If he's an officer and he's in London, then he will be staying at the Stephen's Hotel. Mark my words," the girl had said.

She'd been correct. Emmaline arrived in London that morning and by afternoon she had found him. And lost him again.

Now what was she to do?

An idea occurred to her. If Gabriel was at the Stephen's Hotel, maybe Edwin Tranville was there, as well. *Non,* if that were so, surely Gabriel would have told her. Besides, if Tranville were so easy to find, Claude would have killed him already and her strong, handsome son might already have hung by the neck for it.

Claude had grown strong again, even though it had taken him two years to fully recover from his wounds at Waterloo. As his strength grew, so did his restlessness. He finally asked to travel to Paris to visit her parents. Emmaline had agreed, hoping a change in scene would be good for him.

But he had never arrived in Paris. Instead a letter came, explaining his true destination and his avowed intent.

That had been a month ago. Where was he now? And how would she find him?

She came back to Gabriel.

She must think of a way to make him agree, though why should he help her when she had rejected him so cruelly?

She flung an arm across her face, trying to hold off the despair that threatened to completely overwhelm her.

She'd give anything to keep her son from throwing his life away.

Anything. But what did she possess that would entice Gabriel to help her?

Emmaline sat up.

She had said she would give *anything* to save Claude. Well, she would do more. She would give Gabriel *everything.*

Everything.

He would not refuse.

Chapter Eight

Gabe descended the stairway to the hotel's dining room, deciding he might as well distract himself and eat. Staying alone in his room had been no help. One minute he had surged with anger at Emmaline for coming back into his life and re-igniting his need for her, the next minute he knew he must help her. It would require no effort on his part, after all.

He knew where to find Edwin Tranville.

Mere weeks ago he'd been thrown into Edwin's company. He'd run into Allan Landon, his friend since Allan had been his lieutenant in Spain. Allan was no longer in the army, but was working for Lord Sidmouth and the Home Office, as was, astonishingly, Edwin Tranville. They were charged with combating seditious acts. Allan had learned that a group of soldiers planned to gather to protest against unemployment and high prices. He wanted to stop the protest before the soldiers risked arrest. Gabe had run into Allan when Allan was searching for Edwin, who knew where the gathering was to take place. Gabe helped him search. They found Edwin in a tavern, drunk as usual. Allan quickly left to stop the march and Gabe wound up playing nursemaid to Edwin.

No mention of the soldiers' march ever reached a newspaper, so Gabe surmised Allan must have been successful.

Luckily Edwin had apparently been too drunk to remember

Gabe's interference. Gabe had no wish for Lord Tranville, Edwin's father, to learn he was in London seeking a new commission. Lord Tranville would certainly foil any chances Gabe possessed.

Gabe approached the door of the dining room. The Stephen's Hotel was a popular place to dine and almost like a club for officers who could not gain admittance to White's or Brooks's.

No sooner had Gabe entered the dining room than he was hailed by the three officers who accosted Emmaline. They waved him over to sit with them. Gabe shrugged. They'd done her no real harm, nothing any man with a little drink would not have done when encountering a beautiful, unaccompanied woman. Besides, it would be advantageous for him not to be alone with his own thoughts.

"We are making a wager," Irishman said, "with Webberly's timepiece—how many minutes until the fried soles are served? Are you in?"

"I never wager." Gabe lowered himself into a chair.

Hanson immediately poured Gabe a glass of wine. "There's the pity of it. We could have a game of whist after dinner if you were a gambling man."

Gabe scanned the room. "I trust someone here would accept."

Irishman drummed his fingers on the table. "We sat down not more than ten minutes ago, and the servant brought the wine immediately—"

"And thereby earned my eternal gratitude," interrupted Webberly.

Irishman went on. "So, I estimate it should be another ten minutes at least,"

"I wagered another twenty minutes," Hanson said.

Webberly lifted a finger. "And I, fifteen."

Unimaginative lot, thought Gabe. They all bet in equal segments. Likely the food would come on some other point of the clock, like eight minutes or thirteen.

At that moment the soup arrived and they fell silent, except for some audible slurping. No sooner were they done with the soup than the fried sole was served.

Irishman jostled Webberly. "How much time? What does your timepiece say?"

Webberly picked up the gold watch from the table and pressed the button to open it. "What time did the wager start?"

His two friends looked at him blankly and all three burst into laughter.

Irishman lifted his glass of wine. "'The better the gambler, the worse the man!'" A quotation by Publius Syrus, Gabe recalled from his school days.

"Then we are the best of men." Webberly took a gulp from his wine glass.

Their dinner conversation drifted into more serious matters, such as who among their acquaintance had found commissions, who was still looking, and who might become desperate enough to accept a place in the West Indies.

The conversation was not enough to keep Gabe from being haunted by the memory of Emmaline's desolate expression when he sent her away. He pushed around slices of scalloped potatoes and finally jabbed at his fried sole.

There was only one way to exorcise himself of her image. Do as she wished. Find Edwin, warn him, and be done with it.

In the morning he'd visit the Home Office, perform this one more service for her, and maybe purge her from his mind for ever after.

The next morning Gabe set out early, planning to walk the distance to the Home Office because the weather was so fine and the exercise would calm him.

He turned on to Bond Street. And saw Emmaline.

She walked towards him with a determined, yet graceful step, and he disliked that her mere appearance affected him so strongly. This day she wore pale lavender and the mere hue of her clothing brought back to him the lavender scent from the lace shop, the scent that always wafted around her.

She, too, caught sight of him. As she drew nearer, her pace remained carefully even.

"Good morning, Gabriel," she murmured when they were in earshot. She looked directly into his eyes.

"I am surprised to see you, Emmaline." She appeared to be walking back to Stephen's Hotel to seek him out again.

Gabe had not expected or intended to lay eyes on her again. After warning Edwin, he'd planned to write her a letter and have it delivered to her hotel.

"I still have hopes to convince you to help me." She lowered her gaze. "May I have a moment of your time to speak to you?" She spoke so carefully, so hesitantly.

He paused. "Walk with me."

They walked in silence, crossing Piccadilly and making their way towards Green Park.

"I have a new proposal to present to you," she said to him, breathless from keeping up with his long strides. "Could we not stop so I may tell you of it?"

What would she offer now? More money? Or merely play upon his obvious regard for her? He did not wish to hear more from her.

Still, he seemed unable to refuse. "We will stop in the Park."

They could cross through Green Park to reach the Home Office. There would be benches there where they might sit, where she could catch her breath and spill out this new proposal he had no wish to hear.

The Park was fragrant with blooming flowers and the scent of leafy trees and sprouting grass. Warm breezes whispered through the shrubbery, and Gabe for a moment was transported back to the Parc de Brussels where he and Emmaline had strolled in happier days.

They came upon a bench and he gestured for her to sit. "Say what you need to say."

She lowered herself on to the bench and looked disconcerted when he remained standing. Her hand fluttered to her face. "How to begin…"

Gabe gazed through the trees, his insides seared by memories and false hopes.

She fingered the front of her dress. "You once seemed to have a regard for me, is that not so, Gabriel?"

"Once." He refused to admit more.

"We did well together, *non?*" She smiled, but her lips trembled. He merely stared at her.

"You proposed marriage to me, *non?*"

He still did not speak, not knowing where she was leading, surmising it would cause him pain.

She took a breath. "I will marry you now, Gabriel." She waved a hand. "If—if you help me find Claude and stop him from doing this terrible act, I will marry you and go wherever you wish and do whatever you say." She made a quick, decisive nod, as if convincing herself that she could indeed perform such a distasteful task.

Gabe gaped at her. "Marry me? What of Claude, then? Will he cease to despise me if I stop him from what he wishes to do?"

A great sadness filled her eyes, but her chin lifted in determination. "He will probably hate you the more for it, but that cannot be as important as him being alive. It is better for Claude to live and have a chance for happiness, even if he chooses to exclude me from his life."

Her son's life. To save it, she'd agree to anything. Even to marry Gabe.

It felt as if she had now twisted the knife she'd plunged into his chest two years before. Did she think he wanted her to give up the most important part of her life for him?

When he'd proposed to her in Brussels, he'd meant their marriage to be a pledge of love and fidelity between them, not a contest between him and Claude. *You win, Gabriel. I'll marry you.* That had not been what Gabe meant about wanting to win her hand. Possession of her company was not the prize, winning her away from her son was not victory. Spending his days and nights with her, sharing their dreams together, that was the prize, much more valuable. Gabe wanted to grow old with Emmaline, but not at the expense of her attachment to her son. What kind of man did she think he was?

She gazed back into his eyes, her expression tense. "Well, do you agree? Will you help me?" Her voice wobbled.

This offer of hers—this *sacrifice*—stung worse than her initial rejection, which, even though he did not like it, he'd understood. God help him, he had even envied the devotion she bestowed on her son. He'd never been that important to his own mother, not with all his brothers and sisters needing her more, but this was not about his needs. It was about Emmaline. She needed her son like she needed air to breathe. As painful as it was, Gabe would never take away her life's breath. He refused to be the sacrifice she must make, the price of saving Claude from his own folly.

"Gabriel?" she asked anxiously.

He could at least force her to explain. "I thought you did not want to marry a man your son would despise."

Panic flickered in her eyes. She glanced away. "I never despised you, though. We—we were good friends, were we not?"

Good friends. Such a far cry from being her life's breath.

She went on, "It will be enough to know Claude is alive. I…I will even—how did you say it?—follow the drum with you when you return to the army."

"You will marry me and travel with me as a soldier's wife?"

She'd hated such a life when her husband had demanded it of her. More sacrifice she was willing to make, for the sake of her son.

She blinked. "If you are able to prevent Claude from murdering, yes, then I will marry you." She looked up again. "I will gladly marry you."

"What a compliment to me," he murmured.

"Qu'est-ce que tu as dit?" She shook her head. "I mean, what did you say?"

"It is of no consequence." He gestured to the path. "Shall we be on our way?"

She rose and clutched his arm. "You did not answer me."

There was no more than an inch separating them. The sun lit her anxious face and the lavender scent he'd imagined became real. At the Parc de Brussels they'd stood together just like this, sheltered from view by a large allegorical statue. He'd leaned down and tasted her lips that day and held her in his arms.

The urge to kiss her and hold her again was unabated even though *he* was the sacrifice she would make to save her son from a hanging. He leaned closer and she rose on tiptoe, so close their breath mingled.

"Your answer?" she whispered.

He stepped back. He ought to let her think he'd go along with making her choose him over her son. It would serve her right for thinking so little of him.

He was no card player, but he could bluff like one. "Very well, Emmaline. I will hold you to your promise. I will prevent Claude from murdering Edwin Tranville and you will marry me."

Her lips trembled again, but she nodded, her hand pressed against her chest.

He started to walk and she skipped to catch up to him. "Where are you going?"

"I am headed to the Home Office," he said.

"The Home Office?"

He set a fast pace. "The place where Edwin Tranville is employed."

She strained to keep up with him. "You know where he is?"

"I always knew where he was."

She sounded angry. "You were going to warn him? Even before I spoke today?"

He stopped and faced her. "That is correct, Emmaline. I was planning to do that much for you, but you made a new bargain. After I speak to Edwin today, I'll proceed to where I might obtain a special licence so you and I can be married right away."

She gazed straight ahead. "Do not forget you must ensure that Claude does not kill this man. Then I will marry you."

He gave her a sardonic smile. "That is our bargain."

They did not speak until the buildings on Whitehall came into view.

"We are near," Gabe said.

When they approached the Home Office building, Emmaline shrank back. "Must I see him?"

"See who?"

"Edwin Tranville." Her voice turned low and shaky.

He'd forgotten. She did not know Edwin as a drunken coward, but as a dangerous man who'd tried to rape her and kill her son.

He put his hand over hers. "Do not fear," he murmured. "He cannot hurt you."

She looked up into his eyes and he could almost think that the connection he'd believed they had in Brussels had returned and was real.

He led her through the hallways to the rooms housing the Home Office. She shrank back as he opened the door.

A clerk sat behind a desk, looking very much like the clerk who sat behind the desk in the War Office. The man raised his eyes. "Yes?"

Emmaline stood behind Gabe. He could feel the stiffening of her muscles. She was bracing herself to see Edwin again.

Gabe inclined his head. "Edwin Tranville, please."

The clerk glanced down again. "Edwin Tranville is not here."

"When might we expect him?" Gabe asked.

"Never," the clerk said. "He will not be back."

Emmaline moved forwards. "Did something happen to him?"

"No." The man regarded her with a puzzled but admiring expression. He glanced down again and restacked the papers in front of him. "Lord Sidmouth gave him the sack."

Emmaline looked at Gabe. "What does this mean, 'gave him the sack'?"

"Terminated his employment," the clerk answered. "Mr Tranville failed to fulfil his responsibilities."

Somehow this was not a surprise. It was more bewildering that Sidmouth had hired Edwin in the first place.

"Is Mr Landon here, then?" Perhaps Allan would know where to find Edwin.

The clerk laughed drily. "Not since he married an heiress and no longer needs to work."

Allan married? And to an heiress? Lucky woman. He was the best of men and would make the best of husbands.

"Do you know where I might find Tranville?" Gabe asked. "Does he reside with his father, Lord Tranville?"

The man shrugged. "He lives at the Albany."

"Thank you." Gabe nodded to the man.

When they walked out the door, Emmaline seized his arm. "Gabriel, is Edwin Tranville's father a lord?"

"He is."

She whispered, "This makes it worse for Claude."

Always Claude. Anger twisted inside Gabe and he hated feeling it. He did not wish to feel a rivalry with her son.

"Will we go to this Albany?" she asked.

He shrugged. "It is a logical next step." And not too much more exertion on Gabe's part, before he could end this charade.

Their walk to the Albany on Piccadilly reminded Gabe of their strolls through Brussels' streets, but only in contrast. Gone was the ease between them, the pleasure of merely walking at her side. Still, he was struck with the odd feeling of how right it seemed that they walked together again.

He must take care. It was startling how easily his fantasies about her grew. He must not forget that her sole purpose was to save her son and she would do anything to rescue him from his folly.

Even marry.

Gabe tried to keep that thought in his head. It helped ward off fanciful musings.

The Albany was a popular bachelor residence for the aristocracy, so it stood to reason top-lofty Edwin would live there.

When they reached Piccadilly, Emmaline remarked, "There are many shops here."

Gabe made a sarcastic smile. "Did not your Napoleon call England a nation of shopkeepers?"

"He is not my Napoleon," she snapped. Her voice turned low. "Never *my* Napoleon."

The Albany was set back from the street, a three-storey house flanked on two sides of a courtyard by wings two storeys high. They crossed the courtyard, Emmaline receiving curious and appreciative glances from the young gentlemen they passed. Gabe disliked their open admiration.

He led her through the main doorway and found a servant attending the hall.

"Is Edwin Tranville here?" Gabe asked the man.

"Cannot say," he answered. "I do not know of all the comings and goings. Shall I send someone to his room?"

"Please," Gabe answered.

The man made a vague gesture towards the wall. "You may wait here."

Gabe endured Emmaline receiving more leering glances by men who passed by. She nervously fingered the front of her dress, which did nothing to keep him from thinking about how pleasurable it had once been to undress her.

"I do not wish to see him," she murmured.

Gabe's compassion was sparked again. "If you like, I can escort you back to your hotel and return here later."

She shook her head. "I do not wish to delay."

Two men crossed the hall and this time their glances at Emmaline were plainly lascivious. Gabe nearly stepped forwards to defend her.

He controlled the impulse. It would help nothing to engage impertinent young men in fisticuffs.

Finally the servant returned, another man accompanying him. This man approached them. "You asked for Mr Tranville?"

Gabe nodded. "We did."

"Mr Tranville is not here. I am his man. May I ask the reason you are calling upon him?"

Gabe responded, "I served with him in the Royal Scots."

The valet looked at Emmaline and raised his brows.

Good God. Even a valet was being insulting. Gabe glared at him. "My betrothed accompanies me at my request. Do you have some objection?"

The valet's cheeks turned bright red. "I beg your pardon, Captain."

"When will Mr Tranville return?" Gabe demanded.

The valet pulled on his collar. "I do not know precisely. He has travelled out of town. I am awaiting instructions from him whether he wishes me to follow him."

Gabe frowned. He should have known Edwin would make this complicated. "Where is he?"

"I do not know precisely," the valet answered. "I am awaiting his direction."

"Non!" Emmaline exclaimed.

Gabe spoke quickly. "Someone must know where Tranville went. Is there anyone here who might know?"

The valet shook his head. "I do not know if he is acquainted with anyone here."

"But we must find him!" cried Emmaline.

Gabe put a stilling hand on her arm. "Is his father in London at present?"

"I do not believe so," the valet answered. "I believe he is at his estate."

Gabe turned to Emmaline. "It is no use."

She looked stricken, but there was nothing more they could do here now. She held back, but finally nodded. She took his arm and they started to walk towards the door.

The valet called after them, "Mr Tranville's cousin resides in London. Perhaps she knows where he is."

Emmaline's fingers squeezed Gabe's arm. Her expression turned hopeful.

"Where may we find her?"

The valet gave them her direction on Bryanston Street. "Her name is Miss Pallant."

Gabe and Emmaline walked out of the Albany and back to Piccadilly Street.

"May we call upon this Miss Pallant?" Emmaline asked him.

He felt as if in a snare, but one he'd chosen to walk into. "We may go there as soon as you wish."

"Now, Gabriel?" Her eyes pleaded.

"Now, Emmaline."

Chapter Nine

Emmaline leaned back against the worn leather of the hackney coach, grateful to Gabriel for hiring it. Her feet hurt from trying to keep pace with him when they walked. When they'd strolled through Brussels he'd never walked so fast.

She supposed she ought not to repine too much about Brussels and how rapturous her time with him had been. Matters were so altered between them now.

His reaction to her bargain to become his wife had not been at all what she had expected. She thought she was offering him what he desired, but it only seemed to make him angrier at her. Did he not know that if it were not for Claude, she would have married him long ago?

She touched the ring she wore beneath her dress, the one that reminded her daily of how important to her he had been.

And still was.

Sitting next to him in the carriage was difficult. She could feel the heat of his body, inhale his scent, feel every breath he took, every flexing of muscle. Being so close reminded her of tangled sheets and naked skin and the glorious nights she'd spent enfolded in his arms.

Now he avoided touching her and the space between them on the carriage seat seemed to crackle with unpleasant emotions.

The coach stopped and he glanced out the window. "We are here."

He opened the door and climbed out, turning to offer her his hand. She felt a shock of awareness when his glove touched hers. Her senses came alive to him and she wished they were still in Brussels, closing the lace shop, crossing the yard to her little house and climbing the steps to her bed chamber.

Instead, he led her to the door of a townhouse, the residence of this Miss Pallant who was Edwin Tranville's *cousine.* The town house was built of dark-grey brick with a red-brick fan design above windows with white sashes. What would an English house look like inside? What would the mistress of such a house think of a Frenchwoman whose son planned to kill her cousin?

She shuddered.

Gabriel sounded the knocker and after a few minutes it was opened by a large man who looked more like a soldier than a servant.

Before the man could speak Gabriel cried, "Good God. Reilly?"

A wide smile lit the man's face. "Captain Deane!"

The two men shook hands like long-lost brothers.

"Come in. Come in." Reilly stepped aside. "It is a pleasure to see you, sir."

"What the devil are you doing here?" Gabriel ushered her inside.

Reilly laughed. "I'm the butler here, if you can believe that."

"The butler?" Gabriel shook his head.

"My lady found me when I was as low as a man can get. No job. No food. Thinking of turning to thievery, I was." He paused. "But never mind that. I expect you are here to see—"

At that moment another man, more finely dressed, entered the hall. "Who's come, Reilly? I heard voices."

"Allan?" Gabriel sounded shocked.

"Gabe!" This man rushed forwards and embraced Gabriel. "Thought I'd lost track of you. But you found me. I'm so pleased."

"Indeed."

This appeared to be a joyful reunion, so Emmaline was happy for Gabriel. She just hoped it would also mean they would find the cousin who could lead them to Edwin Tranville.

Gabriel's friend glanced at her with a curious expression and Gabriel seemed to belatedly remember her presence.

He took her arm and presented her. "Allan, this is Madame Mableau."

Allan looked even more curious. *"Madame."* He bowed.

"Do you not recognise her?" Gabriel asked.

Emmaline's brows rose. Was she supposed to know this man?

Allan shook his head.

Gabriel darted a glance towards the butler before turning back to his friend and speaking in a low voice. "She is the woman from Badajoz." He turned to her. "Emmaline, this is Captain Allan Landon. He was there."

She gasped. In Badajoz. He must have been the one who carried Edwin Tranville away. "Captain Landon."

The Captain's eyes widened. *"Madame!* My God. I hope you are well—" He examined her again. "But you must be well. You look so lovely. Why are you here?"

"I fear we are in the wrong house." She wanted to find Edwin Tranville's cousin, but Gabriel was so happy to see his friend. If she knew the correct house, she would call upon the cousin alone.

Gabriel explained. "We thought this the residence of Miss Marian Pallant."

Landon looked even more puzzled. "It is, but—" He tapped his forehead. "Forgive me. Let us sit. Have refreshment."

"I'll tend to it, Captain," Reilly said.

Landon offered Emmaline his arm and led them to a drawing room, a comfortable room, with upholstered sofas and chairs of the best brocade. Porcelain figurines, a matched set of a shepherd and shepherdess, decorated the mantelpiece. They might have come from the finest china shop in Brussels.

"Please sit," Landon said, leading her to a sofa. Gabriel remained standing.

She did not want to sit or have refreshment. "Please. Is Miss Pallant here? It is urgent that we speak to her."

"Urgent?" Landon frowned. "What is this about?"

She turned to Gabriel. "How much may we tell him?"

Landon stiffened. "By God, you will tell me all of it if it involves my wife."

"Your wife?" Gabriel blinked.

Landon fixed his gaze on him. "I am married to Marian Pallant."

"The heiress." Gabriel nodded. "Yes. They said at the Home Office you had married an heiress."

Landon folded his arms across his chest. "Why were you at the Home Office and why was my wife being discussed there?"

"Do not tell him." Emmaline rose. "Perhaps we cannot trust him."

Gabriel put his hand on her arm. "Allan, we are looking for Edwin. His valet sent us here."

Landon's eyes narrowed, his expression angry. "Edwin." He looked at Emmaline. "Why do you wish to see Edwin? After what he did—"

Gabriel answered, "We are attempting to prevent a wrong. Emmaline's son has vowed to revenge himself on Edwin and we are trying to intervene."

Emmaline held her breath, carefully examining Landon's expression to see if he would act as friend or foe.

"God knows Edwin deserves it." Allan expelled a breath. "I presume you spoke to his valet at the Albany. Edwin was not there?"

"Out of town, apparently," Gabriel responded. "We were hoping his cousin—" he smiled "—*your* wife would know where he had gone."

"Is she here?" Emmaline broke in. "May we speak to her?"

Landon looked at her with kindness. "She is not here."

Emmaline averted her gaze, disappointed tears stinging her eyes.

"Madame." Landon's voice was soothing. "She will return later this day."

There was a knock on the parlour door and the butler entered with a tray with a carafe, glasses and tea things. "Brought both, Captain," Reilly said. He bowed out.

"Sit, now," Landon said. "Gabe, I suspect you would rather have the brandy."

"Indeed."

Landon told them about meeting his wife during the battle of Waterloo and again when the war was over. They'd been married only a few weeks. "I cannot say if Marian knows Edwin's whereabouts or not."

They all fell into silence; Emmaline sipped her tea while the men drank brandy.

Alan drained his glass and set it on the table. "I have an idea, but I need time to work on it. You both must come for dinner tonight at eight."

"Your wife will not mind?" Emmaline asked.

"Not at all." His expression turned proud. "She is an exceptional woman. She will assist you if she can." He smiled. "And she will enjoy having you as our guests for dinner."

Enjoy it? Emmaline could not imagine that a lord's niece who owned such grand things would enjoy dining with a shop girl. There was no *égalité* in England, it was said. But, then, the English did not use the guillotine; that was to their credit.

The rope, however, could be equally as lethal.

When she and Gabriel left and were seated in another hackney coach, she asked him, "Are you certain I should attend the dinner?"

He looked puzzled. "Why would you not?"

"I work in a lace shop."

He shrugged. "What does that matter? This is about locating Edwin's whereabouts."

She sighed. He did not understand.

He walked her to the door of her hotel. "I will have a coach here at seven-thirty." He bowed and walked away.

Emmaline descended the stairs and entered the hall of her hotel just as the clock sounded quarter past seven. If she had stayed one more minute in her room, she'd have perished from nerves. Once more she looked down at her dress and smoothed the skirt. Ladies dressed formally for dinner, she'd heard, but she had nothing like that to wear. Except for the dress she'd worn while travelling, Emmaline only had one more dress that Gabriel had not seen, a rather plain walking dress, but it was a pretty deep-rose colour. She'd quickly embellished the neckline with a lace ruff and added a peek of lace at the cuffs. She hoped it would be enough.

Gabriel was already waiting and stared at her as she crossed the hall to meet him at the door.

"Is my dress acceptable?" she asked him.

"Yes." His gaze flicked over her again. "It is acceptable." His voice was rough.

His reaction did not much relieve her mind.

A hackney coach waited on the street and Gabriel escorted her to it. The sky was still light and the evening as fine as ones they had shared in Brussels, but his company, much as she desired it, lowered her spirits.

As he assisted her into the coach, she set her chin. She must accept these difficult and confusing feelings about Gabriel for

Claude's sake. And she must remain hopeful. This night she would meet Edwin Tranville's cousin and they would discover where to find him. Once Tranville was warned, they could work on finding Claude.

Claude would give up this foolish plan of vengeance for her. He must!

Her thoughts filled the time it took the coach to take them back to Bryanston Street, which was a good thing, because Gabriel did not speak to her.

He looked very handsome in his uniform, with dress trousers and shoes instead of boots. He was freshly shaved and, sitting so close, she could see some pink scrapes on his cheek. She wished she could soothe them with her fingers.

She sighed.

"What is it?" Gabriel asked her.

She nearly jumped. "I did not speak."

"You sighed." His voice was low. "Were you thinking of Claude?"

"No."

He gave her answer no heed. "I suspect Mrs Landon will know how to locate Edwin, if that is what concerns you."

It was her turn to be silent. What would he think if he knew what had inspired her sigh?

The coach stopped at Bryanston Street and, as he had done earlier that day, Gabriel took her hand to help her out. Their gazes caught and held for a moment. Emmaline's heart quickened.

"Let us go." He made it sound as if she'd deliberately delayed them by gazing into his eyes.

The same soldier-butler opened the door and escorted them to the drawing room. Emmaline heard voices and spied Allan through the doorway.

He strode towards them, gesturing for them to enter. "Gabe! Come in. Come in."

Once they were in the parlour Emmaline's attention was immediately drawn to the two ladies present, both elegantly dressed.

One was exceptionally beautiful, with shining auburn hair and a face that might belong to a portrait at Versailles. The other, a confident, smiling blonde, was already assessing her. Which was Edwin Tranville's cousin? she wondered.

"Look who is here." Allan extended his arm.

A second gentleman stood. "Hello, Captain."

"Vernon?" Gabriel walked up to him, and the two men shook hands. "I am astonished you are here."

Landon grinned. "He is my surprise."

Emmaline knew this man. He also had been at Badajoz. He had drawn pictures of horses to amuse Claude.

He turned to her. "*Madame,* do you remember me?"

She clasped his hand. "I do. You are Ensign Vernon."

He covered her hand with his own. "Now I am Mr Vernon. I sold my commission two years ago."

"Come meet our wives," Allan said.

The auburn-haired beauty was Vernon's wife, who insisted she be called by her given name, Ariana. The blonde, then, must be the cousin.

She did not wait for Emmaline to be presented. "I am Marian Landon." She gave her husband a quick glance. "I am Edwin's cousin."

Emmaline curtsied. "Have you learned why we are here, *madame?*"

The lovely lady looked stricken. "Allan told me. He told me what my cousin did to you and to your son. And that he was with men who killed your husband. I am so sorry."

"Thank you, *madame.*" Emmaline had not been certain she would be received so kindly.

Mrs Landon reached out and touched Emmaline's hand. "Please do call me Marian."

Her husband walked over to a table with a decanter and glasses. "Let us not talk about that now. Dinner will be ready soon. In the meantime, some refreshment." He lifted the decanter. "Claret, everyone?"

They drank claret and the men talked of the army and other officers they had known. The ladies talked of the theatre and the arts, things Emmaline knew little of, but she was not surprised to learn that Madame Vernon was an actress. How ironic that she'd thought the woman as beautiful as a painting, because her husband, the man who'd drawn pictures for Claude, now painted portraits.

At dinner Emmaline learned that Jack Vernon had a portrait of his wife in an important exhibition.

"I need to tell you," Vernon said, "my mother and her husband are in town. They came only a few days ago, for the end of the Season and for the exhibition. But you must know..." He swallowed "You must know that my mother's husband is General Lord Tranville." He looked at Emmaline. "Edwin's father. I might as well add that my mother, before she married Tranville, was in his keeping."

Landon gaped. "No. I do not believe it."

Emmaline turned to Gabriel. "What is this 'in his keeping'?"

He paused a moment before answering. "She was his mistress."

She lifted a shoulder. What was the fuss? In France such would be considered a trivial piece of information. In fact, she had been Gabriel's mistress.

So briefly.

"Is that why you were forced to tell Tranville about Badajoz?" Gabriel asked.

Vernon glanced at his wife. "In part—"

Ariana interrupted. "And in part due to me, I'm afraid."

Gabriel took a sip of the wine and seemed lost in thought.

"We will call upon the father of Edwin tomorrow, will we not, Gabriel?" Emmaline asked him.

"Not you, Emmaline." His voice was firm.

"Why not?" she cried.

"Tranville must not know who you are." The look on his face alarmed her.

"He is right," Vernon agreed. He turned to Emmaline. "I was forced to tell Tranville what his son tried to do to you and your boy. He and I have a mutual agreement not to speak of it. He has good reason not to retaliate against me, but he would feel no such restraint in lashing out against you or your son, if he thought *his* son would be disgraced."

Emmaline's eyes widened. They acted as if this father was to be more feared than the son.

Gabriel set down his wine glass. "I will go alone tomorrow."

"I'll go with you, if you like," Allan offered.

"No." Vernon leaned forwards. "None of you can go. Tranville is shrewd. If he connects you to the incident with Edwin, he'll find some way to silence you. I will go."

Ariana shook her head. "Jack, he will never tell you what you want to know. He never speaks with you unless he cannot avoid it."

Her husband shrugged. "My mother will convince him."

She laughed. "She is more likely to side with him."

"That is true, I'm afraid." He crossed his arms over his chest.

"I should go." Marian straightened. "I am perfect for the task. Uncle Tranville will not question why I am asking about Edwin. I am the only one in existence who might care where Edwin is."

"I shall go with you," Allan said. "We owe your uncle and Vernon's mother a call. It would be the most natural thing in the world for us to do so."

Marian turned to Emmaline and Gabriel. "Come tomorrow for dinner. We will know something then and can decide what to do next."

The ladies retired to the drawing room and Allan, Gabe and Vernon remained in the dining room, drinking brandy.

Gabe absently ran his finger along the rim of his glass, while Vernon and Allan continued to discuss the impending visit to Tranville.

Ever since Emmaline had walked into his life again, Gabe's emotions had been in a muddle. It was best he stay out of Tranville's sights; the man had the power to ruin his chances for a new commission, after all. At the same time, he was having difficulty sharing the task of helping Emmaline, even with his friends.

Vernon pointed a finger at Allan. "Take care you don't even hint why you ask about Edwin."

"We will be careful." Allan smiled. "I'm afraid both Marian and I are well practised in keeping secrets." He turned to Gabe. "What is between you and Madame Mableau?"

Gabe felt his face burn. "There is nothing between us."

Allan persisted. "But she sought you out."

"Who else? She does not know anyone in England." He tried to sound matter of fact.

"I cannot forget those days in Badajoz," Vernon said in a low voice. "It is difficult to blame her son for remembering it with such hatred."

Gabe stared into his drink. "A lot of bad things happened during the war. We must leave it behind us." At least that was what he aspired to do.

Vernon slid cautious glances at them both. "Did any of it ever come back to you?" His tone was hushed. "I had moments when I actually thought I was back there."

"I have had nightmares about it," Allan admitted.

Gabe dreamt of Badajoz as well, but the dreams always were about Emmaline.

How odd it was that one event in Badajoz bound him with Allan and Vernon and that none of them could escape being affected by it still. Even more ironic, they were all connected to Edwin Tranville. At least Gabe did not have to count Edwin among his family. Theoretically, he could walk away from all this and never think of it again.

Theoretically.

He could have refused to help Emmaline. He had no reason to be involved. None of them did, except that they had witnessed Edwin's despicable behaviour and Gabe had learned precisely how acutely it had affected Emmaline and her son.

She had looked more beautiful than ever this night, a worthy rival even for Jack Vernon's wife. The lace on her dress reminded him of the lace shop, of her busy fingers smoothing the delicate creations, folding them or presenting them for display. He imagined her selecting the lace for her collar and cuffs from the strips of lace hanging over rods in the shop. He could see her pleating it and sewing it to her dress, her eyes concentrating on her work, her lips pressed into a line, her fingers as graceful as a ballet dancer as she pulled the needle through. Those same fingers had stroked his naked skin, those lips had showered him with kisses, and her eyes, until that morning when he had proposed marriage, had looked upon him with desire.

"Are you thinking of that night, Gabe?" Allan asked.

He glanced up and realised he'd missed some of the conversation.

"The night in Badajoz?" Not the nights he'd made love to Emmaline in her bed.

Allan's brow creased. "Yes—what were you thinking of?"

Gabe stared into his drink. "I was thinking that we should have killed Edwin that night."

"Gabe!" Allan looked shocked.

Gabe went on. "No one would have known. We would have done the world and ourselves a good turn."

Vernon lifted his glass to his lips. "I'm inclined to agree."

Allan shook his head. "You are speaking nonsense. I know you, Gabe. You would not take a man's life without cause."

"It seems to me we had good cause," Gabe retorted. "This revenge of Claude's, this quest of his mother's, none of it would be necessary had we rid the world of him that night."

How different might it have been if they had put a period to Edwin's existence. Perhaps even Brussels would have been different.

Chapter Ten

The next night they again gathered in Marian and Allan's drawing room, connected by one event, one person, the person Gabe was now duty-bound to find. He glanced at Emmaline as Allan poured glasses of claret and passed them around. She had chosen a chair, not wanting Gabe to sit next to her, he supposed. He envied Jack and Ariana, so comfortable together on the small sofa. But Emmaline did not appear to take heed of them or of Gabe. Her gaze darted from Allan to Marian. Gabe could feel her impatience for them to speak.

Allan's grave expression showed that there would not be a celebratory toast. Gabe sipped his wine and waited.

Allan finally took a seat next to his wife on the other sofa. "I won't tease you any longer. We do have news of Edwin..."

"He is no longer in London," Marian finished for him. "I'm so sorry."

"We do know where he is, however," Allan continued. "He's gone to Bath."

"My uncle sent him there," Marian explained in their seamless joint narrative. "You see, my uncle made a quick trip to town about the same time as the soldiers' march, and he was furious to learn how abysmally Edwin failed in his duties to Lord Sidmouth,

so he banished Edwin to Bath, to the house that was my aunt's."
She turned to Jack. "You remember the house, do you not?"

Jack nodded. "About a mile off the Wells Road."

"That is it." She turned back to Gabe and Emmaline. "Uncle
Tranville told Edwin to stay there and not show his face in town
until his shameful behaviour was forgotten." She made a wry
smile. "That is nearly an exact quote. Minus the malediction."

Allan turned back to Emmaline with a reassuring look. "Bath
is not far. A day's journey by coach on good roads."

"Then I will travel there tomorrow." Emmaline darted a glance
at Gabriel as if unsure that he would accompany her.

"Will you escort her there, Gabe?" Allan asked. It was more
like an order than a question.

Did he think Gabe would leave this task to her alone? She
was wrong to have asked it of him and insulting to offer herself
in marriage as payment, but Gabe was not without honour and
compassion. He'd seen how frightened she was at the prospect of
coming face to face with Edwin.

Gabe met Allan's gaze. "I will take her."

"Tomorrow, Gabriel?" Emmaline still looked tense.

He stood. "Tomorrow. But I need time to make arrangements,
so I'll not stay to dinner."

Emmaline rose.

He barely looked at her. "You may remain, Emmaline. Jack
and Ariana can see you back to your hotel." He glanced at Jack.

"Our pleasure." Jack stood and shook his hand.

Emmaline took a step towards him. "I want to come with you."

He shook his head. "Your company will make it more difficult." Her mere presence made everything more difficult, arousing sensations and emotions that were best buried in the past.

Their gazes caught for a moment, but Gabe quickly turned
away.

"The coaches leave very early. Be ready at four in the morning. I will come to pick you up." He bowed to the others. "Good night."

Allan walked him to the door. "Is there any way we can help?"

"You've already helped." Gabe collected his hat and gloves.

Reilly appeared in the hall and opened the door for him.

Allan walked him to it. "Maybe some day we can all put Badajoz to rest. After this, perhaps."

Gabe shook his hand. "Perhaps."

Gabe stepped out into the night and headed towards Oxford Street in search of a hackney coach to carry him to the Strand and the Angel Inn where passage on a fast coach to Bath could be procured.

At four the next morning, Emmaline waited in the hall of her hotel, her portmanteau, packed with all her possessions, at her feet. As she watched out of the window, she twisted the drawstring of her reticule, fighting an attack of nerves.

She feared encountering Edwin Tranville almost as much as she feared they would find him too late. As if it were yesterday she could feel his hands on her, forcing her to the cobbles, lifting her skirts. She could smell the stink of spirits on his breath, the smell of her husband's blood spilled nearby.

Emmaline shuddered with the memory, enraged tears stinging her eyes. She remembered the knife in her hand, remembered its point piercing Edwin's face, slicing his cheek like a piece of raw meat. If only Gabe had not stopped her. She would have pushed that knife into Edwin's body, stabbed him like the others had stabbed Remy, killed Edwin like the others had killed Remy.

If only Gabriel had not stopped her.

Non. She must not regret Gabriel. He'd hidden her and Claude. He'd protected them, given them money.

And when he'd returned to her in Brussels, he'd shown her a happiness unlike any she'd ever hoped to experience. She let her thoughts turn to the pleasure of being held by Gabriel, of his kisses and caresses, of the intense joy of joining her body to his.

The sound of horses' hooves broke into her reverie. A hackney coach appeared out of the darkness and approached the front of the hotel.

She turned to the hall servant, a young man dozing in a nearby chair. "My coach is here."

He roused himself to unlock the door and open it for her.

As she stepped out into the pre-dawn air, Emmaline saw Gabriel approaching, like an apparition formed from out of the departing night.

She gripped the handle of her portmanteau and met him halfway.

With only a nod for a greeting he took her bag, brushing her hand with his, rousing her body's yearnings, the memories of which had soothed her from more painful ones.

She followed him to the coach. He touched her again to help her inside and she fought the impulse to bury herself in his arms, to press her face against his chest and the strong rhythm of his heartbeat.

Instead she was greeted by Jack and Ariana Vernon.

"We decided to accompany you," Ariana said in her musical voice. "Jack contacted Gabe after we left you last night. It seemed the logical thing to do."

"I grew up in Bath," her husband explained. "And I know Edwin. I am in a good position to help."

Ariana smiled. "And I would not allow him to leave me behind."

Emmaline could not have been more surprised that these mere acquaintances were willing to help a Frenchwoman, someone they could just as easily perceive as their enemy.

Gabriel climbed in and sat next to her, of necessity brushing her shoulder with his own.

"We managed to get seats for all of us in the same coach," Jack went on. "That was a stroke of good luck."

"Do we ride to Bath in this coach?" Emmaline asked, fearful at how much it cost to hire such a vehicle. Her funds were limited.

Gabriel replied, "This takes us to the inn where the Bath stage departs."

The hackney began to roll. Emmaline lost track of where they were headed, but the coach soon pulled up to a busy coaching inn, its sign displaying a picture of an angel. Even at this early hour, the place was a bustle of activity.

They climbed out of the coach. Gabriel took Emmaline's arm and escorted her to a place out of the way of horses' hooves and carriage wheels and men carrying huge bundles on their shoulders.

She managed to ask him, "How much money do I give you for the fare?"

He set down her portmanteau and his travelling bag. "Do not speak to me of money. I can easily afford the cost of this trip for us both."

His tone puzzled her. Why was he so generous to her when he so obviously resented making the trip?

Jack and Ariana joined her; Ariana put a comforting hand on Emmaline's arm. "By tonight we shall be in Bath, and tomorrow Jack and Gabe will find Edwin and all will be set to rights."

Except that Emmaline must still find Claude and convince him to abandon this dangerous vengeance. "Do you know Edwin Tranville?" she asked.

Ariana shrugged. "I have met him, but I can claim no real acquaintance with him. I remember him as a disagreeable man who drinks too much wine." She gave Emmaline a sympathetic look. "Jack told me something of your encounter with Edwin. It was terrible, but I doubt Edwin poses a threat to anyone now."

"Except to my son," Emmaline murmured.

Gabriel returned, and he and Jack picked up their baggage.

"This way," Gabriel said.

Soon they were seated inside a large coach with two other passengers. Gabriel again sat next to her, giving her the window seat, and the Vernons sat across from them. A woman next to Jack carried a large basket smelling of sausage. A man dressed in a shabby brown coat and knee breeches sat opposite her.

With the bleat of a horn and much shouting, the coach lurched forwards, and soon they were on a road headed out of the city.

The sky lightened with each mile of the journey, although a steady drizzle of rain hid the sun. Ariana soon snuggled against her husband and fell asleep. Emmaline wished she could lean against Gabriel in a like manner, to feel him hold her like Jack held Ariana. With the two strangers in the carriage, there was little any of them could say to the purpose of their travel to Bath, so Gabriel and Jack conversed about army matters and other mundane topics. Gabriel said nothing to Emmaline.

At the first stop to change horses, he finally spoke to her. "Stretch your legs while you can."

She did not need to be urged.

She and Ariana used the necessary while Gabe and Jack purchased some food ready-packed for travellers; within ten minutes they were back in the carriage and on the road.

By mid-day, the clouds had cleared and the carriage passed rolling green fields dotted with white sheep and picturesque villages. England was a tidy place, Emmaline thought, watching these pretty scenes pass by. How fortunate these villages were to have escaped the very untidy Revolution.

Ariana, awake now, read a book and Jack busied himself sketching in a small notebook he'd taken from his coat pocket. Emmaline remembered him drawing horses for Claude in Badajoz.

"What do you sketch, Monsieur Vernon?" Emmaline asked.

He smiled at her. "Call me Jack." He handed her his notebook.

On the page was an image of a posting inn complete with carriages and post boys and travellers.

"It is where we last stopped," Emmaline exclaimed. "It looks just like it."

Ariana gave a proud glance over the top of her book.

Emmaline showed it to Gabriel. "Does it not look like the last inn?"

"Very like." His voice was curt, as if he disliked her forcing him to speak to her.

She handed the notebook back to Jack and wondered if she and Gabriel would ever talk easily again, as they had in Brussels.

"May I draw you, *madame?*" Jack asked.

"Moi?" She shrugged. "I suppose. If you desire it."

"Remain still," he said.

It was a curious feeling to have a man look at her so intently. She supposed Gabriel had done so in Brussels, but Jack merely concerned himself with her image. Gabriel's gaze had reached directly into her soul.

Ariana peeked at the sketch and grinned in appreciation. "You've got her!"

Jack continued moving his pencil here and there before he handed the notebook to Emmaline.

She gazed at it in surprise.

Surely he'd made her prettier than she really was. The woman in the drawing gazed with large, expressive eyes fringed with thick lashes. Dark tendrils peeked out of her bonnet and her lips looked full and moist.

"Do I look like that?" she murmured.

Gabriel touched her hand, tilting the book so he could see. "He almost does you justice."

Emmaline's breath caught at his words.

Jack laughed. "That's praise, indeed!"

Her hand trembled as she handed the notebook back to Jack.

He tore the page out and handed it back to her. "For you."

"Merci," she whispered. She held the drawing, trying to think of a place she could put it without wrinkling it.

As if reading her mind, Gabriel reached for it. "Shall I put it in my coat pocket? It will stay safe there."

She released it to him and watched him place it carefully in an inside pocket, directly against his heart.

At the fourth change of horses, the woman with the sausage departed and an eager, fresh-faced youth bounded in. After about ten minutes on the road, the boy seemed unable to contain his chatter. He talked non-stop, asking questions, disclosing the private matters of his family and friends, remarking upon everything he saw out the window. "I see sheep." "Those are mulberry bushes." "The road sign pointed to Bath." After nine hours of travel his fellow travellers were less than appreciative of his commentary, but the lad was too enthusiastic about everything to notice.

He reminded Emmaline of Claude at the cusp of adolescence, in the fresh tone of his complexion and the constant fidgeting of hands and feet. Claude, though, would have been silent and unsmiling, keeping his thoughts to himself.

Emmaline's throat tightened with grief for the life her son had been forced to lead. Not wanting the others to notice, she clamped her eyes shut. Soon the boy's voice lulled her and she finally fell asleep.

When Emmaline woke her cheek was pressed against Gabriel's chest and his arm was around her shoulders.

"Come. We have arrived," he whispered.

For one brief moment she thought she was back in Brussels, back in Gabriel's arms. She blinked the illusion away and allowed him to assist her from the carriage. He and Jack collected the baggage and they all entered the inn.

"I've stayed at the White Lion before," Ariana said to her while Gabriel and Jack spoke to the innkeeper. "It is not a bad place."

Jack walked over to them. "We've procured a set of rooms with a private sitting room. Gabe is having dinner sent up."

A maid came to show them to their rooms and a manservant followed with the baggage. Emmaline's bedchamber was a little room with just a bed and a chest of drawers holding a mirror, bowl and pitcher. A towel hung on a peg on the wall.

At the meal Gabriel shared his plan. In the morning he and Jack would walk to the house off Wells Road and call upon Edwin Tranville. Ariana and Emmaline would remain at the inn.

Ariana protested, "We will not stay cooped up in the White Lion. I shall take Emmaline on a tour of Bath and we will wait for you in the Pump Room."

A pump room seemed a very odd place for a rendezvous. Why would anyone wish to meet in a place where water was pumped? Emmaline merely nodded, however, too exhausted to question anything.

"Emmaline—" Gabriel's voice turned deep "—you must go to bed."

Her heart raced at his words.

"Yes," Ariana agreed. "You look as if you will collapse in a heap at any moment." She stood and put her arm around Emmaline, as if she would need help rising from the chair. "Come. I will help you undress."

Emmaline glanced back to see Gabriel's eyes upon her, his expression unfathomable.

Emmaline woke to a knock on the door. A maid entered, a girl of no more than sixteen with a riot of blonde curls that refused to be tamed beneath a cap.

"Good morning, ma'am," the girl said cheerfully. "I've brought you fresh water and am here to help you dress."

"How kind," Emmaline mumbled.

The maid laughed. "Kind, it wasn't. The officer paid me well for it."

"The officer?" But she knew who the girl meant.

"The one in your party." With that matter-of-fact statement, she emptied the dirty water from the bowl into the chamberpot and placed the jug of fresh water on the chest. "You can wash while I take this out." She lifted the chamberpot. "I'll be right back."

A few minutes later, Emmaline was dressed and the maid, still talkative, was pinning up her hair. "You are French, aren't you, ma'am? I can always tell, because you talk in that French way."

"*En réalité,* I live in Brussels." Emmaline preferred not to think of herself as French anymore.

"*En réalité,*" the girl repeated. "That sounds like French talk."

"Many people speak French in Belgium."

The girl paused. "I never knew that."

Emmaline glanced away. "Did—did you ever hear of a young man speaking in the French way who came to Bath recently?"

"We get lots of them now the war is over," the girl replied.

"He would be just a little older than you and very enamoured of horses."

The girl stuck in another hairpin. "I'll ask my brother. He works in the stables. He might remember if a fellow talked of horses."

She decided to add, "The Frenchman, he might be asking for Edwin Tranville."

"The baron's son?" The girl put in more pins. "Nobody likes him, I've heard, but I don't know why. It was big news when General Tranville became a baron, I remember that from when I was little. People used to talk about that family a lot." She patted Emmaline's hair, signifying she was finished. "There you are. I'm to brush your travelling clothes as well, but is there anything else for me to do? The officer told me to ask."

"*Non,*" Emmaline responded. "Thank you."

The girl smiled and curtsied and opened the door.

"Do not forget to ask your brother," Emmaline added.

"I'll do it, ma'am."

As the maid left, Ariana appeared in the doorway. "I've been waiting for you. Jack and Gabe left a half-hour ago. Come. We shall breakfast on Lunn's buns and you will see something of Bath."

"What is Lunn's bun?" Emmaline asked.

"You shall see!" Ariana said cheerfully.

A few minutes later they were on the street and Emmaline had her first glimpse of Bath.

"Oh, my," she exclaimed.

The buildings were all made of honey-hued stones. They passed one after the other until coming upon a huge church that towered over everything and looked as if it belonged in France. The church was built of the same golden stone as the other buildings. The pavement was paved with flagstone so their shoes and their hems stayed clean. People were already up and about. Young men laughing and ogling young ladies as they passed. Old men in white wigs leaning on canes. Grey-haired dames swathed in shawls and carried about in sedan chairs.

Emmaline kept her eyes peeled for a blond-haired man with a scar on his face. Or for Claude.

They entered a building with a cheerful bow window and sat at a small table. Ariana ordered them both Lunn's buns and coffee.

The buns were round-shaped bread, each filling a small plate. They were still warm from the oven.

"It is a *brioche!*" Emmaline exclaimed.

Ariana frowned at her. "A Lunn's bun is only made in Bath."

Emmaline added clotted cream and jam and took a bite. "It is a very good *brioche.*"

Ariana smiled again. "We shall take a walk after this."

"But when will Gabriel and Jack return? Perhaps we should go directly to this pump room."

"We have time," Ariana said as she nibbled on her bun. "Time enough to talk of you and Gabe."

Emmaline did not know how to talk of her and Gabriel, even if she wished to do so. "I do not comprehend."

Ariana tilted her head pensively. "There must be an attachment, surely."

"Attachement?" Gabriel certainly did not seem to wish for one, although he had accepted her bargain of marriage.

"Emmaline, he looks upon you like a lover might, but there is such a distance between the two of you. What happened?"

Emmaline took another bite of her bun. How long had it been since she'd had a friend with whom to share confidences? Growing up, she'd learned never to share private matters; one never knew what might be construed as treason. She could never share her views about France with her zealous family and her husband had never been interested in what she thought or felt.

Only with Gabriel had she been able to bare her soul.

"I cannot speak of Gabriel." She met Ariana's gaze. "It is for him to tell you, not for me. He must decide."

Ariana shook her head in frustration. "Men will speak of nothing, do you not realise that? They will hold things in until they are destroyed from the inside. I have seen it in Jack, although he manages to release his emotions in paint. He will not even tell me exactly what Edwin did to you and your son, not really."

"I will tell you that much." Emmaline's voice rose. "Edwin laughed when his compatriots stabbed my husband to death in front of my son. He tried to violate me and when my son tried to defend me, Edwin tried to kill him, too. That is the scene your Jack came upon in Badajoz."

Ariana reached across the table and took Emmaline's hand. "No wonder your Claude feels as he does. Jack and Gabe will warn

Edwin, for Claude's sake. And for yours." She smiled in kindness. "Let us finish our Lunn's buns and then I will show you the beauty of Bath."

Emmaline's appetite failed her, but she forced herself to eat most of the meal.

Afterward, true to her word, Ariana refrained from asking more about Gabriel or Edwin Tranville. She led Emmaline through the hilly streets of Bath, promising to show her a grand sight. Emmaline pretended to enjoy the walk, even though her shoes pinched her feet and she worried the whole time that they would not reach the pumps in time to meet Gabriel.

"What is it you wish to show me?" Emmaline asked again, although Ariana had already told her she must wait and be surprised.

Finally they came upon a row of buildings that formed a huge circle, all built with the honey-coloured stone. They walked to the centre of the paved courtyard that the buildings surrounded. Emmaline twirled all the way around to see them.

"This is the circus," Ariana said. "But come."

"There is more?" Truly, she just wanted to go to the room where the pumps were, even if they arrived early.

They crossed the courtyard and came on to a more ordinary street, but, as they continued, another marvellous sight appeared before them.

"Oh!" Emmaline exclaimed. The view was majestic.

"The Royal Crescent!" cried Ariana. "Bath is famous for it. I wonder you have never heard of it."

"We never heard much of England," Emmaline explained.

This time the golden buildings were curved in a crescent and faced a fine park. The sight of them was like nothing Emmaline had seen before, both unexpected and interesting. Even so, she could admire them only so long before she felt impatient to be off.

Finally her guide said, "Let us go to the Pump Room."

Emmaline expected them to proceed to the river where a pump would likely be placed, but instead they entered a building near the big church and walked into a very elegant room with several people standing about.

"Do you see them?" Ariana craned her neck and surveyed the room.

"This is the Pump Room?" It looked more like a very elegant assembly room.

Ariana still searched the room. "Yes. You can take the waters if you like." She pointed to a counter where capped maids handed small glasses to the people flocked around it.

"Take the waters?" This was making no sense.

"From the springs," Ariana explained in an incredulous voice. "Do not tell me you have not heard of the therapeutic waters of Bath?"

"Ah." She finally understood. They pumped therapeutic waters into this room. "It is like *Les Eaux-Chaudes* in France." The waters of *Les Eaux-Chaudes* were supposed to be healthy to bathe in and to drink.

Ariana was no longer listening. "I see someone."

"Edwin?" Emmaline's heart beat faster.

"No, but someone who might know him." Ariana pushed through the crowd and, before Emmaline could follow, disappeared.

Emmaline's knees shook. Suppose she encountered Edwin Tranville all alone? If only Gabriel were with her, she would not be afraid. She stood on tiptoe and scanned the throngs of people in the room, looking for him. Gabriel would be taller than most of them, more easily seen.

Some people shifted and she saw Ariana, not far away, speaking to an older gentleman. Relieved, she turned towards the door so she might see Gabriel when he walked in.

She caught a glimpse of red. Gabriel's coat. He stood near the doorway, sweeping his gaze around the room. He searched for her, she knew. Her heart raced again, but not in fear. It was the excitement of merely seeing him.

She hurried to him through the crowd. "Gabriel!"

Gabe turned at the sound of her voice.

She advanced towards him, hands extended. "Did you find him?"

The hopeful expression on her face touched at his guilt. His failure.

He stepped back and averted his gaze, not wanting to witness her disappointment. "Edwin has left Bath. We have not yet learned where he went."

She lowered her head and he resisted the urge to touch and comfort her. "I am sorry."

Ariana walked up to them. "What news?" she asked him. "Where is Jack?"

Gabe turned to her. "Edwin has left Bath. Jack is asking among old acquaintances for news of his whereabouts."

Ariana made an exasperated sound. "I will wager Jack discovers Edwin has been gone a week. I've spoken with Lord Ullman. I knew he was acquainted with Edwin." She touched Emmaline's arm. "Lord Ullman is the older gentleman with whom I was speaking just now. He saw Edwin a week ago, but not since. Edwin was in the company of other men. One of them was named Nicholas Frye, the other, a Mr Stewel. Lord Ullman has not seen any of them for a week and believes they left Bath together."

The two beautiful women were drawing curious glances from people standing near them. Gabe did not like it. "Let us return to the inn. Jack will meet us there. With any luck he will know where Edwin has gone this time."

Once outside, Ariana halted. "Let me visit the theatre. I still know people there and perhaps they have heard something." She shooed them forth. "You go on. I'll come to the inn afterwards."

Emmaline did not take Gabe's arm as they walked back to the inn. She avoided touching him or speaking to him. Gabe suspected she was bitterly disappointed that he had again failed to find Edwin.

When she had reached for him in the Pump Room, he'd again felt that bond between them, the one created from endless conversations and passionate lovemaking. The moment passed as swiftly as it had come and must have been illusion. Gabe gritted his teeth. He must remember that his importance to Emmaline was connected to the successful rescue of her son. Nothing more.

But could he find Edwin fast enough to warn him before Claude made good his vow of vengeance? With each step the task became more difficult, more impossible.

Gabe could not blame Emmaline for losing faith in him. He felt it in the increased tension in her muscles, the worried set of her mouth, the despairing expression in her eyes.

He glanced away from her, hating his acute awareness of her every breath, of every twinge of her anxiety. He knew she was thinking of Claude, fearful that he had reached Edwin, fearful that he'd already murdered him.

Gabe thrust aside his own concerns and tried to reassure her. "Just because we have not found Edwin does not mean Claude has found him."

She merely glanced at him, her eyes wide and in pain.

He tried again. "It should be easier for us to find Edwin than for Claude to do so. Claude has no contacts, no friends here in England."

She gazed up at him. "But he has been looking for much longer."

They reached the inn and climbed the stairs to their set of

rooms. In the hallway, the maid with the unruly blonde hair broke into a grin when she saw them approach.

"Good day to you, sir," she said brightly. "And to you, ma'am."

He and Emmaline murmured a greeting and passed her.

"Oh," she called to them, "I talked to my brother."

Emmaline seized his arm so he would stop. She turned. "What did your brother say?"

Even a clod could not miss her intense interest.

The maid glanced first at him, then smiled at her. "You were very right. There was a Frenchman asking about Edwin Tranville in the stables. My brother remembered him because he knew a great deal about horses."

Emmaline tightened her grip on Gabe's arm. "What else?"

The girl shrugged. "That was all, ma'am."

"When did this man speak with your brother?" Gabe asked.

She became more animated. "It happened about a week ago, my brother said."

Gabe fished in his pocket and found a coin. He handed it to the maid, who grinned and curtsied. "Thank you, sir!"

Emmaline walked to the door and waited there until he joined her and unlocked it. He could feel her distress escalating even higher.

Once inside he gave in to his desire and reached for her. She collapsed against him. "Oh, Gabriel," she cried. "Claude is ahead of us. He is ahead of us in finding Edwin Tranville."

Footsteps sounded in the hallway and the doorknob turned. Gabriel released Emmaline and she stepped away from him.

Jack entered the room. "I have discovered where Edwin has gone!" He paused a moment to catch his breath. "To Blackburn for the cock-fighting."

Chapter Eleven

One brightly plumed cock lunged at another, drawing blood with his sharp beak. Feathers flew, and the other bird, a black-breasted red, lashed out with silver spurs affixed to its clawed feet.

"That's the way!" one man yelled while he stared down into the pit. "Kill the bloody fowl!"

Another man shoved him. "My bird's not done for yet."

The brightly plumed cock shrieked and lashed back, wings flapping, dust rising. More blood splattered on the dirt beneath their feet.

A roar broke out in the crowd, and several red-faced, sweaty men threw down bets.

"Kill him! Attack!" The shouting continued.

Claude Mableau stood at the edge of the crowd, heedless of the sound and caring nothing about the two cocks locked into a battle to the death. Claude's attention was consumed by only one man.

Edwin Tranville.

Claude watched Tranville's eyes flash with excitement as he devoured the violence in front of him and swigged from a leather-sheathed flask. His shrill laughter rang in Claude's ears.

Claude had seen that same expression on Tranville's face once before, heard that same macabre laughter. It had been years ago at Badajoz when Tranville watched Claude's father being stabbed to death. Like the cocks now jabbing with beaks, two English soldiers had plunged knives into Claude's father until he fell to the cobblestones and his blood pooled around him.

The scent of burning wood and gunpowder and fear again filled Claude's nostrils, scents belonging to that earlier time, that other place of violence and death.

He'd been a boy then, too afraid to come to his father's aid. He was no boy now. He stood inches taller and weighed a good two stone heavier than the scar-faced man who'd invaded his thoughts so vividly throughout the years.

The other two men were a blur in his memory. That night they'd been shrouded by shadows, but Claude had seen Tranville so clearly the man's image was etched on his brain.

Claude had been searching for weeks, and finally he was close to Tranville, the man who'd celebrated Claude's father's death by trying to rape his mother.

Claude took a deep breath and the knife hidden under his coat pressed against his chest. He slipped his hand inside and curled his fingers around its hilt. The handle fit Claude's hand to perfection. Its blade was thin and sharp. All Claude needed to do was sidle up to his enemy, slip the blade from under his coat and jab it into Tranville in any number of lethal spots that would guarantee his death. Claude could slink away before the cock-wild crowd would even notice.

He tasted the prospect of success and moved closer, reaching a spot behind Tranville, so close he could smell Tranville's unwashed hair and the brandy on his breath.

Claude's fingers closed around the knife's handle.

One of Tranville's friends, the one called George, pushed his way between them. "Come on, Edwin. Out now." George pulled Tranville off the wooden bench and dragged him towards the door.

Claude's heart pounded. He froze for a moment, thinking the

friend had guessed what Claude had been about to do, but the man took no notice of him.

Bitterly disappointed at being even unwittingly thwarted, Claude followed Tranville and his companion out of the building and into the drizzle of the early evening. Keeping to the edge of the path, Claude bent his head low to look as if he were paying Tranville and his friend no heed.

"I wanted to see the end!" Tranville protested. "It promised to be a battle to the death."

"Did you have money on it?" George asked.

"No," Tranville admitted.

"Never mind, then." George waved to Tranville's other two companions, Harry, with blond hair so light it looked white, and Nicholas, whose red hair and spindly legs made him resemble the cocks in the pit.

These *messieurs élégants* had never been soldiers, Claude was certain of that. In fact, if Claude had not recognised Tranville's scarred face, he would never have guessed Tranville to be a soldier.

Claude ducked into the shrubbery so he could make his way close enough to the men to hear what they said to each other.

Harry called to Tranville as he approached, "We need your blunt. The innkeeper is demanding his money for the rooms and the damages."

"Damages?" Tranville looked puzzled.

Nicholas clapped him on the shoulder and laughed. "You were too deep in your cups to remember. We sported a bit with his daughter; it is not our fault that some of the furniture and crockery was broken. The damned man says he'll go to the magistrate unless we pay."

Tranville fished in his pockets and drew out a purse. "I have a little left."

"The rest of us are all done up," George said. "We'll have to rusticate at my family's estate for a while. I sent a message for the coachman to pick us up tomorrow."

"Sounds like a dead bore," Tranville said.

They walked towards the inn and their voices faded, but Claude had heard enough. He would discover more at the inn's public rooms that evening and the stable in the morning. Wherever he went he befriended stable workers, who always could tell him what he needed to know in order to track Tranville.

Perhaps it was for the best he had not killed Tranville this day. Better to confront Tranville and compel him to disclose the names of the two men who'd actually killed his father. Claude liked the idea of facing Tranville, eye to eye. He wanted Tranville to know who murdered him and why.

Claude took a breath and reached into his coat and again felt the warm metal of the stiletto.

If no opportunity afforded him to kill Tranville tonight, he'd follow him to the next destination. No matter what, Claude was certain to eventually devise a way to confront Tranville alone.

And finally avenge his father's murder.

The next day Gabe and Emmaline set off for Blackburn while Jack and Ariana returned to London.

It took Gabe and Emmaline three days to reach Blackburn from Bath, in Gabe's mind a journey more difficult than a fortnight's march through the hills of Spain. Indeed, Gabe would have preferred a hard ride on horseback instead of this cushioned coach, sitting next to Emmaline. He was forced to remember how it had felt to hold her, to make love to her.

How had he come to spend so much time in her company, to be so constantly reminded of the past, so frequently tempted? He felt trapped in a vortex, spinning deeper and deeper. True, he could escape her at any time, merely by refusing her request to

find Edwin and save her son. He ought to do that very thing: return to London and continue the search for a commission.

But that would mean abandoning her. He could no more abandon her than he could require her to for ever be separated from
her son.

He ought to be wishing she'd never come back to turn his emotions into complete disorder, but even in this misery of confusion,
he relished her company.

Once being seated beside her had seemed like a joyous gift.
Now each turnstile they crossed, each village they passed, merely
intensified the unease between them. They spoke as little as possible to each other. Even when others were not present and they
could talk freely of their search, there was little new to be said.

To make matters worse, the journey turned into a familiar one.
The Bath coach eventually travelled to Manchester and they were
required to wait several hours in the inn there until the stage to
Blackburn arrived. All the while they remained in Manchester
Gabe worried he might happen upon someone who knew him.

There was little reason to think he'd be recognised. His appearance was so altered by his years in the army that his only
real danger was if a member of his family happened to come into
the coaching inn. To limit that slim possibility Gabe secured a
private dining room so that he and Emmaline could wait out the
time alone.

That came with its own dangers. To be alone with her, just the
two of them, intensified memories of the intimacy they'd once
shared.

After what seemed an eternity, they climbed in the coach to
Blackburn. Gabe breathed another sigh of relief that none of his
brothers were also making the journey. In his childhood, frequent
trips to the then-new textile mills in Blackburn were a part of his
father's business. As a boy, he'd sometimes accompany his father

and brothers, but he was needed only to carry bolts of cloth. Gabe mostly felt in their way.

Sometimes, if lucky, he'd been able to go off on his own and explore Blackburn as much as he wished.

When the stagecoach finally reached the outskirts of Blackburn, the afternoon was well advanced. Luckily the posting inn was close to Miller's blacksmith shop where Jack had learned Edwin and his companions were bound. Miller was well-known for his cock fights. Gabe had even sneaked into Miller's on some of his boyhood expeditions.

After securing their lodging, Gabe asked the innkeeper whether Edwin was a guest. Why not? Maybe their luck would change. Maybe they would find Edwin this day and Gabe's duty to Emmaline could be discharged and he would part from her once more.

The innkeeper slid his finger up and down the pages of his register book. "What name again?" the man asked.

"Edwin Tranville."

Emmaline stood behind Gabe and he sensed her tension, as if her nerves were connected to his own.

The innkeeper turned back another page. "There have been several comings and goings." He glanced up. "The cock fights, you know."

"If he did not sign the book, perhaps you will see the name of one of his companions, Frye or Stewel."

The innkeeper's brows shot up. "I remember those two. Frye and Stewel. Troublemakers. I tossed them out—good riddance to them!"

Gabe frowned. "They are no longer here?"

"Gone several days already." He tapped on his book.

Emmaline made a small cry. Clutching Gabe's arm, she asked,. "Did Edwin Tranville stay?"

The innkeeper pointed to names on the page. "I cannot read

the names. There were two others with that lot, though, come to think of it. Can't say if the fellow you are seeking was one of them."

Gabe peeked at the page. The signatures indeed looked like scribbles.

Emmaline spoke up. "He would have a scar."

The man raised a finger. "Ah, yes! Scar on his face from here to here?" He pointed from his temple to his mouth.

"That is the one," Gabe responded. "What can you tell us of him?"

The innkeeper laughed. "I can tell you he depleted my stores of brandy. More than that I do not know. He and his friends left the same day, thank the Lord." He shook his head. "You could ask in the stable. One of the workers might know more."

"We will do that." Gabe gestured to their baggage. "Can someone take our things up to the rooms? We'll go to the stables now."

The innkeeper called to a boy in the other room and told him where to take the luggage. Gabe gave them both coins in exchange for their assistance. He and Emmaline hurried to the stable.

"I recall them," one of the stablemen said. "They left in a private carriage. It came and fetched the lot of them and carried them away after the horses rested."

Another man spoke up. "There was a crest on the side of it. With a bird, I think."

"Do you know where they went?" Gabe asked.

The first man scratched his head. "Can't say I do. The coachman waited inside the inn. Did not pass the time with anyone here." The other shrugged in agreement.

"*Pardon,* sir," Emmaline broke in. "Was there a young Frenchman here at that time? He would have been a *connoisseur* of the horses."

"Mableau?" He grinned. "Nice fellow. Not French, though. Said he was from Brussels. He left about the same time as that other lot, come to think of it, but I did not see him go."

The other worker also shook his head.

"Thank you." Gabe tipped both stable workers. "We are staying at the inn. I would be grateful if you would come and tell me if anyone else knows more."

As they walked out Emmaline grabbed Gabe's arm. She needed steadying. "What do we do now, Gabriel?"

What, indeed? Gabe had no notion of how to look for a group of young men who had left in a private carriage. They could be anywhere.

"We go back to the inn." What else could they do?

She stepped in front of him and clutched at the lapels of his uniform coat. "We cannot give up! Claude has followed them. We must find him before it is too late!"

He dug his fingers into her shoulders, not knowing whether to push her away or to enfold her in his arms and comfort her.

He released her, now pulsing with desire and resentment. It was madness to feel attached and distant at the same time.

By all rights he should abandon this charade. He needed to return to London, to be present if word came of a commission. If an opportunity presented itself, he had to pounce on it or lose it to one of the countless other men eager to return to full military service.

He opened his hands as if telling himself he would not touch her again. "We will walk back to the inn where you will stay. I will go to the cock fights and ask among the spectators. Perhaps someone will know where they were bound."

Her eyes met his and roused his tenderness again. "I want to go with you."

He turned away and started walking. "Not to a cock fight."

She said nothing else to him as he escorted her back to the inn and arranged for a meal to be sent up to her room.

* * *

Gabe spent a good two hours watching birds attack each other so men could bet on them. When a boy, watching the fights held all the excitement of the forbidden, but now it disgusted him. He'd seen too much bloodshed during the war. Watching birds jab and slash each other held no amusement.

He did manage to engage a few men in conversation. Some recalled seeing Edwin but only now noticed he and his friends were gone. Gabe found no one who knew where they might have travelled next.

"They lost a great deal of money," one man said, patting his coat pocket. "I know because I profited nicely from it."

Where would spoiled young gentlemen go if low on funds? Gabe had no idea. He checked in a few nearby taverns before making his way back to the inn. These Blackburn streets were both familiar and strange. Like his home town, Manchester, Blackburn, too, had changed. The mills had multiplied. A canal had been built. More people crowded its streets. Dusk had fallen and Gabe imagined they were bound for their homes and families. He fancied they'd settled into a life where they could predict what would happen one day to the next. He did not know whether to envy or pity them.

With the inn in sight, Gabe stopped. All he had to offer Emmaline this night was more disappointment. How long could he continue to search, especially with no clues at all of where to look next?

He must eventually face the fact that he could not help her.

Gabe pressed his fingers against his forehead. He needed a drink. Or two. Or three. He turned around and went back to the tavern he'd just left.

Seating himself in a dark corner, he signalled the serving maid. "Brandy," he ordered.

* * *

"Open the door, Frenchie!" The man's voice was slurred and Emmaline heard one of his companions laugh, as if those words were very droll.

He pounded on the door again and the wood bent with the force.

Emmaline jumped back and hurriedly dragged a wooden ladderback chair to wedge under the doorknob. Remy had taught her the trick many years before. It was her husband's version of protecting her when he marched them into places of danger.

"Let us in!" the man growled. "You know you want us."

That brought more laughter.

She feared no one would hear them. Her room was a considerable distance from the stairway, at the end of a long hall and around a corner from Gabriel's.

Gabriel.

Where was he? He'd been gone for hours. Had something happened to him?

"Open, woman! No more teasing." The door bowed again under the man's fist.

Emmaline dug into her portmanteau for her sewing scissors, securing it in her hand so that its point made a weapon. If the men broke in, she would scream. She would fight. She would stab.

She'd done it before, the day Gabriel had encountered her in Badajoz and prevented her from killing Edwin Tranville.

Where was Gabriel?

"Frenchie!" the man called again.

Suddenly a new voice roared, "Stay away or you'll answer to me!"

Gabriel!

Through the door Emmaline heard sounds of a scuffle. Gabriel was only one man against three. She must try to help him. Still gripping her scissors, she pulled the chair away and flung open the door.

Two of the men were already fleeing down the hall. Gabriel lifted the remaining one by the collar and tossed him after them like a sack of flour. The man scrambled to his feet and scampered away.

Gabriel turned to her, his eyes still flashing with violence. He breathed hard as he took one step towards her. "Are you injured?" His voice was rough and it frightened her.

"Non," she managed.

He advanced closer and she backed into her room.

"You will wish to know what happened," she said quickly. She'd been foolish and had not heeded his orders. He would be angry at her. "I did not stay in my room. I went below to ask about Claude in the public rooms. Those men followed me back here."

His gaze bore into her, too much like a jealous Remy when he thought another man had taken notice of her.

She raised her palm and continued to back away. "I did nothing to entice them. I did not even speak to them. They would not leave me alone. I left when their attentions became unseemly."

He leaned closer to her. "I told you to stay in your room."

Emmaline felt transported back in time. How many times had she played a scene like this with Remy? Next she would admit her mistake, promise never to defy him again, beg his forgiveness.

She stopped herself. This was Gabriel, not her husband. She could speak her mind to Gabriel.

She lifted her chin. "How many hours were you gone, Gabriel? I thought something bad had happened to you." He smelled of spirits. "I did not guess you would spend the hours in a tavern."

He glanced down for a moment before raising his eyes to her again. "No matter. You should not have left your room." A line creased his forehead. "What if I had not come upon them when I did?"

She lifted her hand, still holding the scissors. "I armed myself."

He stared from her hand to her face and his angry expression dissolved. Bracing himself against the bedpost, he swept his arm toward her portmanteau. "Pack your scissors and other things. You will stay in my room tonight."

A thrill rushed through her.

He had never shared a room with her, not since Brussels. At every inn along the road he'd secured separate rooms. When her room was next to his, she would be so lonely for him she would press her ear against the wall and listen to him moving about. When his bed creaked beneath him, she longed to be lying beside him, returning to those nights of lovemaking they'd once so happily shared. Alone in her bed, she'd yearned for his arms to comfort and protect her when she woke in terror from the nightmare, the one that placed her back in Badajoz, Edwin laughing at her husband's death, Edwin forcing himself on her, the stench of spirits on his breath.

Emmaline packed swiftly, aroused that his gaze followed her every move. Closing the buckle on her portmanteau, she said, "I am ready."

He reached for the bag, brushing against her, her skin delighting in the contact. It was all she could do not to skip down the hall after him.

They turned the corner and stopped at the door to his room. He fumbled with the key, but finally gained them entry. The room was nearly identical to hers in its furnishings and space. The bed was as small, but she did not mind that. It meant sleeping close to him.

Maybe if they shared lovemaking again, he would talk to her again instead of merely barking instructions. Maybe if she joined her body with his, they would both rediscover a piece of the bliss they'd shared at Brussels.

He placed her bag on a stool near the window and turned to her, his eyes raking her from her head to her toes.

Her breath quickened and she waited.

He crossed the room to her, stopping inches from her. He took her hand and lifted it.

And placed a key in her palm. "Lock the door behind me."

She gaped at him. "You are leaving?"

He gazed down at her and her senses filled with him, making her ache for wanting him. He leaned closer, his lips nearing hers.

He straightened. "I will sleep in your room."

He turned to pick up his own bag.

Emmaline's voice trembled. "Do not leave me alone."

With a resolute look, he headed towards the door.

She felt sick inside, bereft that he did not wish to be with her, that he no longer desired her as she desired him. It made her despondent at what this boded for their bargain, their eventual marriage.

He placed his hand on the doorknob.

"Gabriel!" she pleaded.

He turned back to her.

Chapter Twelve

Gabe knew he should not have turned back. Her face was flushed, her breathing rapid, her eyes pleading with him to stay. *Do not leave me alone,* she'd begged.

How heartless could he be? She'd nearly been attacked by drunken men. She'd endured that horror before at Badajoz.

But how could he convince her that at the moment *he* was not safe, not when the blood was surging through his veins from tossing those men away from her door, not when the sight of her now aroused him into a fevered state.

"No harm will come to you here," he forced himself to say. "If those men dare return, they will find me in your room, not you."

Her hand trembled. "I want you to stay. I do not want to be alone."

He still gripped the doorknob. "I have been drinking, Emmaline. So much that I cannot trust myself with you."

She walked towards him. "But I trust you, Gabriel."

He held up a hand for her to stop. "I am as dangerous to you right now as those men."

She came closer. "What would you do to me, Gabriel, that I would so dislike?"

He stiffened while desire coursed through him. He longed to tear the clothes from her body, to feel her bare skin beneath his fingertips. He longed to taste of her dark-rose nipples, to bury himself inside her.

She extended her hand to him. "Stay."

He dropped his bag and seized her by the shoulders. "Emma-line—"

She winced and he loosened his grip. He had not meant to cause pain. The brandy had eroded his control—could she not see? It muddled his thinking. "You want this?" he rasped.

She nodded and her eyes flared with a desire that seemed to equal his own.

His body reacted as if she really wished to bed him, but why would she do so now? She was with him out of desperation, not choice. And she would marry him out of that same desperation.

"It is what I want." Her voice was husky, unhesitant. She turned away and pulled a chain over her head, a necklace he'd not re-alised she'd worn. She set it aside and turned back to him, rais-ing her arms and running her fingers through his hair.

His hand slid to the smooth column of her neck. His fingertips felt the rapid beating of her pulse. She responded to his touch by tilting her head like a cat wanting to be petted.

"I do most certainly want this," she whispered, her voice like a fleeting summer breeze.

She twined her arms around him and pulled his head down until he could no longer resist tasting her lips again. He crushed her mouth against his, a man starving for want of tasting her. She tasted of heaven, of warm nights and peaceful days. This was what he'd lost, what he would lose again. Losing her the first time had almost crushed his very soul—what would happen when he lost her again?

Pain be damned. She was here now, willing to let him love her again—no, *wanting* him to make love to her again. She wanted that pleasure again. The brandy he'd consumed had not addled his thinking to that degree. She *wanted* this.

So, why shouldn't he? Men made love to willing women all the time. He'd done it. Many times. Why the devil stop now?

Still kissing him, Emmaline began to work the buttons on his coat. He quickly shrugged it off and tossed it aside. She stepped back to unfasten her dress and his fingers flexed with the impulse to rip the fabric away.

Her dress dropped to the floor and she backed him towards the bed, kicking off her shoes. "I will remove your boots."

He sat upon the bed while she pulled off his boots, then he drew her close so he could untie the lacings of her corset. His hands shook with impatience as he worked the knot.

When he finally freed her from the garment, she unfastened the fold of his trousers. He pulled off his shirt.

They'd undressed like this in her Brussels bedroom many times, only this felt different to him, more urgent. But then the brandy made everything seem more than it was. The brandy made him hurry. The brandy made him willing to think only of this moment and nothing more.

Soon they tumbled together on the bed, freed of clothing and restraint, skin against skin. He'd forgotten how beautiful she was, how narrow her waist, how flawless her skin, how full her breasts.

No, he'd really not forgotten; he would never forget anything about her. He'd merely tried to force her from his mind. But now she was with him again, in the flesh. In the warm, smooth, erotic flesh. He inhaled her fragrance, linen and lavender, so familiar, as if she for ever carried the scent of the lace shop with her. Even the sound of her breathing was familiar. He hated to admit he felt more at home at this moment than he'd felt when visiting the house of his birth, the family who shared his blood.

Rational thought tried to poke through his reverie, but he pushed it away. He did not care that she wanted his hands on her merely out of carnal desire. His carnal needs drove him, as well. He did not care if she did this merely to keep him from abandoning the search for Claude—

He pulled away.

"*Qu'est-ce que c'est?*" she asked, then shook her head. "I mean, what is it? What is wrong?"

He could no more accept her lovemaking as payment than he could accept marriage.

"I need to know if you want this, Emmaline." His voice came out too loud, too rough. "Do you want this?"

Her breath accelerated. "You must ask this again? I have never stopped wanting this."

She reached for him and he rose over her, convinced that her fever was running as hot as his own. Her legs parted for him and he thrust himself inside her, rushing in spite of himself, as if he could lose everything if he did not seize this moment.

Miraculously, she did not cry out in pain, but in passion, and immediately she moved with him, as fast as he moved, as force-fully as he pushed. He felt everything in the moment. All his long-ing for her, all the delight in joining with her again, but that was not the total. He also felt the agony of her sending him away, the rage at her bargain with him, the cold realisation that he would part from her again.

His body chased emotion and thought away, replacing them with a pure physical need, the need nature supplied every crea-ture, the need that promised man indescribable pleasure. Every muscle, every nerve, every part of him embraced the pleasure, and every part of him raced to the culmination, the climax.

She stayed with him on this frenzied journey, as if her every muscle, nerve and limb were as much a part of him as his own. They even breathed in unison.

The moment came.

Together they cried out. Together they convulsed with pleasure.

Together they suspended time. All that existed was here, now and each other.

Their lassitude came in unison, as well. Gabe relaxed beside her, holding her close as if otherwise she might evaporate like dew on morning grass. She snuggled next to him, entangling her legs with his so that even now he felt connected to her.

"I have missed that," she murmured.

He was surprised he had lived without it.

As the sensation ebbed, he wondered how long it had been since she'd lain with a man. It was inconceivable to him so passionate a woman could deny such needs, especially when her beauty no doubt attracted many willing men. Who could blame her? After all, he'd not been celibate since Brussels.

Although, if he were honest with himself, any release he'd found among the willing Parisian courtesans had meant nothing to him.

He firmed his resolve. This must mean nothing as well, mere physical release.

She rose on one elbow and looked down at him. "What is it, Gabriel?"

He had not even moved. "What? Nothing."

"Something upset you suddenly."

Her hair was all a-tumble, distracting him with its sensual beauty.

"A stray thought, nothing more." He brushed her locks away from her face. "We forgot to take down your hair."

She sat up and felt for her hairpins, pulling them out so that her hair fell over her shoulders and down her back.

Gabe combed the tresses with his fingers. "Still as lovely," he whispered.

She leaned down and placed her lips on his, her hair tickling his chest, her kiss arousing him once more.

To the devil with the past and the future. What did a soldier care for such things? Reach for what was within grasp.

She broke off the kiss and climbed atop him, speaking the words that were in his mind. "I want you again," she murmured.

When dawn flooded the room with light, Gabe made love to her again, as aggressively as the night before, lest daylight change everything. Nothing gentle between them, they grabbed at the pleasure, demanded it of each other and built it to an explosive force.

Afterward, as she lay in his embrace, he sensed the moment her lassitude turned to tension again. "What do we do now, Gabriel?"

To find Edwin and stop Claude, she meant.

He should tell her now that it was no use. There was nowhere to search, no clue to explore. He must return to London.

He composed the words in his mind and pictured himself telling her. He imagined her face when he dealt the crushing blow. It pained him as much as if he were inside her skin, enduring her disappointment and fear. Could he truly wound her in the way that would hurt her the most, by saying there was no way to save her son now?

He could not.

"I was thinking," he began, stating a plan that would sound as if he'd deliberated on it all night long instead of making it up as he spoke. "We should rent a horse and carriage, something I could drive myself. We can head out in some direction and ask about Edwin at the posting inns. If one direction fails to find someone who has seen them, then we'll backtrack and start in another direction."

"You will do this, Gabriel?" She sat up and her smile rivaled the sunshine. "*Très bon.* We will find someone who remembers seeing them. I know we will!"

She lowered herself to kiss him again, a kiss filled with relief and gratitude for a decision he might very well regret later.

Reluctantly he broke off the kiss. "Let me dress and go out now to see what I can arrange."

It took some time to track down an available carriage. After asking at several posting inns, Gabe finally found someone willing to rent him a gig. The one-horse vehicle was not as fast as a curricle with two horses, but it would have to do. He had no wish to search for something better all day and lose the time on the road.

When he returned, Emmaline had their bags all packed.

"Let us eat breakfast, enough to last us most of the day," he told her. After a hearty breakfast they would leave on this next, probably hopeless, leg of their journey.

Soon they sat in the public room, drinking mugs of hot coffee and eating slices of ham, cheese and bread. Their table was located in the path most patrons needed to pass to be seated, so their conversation was frequently interrupted. Not that there was much conversation between them. What was he to say to Emmaline after their impassioned night together?

As they ate, a man bumped into Gabe's chair. He looked to see who it was.

"Beg pardon," the man said.

Gabe spoke to Emmaline after the man passed. "Are you concerned that the men who accosted you will show up here?"

She shook her head. "Not at all. They will see you first and avoid you, I am certain."

Another man walked by, nodding a greeting. Gabe recognised him as one of the men he had questioned during the cock fight.

He glanced back at Emmaline and their gazes caught. Something had changed between them, he had to admit.

They were carnally aware of each other once again.

Emmaline blinked, and her expression turned to worry. "Where do we begin to look?"

Gabe shrugged. Perhaps it was only he who was preoccupied by their lovemaking. Her son consumed her thoughts. As always.

"We can toss a coin," he suggested.

"Toss a coin?" Her brows knit in confusion.

He waved a hand. "We can go in any direction. One gives us as much a chance of succeeding as another."

He took a sip of coffee, glancing up as yet another man walked by.

The man stopped. "Gabe?"

Gabe felt the blood drain from his face. It was his brother Paul.

His brother made a surprised sound. "Gabe! By God, it is you!"

Gabe rose and his brother enveloped him in a rough hug. "It is prodigious good to see you, but what the devil are you doing here?"

What spate of ill luck brought Paul here at the exact moment Gabe was sitting with Emmaline?

Without waiting for Gabe's answer, Paul looked from Emmaline to Gabe, a question in his eyes.

Gabe moved closer to her. "Emmaline, may I present my brother, Mr Paul Deane. Paul, Madame Mableau."

Emmaline extended her hand. "It is a pleasure to meet you, sir."

Paul clasped it. "You are French!" His eyes widened and he slid a very curious glance towards Gabe.

"Belgian," she said.

Two other men had to squeeze by, and the serving girl stood with a tray full of food. "Your breakfast, sir," she said to Gabe's brother.

Gabe pulled out a chair. "Join us, will you?"

He signalled the tavern girl to put the food on the table.

His brother sat, but looked from Gabe to Emmaline instead of at his food. "What are you doing in Blackburn, Gabe? Are you billeted here?"

"No," he replied. "I am still awaiting a commission."

Paul did not even seem to hear him. His brow was creased and he looked at Emmaline, trying to puzzle out who she was and why she was sharing breakfast with Gabe.

Suddenly Paul's eyes widened as if understanding dawned at last. His face immediately flushed red.

"What goes here?" he whispered to Gabe, inclining his head towards Emmaline.

She was witnessing all this, of course.

Paul's disapproving expression looked so much like their father's that Gabe was taken aback. Paul always had been a strait-laced prig. No doubt he'd concluded that Gabe and Emmaline had shared a bed as well as breakfast. He acted as if Gabe were seventeen and caught in a peccadillo, instead of a man in his mid-thirties who damned well could bed whomever he wished and didn't need an older brother to pass judgement on him.

Or on her. It was unspeakably ill mannered of Paul to gesture and whisper and eye Emmaline so blatantly. He might as well point to her and yell, "Harlot!"

Emmaline had already blushed. Gabe was certainly not going to embarrass her more by giving his brother what for.

He made his voice mild. "To answer your questions." Both the spoken one and the unspoken one. "Madame Mableau and I are in Blackburn on business, a private family matter that will not concern you—"

Paul's brows rose as if waiting for more.

"I will lay your suppositions at rest and tell you what I intended to keep private a while longer—"

Paul's expression turned smug. Emmaline stared down at her plate.

Gabe reached across the table and covered her hand with his own. He'd be damned if he let Paul shame her one second longer. "Emmaline and I are betrothed."

Chapter Thirteen

Emmaline's gaze flew to his face. "Gabriel," she mouthed.

His brother Paul released a laugh and rose to clap Gabriel on the shoulder. He took her hand from Gabe's and shook it again. "That's the stuff. Delighted for you. Can't see all the secrecy—"

"None the less, you will respect our wishes," Gabriel intoned.

She had felt such humiliation when Gabriel's brother so obviously disapproved of her. These English were such *moralistes* about such matters.

She did not wish to feel shame for bedding Gabriel. She had never experienced such desire for him as she had the previous night. Never, not even during their happy nights in Brussels. It was as if all her anxieties for Claude, her fear of the drunken men and Gabe's battling with them had transformed into passion. Even now her senses flared with the memory of its intensity.

Gabriel's brother returned to his seat. "When are you planning to tell our mother this happy news? Are you returning to London after this? You should stop in Manchester on the way. Introduce her to the family."

"We are not returning to London," Gabe answered him.

"No? Where are you headed?" His brother slapped his forehead. "Of course. To our uncle's. You are planning to pay him a visit."

In Brussels Gabe had spoken of an uncle who lived on a sheep farm, but she did not know if this was the uncle his brother meant.

"Yes," Gabe responded so quickly it took her aback. "We intend to call upon Uncle Will."

Emmaline gaped at him. Did he mean that? What about Claude? Tranville? "Gabriel, you said—"

"Never mind what I said." He silenced her with a firm gesture and a stern look. "We are visiting my uncle and announcing our betrothal to him."

Not searching for Tranville? Not stopping Claude? Emmaline's insides twisted into a knot.

She'd felt hopeful for a moment. She'd begun to believe in Gabriel, that their marriage might not be so grim, not with nights filled with lovemaking like they'd so recently shared. And then he abruptly changed what he'd promised to do.

How quickly her disquiet returned.

Gabriel behaved as Remy would have done, making plans and pronouncements without a word to her, without a moment's consideration of her wishes. By the time Remy thought to tell her of where they would march or where they would live, it was a *fait accompli,* as autocratic as Gabriel with this visit to the uncle.

She trembled with anger. "Why not ask your brother to accompany us to this uncle?"

Gabriel shot her a surprised look.

Paul seemed to notice nothing amiss, however. He patted her hand. "Cannot do it. I'm off today. Taking the canal to Liverpool. I'm riding the barge with the goods we purchased here. It is a slow trip, you know, but pleasant."

"*Quel dommage.* What a pity," she responded with false emotion.

Paul rubbed his lip. "Dashed if I don't feel guilty now. Uncle Will is so close; I ought to have called on him." He dived into his plate of eggs. "Too late now."

"What news of the family?" Gabriel asked. Apparently he'd dismissed her chagrin. That was like Remy, as well.

But she was acting like Remy's wife, not speaking directly, relying on sarcasm that men seemed too obtuse to realise. *Alors,* this behaviour was exactly how she'd put Claude in danger all those years ago, when she hadn't refused to follow her husband to Spain. She had not learned the lesson, had she? To confront, to defy, to demand.

Emmaline tried to act as if she were listening politely while the two brothers spoke of their large family, people she did not know. She must explain to Gabriel that she had no wealth of family. She had only Claude to be precious to her. Surely stopping Claude from committing murder was more important than visiting an uncle?

She shuddered, remembering the stable worker had said that Claude had left Blackburn the same day as Edwin.

She pressed her hand against her stomach. What if Claude had already found Edwin? What if he was lying in wait, ready to strike Edwin dead? What if a delay to visit this uncle kept them from finding Claude and stopping him in time?

The hand holding her fork began to shake.

Louisa Finch strode out of Rappard Hall, glad to escape its walls and breathe in the fresh morning air. On a routine day she savoured the singular pleasure of a morning's ride. It gave her some respite from the duties she'd assumed at the Hall. On horseback she could forget she was a poor relation, lucky to have a roof over her head, food to eat and clothing on her back. Lady Rappard was her late mother's cousin and Louisa's closest living relative. Louisa was glad to show her gratitude to Lady Rappard by assuming the running of the house in her absence and by taking over the housekeeper's duties. Poor Mrs Dart. Louisa supposed when Lord and Lady Rappard finally noticed the poor lady was too feeble and forgetful to complete her duties, they would pension her off to a cosy retirement. Then would Louisa become the housekeeper? To slip irrevocably into servant status was what she most dreaded.

She tried to shake off that thought.

It would be fortunate for her to have such respectable employment, but, at seventeen, daughter of an aristocratic family, she yearned for more than being buried on a country estate.

Louisa laughed out loud at herself. She was happy enough at Rappard Hall. The servants were like family to her, and she had Pomona, her lovely horse. Lord Rappard had allowed her to keep her horse, an expense she certainly could not bear on her own. Riding in the morning, useful work in the day, leisure in the evening. It *was* enough.

Her disquiet must be due to her cousin George and his friends descending upon the house. They were noisy and dirty and rude, and that Nicholas Frye was forever uttering suggestive remarks and giving her leering stares. He made her exceedingly anxious, especially because she must be constantly vigilant lest Nicholas and the other two guests bothered the maids in such a manner. George certainly was turning a blind eye to his friends' antics.

She reached the stable and entered its wide doors, greeted by the scent of hay and leather and horse.

Mr Sellars, the stablemaster, walked up to her, wiping his hands. "Good morning to you, Miss Finch. You are here to ride today, eh?"

She smiled. "As always, Mr Sellars, if it is not too much trouble. I hope you are in good health today."

"Fit as a filly. Thank you for asking," the man responded. "I'll get someone to saddle Pomona for you." He gesture to a nearby groom. "Saddle Pomona for Miss Finch, lad."

The young man turned and nodded.

"Is that your new worker?" she asked Mr Sellars. "How is he faring?"

"Never saw a lad so good with horses," Mr Sellars responded with a satisfied look. "I tell you, it was a stroke of luck your cousin allowed John Coachman to give that lad a ride, else I would never have found him for hiring. He's a hard worker. Takes the filthiest job without complaint."

Mucking out the stables, she presumed. She glanced at the new worker curiously. He was lean and only a few inches taller than herself. She could not see his features clearly, but he looked to be around her age.

Mr Sellars went on. "I believe I'll let him accompany you."

She pursed her lips at him. "Now you know I feel perfectly comfortable riding alone. There's no need to take a worker away from you."

He shook his head. "Won't hear of such nonsense. Would never forgive myself if something happened to you out there alone." He turned and raised his voice. "Saddle a horse for yourself, lad. You'll be riding with Miss Finch." He gave Louisa a conspiratorial wink. "Mark my words. He'll choose the horse that most needs a long ride."

A few minutes later, the young man led a saddled Pomona and a spirited black gelding named Apollo, who indeed looked as if he were champing at the bit for a good run.

Louisa liked the looks of this new groom. He had dark hair in need of a trim poking out from under his cap. His face was clear and his large eyes were a vibrant blue, framed by dark thick brows. What's more, there was a touch of sadness in those eyes and a melancholy turn to his full lips. Perhaps that was why she felt an inexplicable kinship.

Mr Sellars nodded and walked away without introductions. The young man held out a hand to assist her on to the mounting block.

She looked into those blue eyes as his strong hand gripped hers. "You are the new groom. Welcome. I am Louisa Finch."

He released her and glanced away as she finished mounting. When she was in the saddle, his eyes met hers again.

He removed his hat and bowed his head. "I am Claude Mableau."

Chapter Fourteen

Claude mounted the fine black horse that so reminded him of his own lost Coco, although this steed was undoubtedly of a finer pedigree. He could not help feeling excited to be riding such a horse, even if riding with this young lady unsettled him.

She looked to be a girl in the first bloom of womanhood, perhaps no more than two years younger than his eighteen years. Her cheeks were creased by dimples, created by a smile that seemed to bring sunshine into the stable with her.

Merely to glance at her made it hard for him to breathe.

Who was she? He'd heard of Lord and Lady Rappard, now summering at Brighton, and knew of their son, George, one of Tranville's friends. No one had spoken of a girl living at Rappard Hall. Was she a member of the family or a servant?

Her riding habit did not look as fine as some ladies' dresses he had seen since being in England. Perhaps she could be a servant. But what servant would have permission to ride such a fine horse as Pomona?

English people were such a puzzle.

She spoke, her voice as light and carefree as a summer breeze. "I hope you do not mind riding with me."

Mind? To be on horseback? To be near her for a time? It would be a joy.

"I do not mind," he responded.

They rode out of the stable and into the bright sunshine.

"You are French!" She sounded as if she was pleased by the notion.

Still, he'd learned it was not prudent to admit to his true nationality. "I am from Brussels."

"How exciting that is." She led them behind the stables where the paddocks were. The few other workers toiling there seemed to take little notice of them.

"Where do you wish to ride, miss?" he asked as they faced empty fields.

She laughed again, this time a throaty sound that made his male parts stir. "As far as we can go!"

She urged her horse into a gallop. It took him a stunned moment to follow. They whipped through thick green grass towards hills dotted with white sheep. Pomona ran with relish. Apollo galloped as if set free from a long confinement.

Claude felt almost happy.

When they approached a low hedge, he started to shout a warning to her, but Miss Finch jumped it with ease. He laughed aloud as Apollo sailed over behind her.

Miss Finch called to him as they charged on, "Glorious, is it not?"

It was not good for the horses to run full out for too long. He sensed it was time to slow down and was about to tell her so, when she pulled on her reins.

She signalled Pomona to walk. "We should rest the horses. There is a stream nearby. They can drink."

The stream was a short distance away, nestled between lush green-leafed trees shading each bank. When they came closer, Claude heard the tinkling of the water running over rocks. It was like music. On the other side of the stream's banks, black-faced sheep gazed at them curiously from their green pasture.

"Is this not a pretty place?" Miss Finch exclaimed.

He did not wish to admit that any place in England was pretty, even if this spot seemed as idyllic as if appearing in a dream.

Without answering, he hurried to assist her to dismount and led the horses to a spot where they could easily dip their muzzles into the water.

Miss Finch lowered herself gracefully to a grassy spot. "Come sit with me, Claude."

He hesitated. What was proper in England for a stable worker to do?

What did he care? He was French and equal to any man...or woman.

He sat next to her.

She smiled over at him. "Tell me about Brussels and why you left your home to come here."

He shrugged. "I wanted to travel."

"I would love to travel!" She laughed softly. "Although I am not certain I would pick Lancashire to visit. I cannot imagine what attracted you to this place."

One man attracted him to this place, but he could not explain that to this pretty girl. "Is Lancashire your home, miss?"

She averted her face, but not before he saw her expression turn solemn. "I grew up in Sudbury." She turned back to him. "It is not far from Newmarket."

"I have heard of Newmarket." Newmarket was a place for horse breeding and racing, too. Claude knew of such places.

"But I have lived here at Rappard Hall for two years," she went on, her expression composed now. "I am what we English call an impoverished relation. Lady Rappard, my mother's cousin, was kind enough to give me a home."

His brows knit. She was a member of the family.

She lifted her chin. "Oh, but you must not feel sorry for me. I am quite fortunate. Besides, Lady Rappard needs me. Mrs Dart, the housekeeper, is so old that she requires my help to properly run the house."

"You are the housekeeper?" he asked, confused again.

She shook her head. "It is merely how I repay Lord and Lady Rappard for my livelihood."

He did not know what to say. It seemed she was neither family nor servant, but something in between. He still did not know if he risked being sent packing for talking to her.

"It is not a bad thing!" Her cheerful tone seemed forced. "Of course, with my cousin George and his companions in residence, there is quite a bit more to do."

Cousin George. His companions included Edwin Tranville. The man Claude had come to murder.

A cloud covered the sun and the stream no longer sparkled. Claude reminded himself he was not here to become enamoured of an English girl, no matter how prettily she smiled at him.

"I rode atop their coach, but that is all I've seen of the young gentlemen," he said.

There was much more he wished to know about them, however. Such as, what time did they retire at night? Which bedchamber was Tranville's?

She frowned, then glanced up at the clouds and stood. "Perhaps we should head back."

He hurried to bring her horse to her and to help her mount. This time his thoughts were not consumed with how delicate she felt or how his fingers tingled from merely touching her. Tranville had intruded into his thoughts and his mind was filled with how he might find him alone.

They took a slow pace back to Rappard Hall, a pace that gave Claude more time to think about his quest for revenge. He lagged half a length behind her, and they did not speak. Still, he admired her confident handling of the horse, her comfort in the sidesaddle.

When Rappard Hall came into view Claude looked upon it with

disdain. A *château,* it would be called in France, although certainly a French *château* would be grander. The house was large enough, but boxy in shape and constructed of red sandstone over which ivy and moss had grown. It had one large tower perched on top of its three storeys, as if it had been stacked there like a child's set of blocks. The windows, however, were what most interested Claude. Which one would reveal Tranville?

"I will ride you to the door and take Pomona back to the stables for you."

She smiled at his offer, as if it had been an unselfish one. "That would be so kind, Claude."

He was not kind. He was a miserable dog. His intent was solely to more closely examine the house, to see where he might enter it, to discover where he might finally confront Tranville.

And kill him.

Gabe stowed the luggage in the gig and glanced at Emmaline. She stood stiffly, her face averted. He could almost feel the tension inside her. He'd been acutely aware of it ever since his brother had joined them at breakfast.

Cursed luck. What were the odds that a member of his family would visit Manchester at the same time, stay in the same inn and walk into the public rooms at the precise hour he sat there with Emmaline? Now it was almost noon. Paul's appearance had delayed their departure. Half the day was nearly gone.

Even worse, Paul had gaped at Emmaline as if she were merely some doxy with whom Gabe was trifling. Gabe had seethed at the knowing look Paul had given him and at the tone of disapproval in Paul's voice.

He frowned with the memory and raised the hood of the carriage so Emmaline would be shaded from the sun and protected from any sudden shower. He turned to help her into the seat.

Emmaline stepped back. "How could you do this to me, Gabriel?"

How was he to answer? His brother's presumptions about her were rude, but not entirely incorrect. He and Emmaline were lovers, after all. The previous night proved that.

"My brother's appearance was unfortunate—" he began.

She waved a hand. "Do you think I care about that? You broke your word to me! That is what I care about. You dictate a visit to this uncle when you know all I want to do is find Claude and stop him."

He was shocked. "You think I broke my word?"

Was her opinion of him so low that she thought he would forget their purpose of being together or the promise he'd made to her about continuing the search?

"What else can I believe when I heard you with my own ears?" She crossed her arms over her chest. "I do not wish to visit this uncle, Gabriel. I will not go with you."

The horse shuffled, as if impatient to be moving. So was Gabe. His bargain with her was to prevent her son from murdering Edwin Tranville, and, even though his chances of success were now exceedingly slim, he intended to try every means he could think of to accomplish that feat.

He looked directly into her eyes. "We search for Claude, Emmaline. What I spoke to my brother was fiction. What I said to you was truth." He paused. "Unless you would have preferred I explain to him we merely shared a bed during our quest to keep your son from murdering a baron's son?"

She looked down at her feet. "I did not realise."

He extended his hand and this time she allowed him to lift her up to the gig's seat. He climbed up beside her and signalled the horse to begin moving. Though he could not remember when he'd last driven a carriage, the skill came back readily and he eased the horse into the traffic on the road.

She was silent, but subdued. How easily she had misjudged his character.

And his feelings towards her.

As he drove he spoke, "My uncle is to the north-west. We will head south. Towards London. London or Brighton seems their most likely destination."

The horse faltered as other carriages, wagons and riders clogged the road out of Blackburn. Gabe pulled on the ribbons to keep the horse steady.

"I am sorry, Gabriel," she murmured.

Her wounding words still stung, no matter her apology.

She turned to him and he caught her earnest expression. "Why did you tell your brother we were betrothed?"

She did not understand? He gritted his teeth. He gave her a scathing look. "I had the frivolous notion to protect your reputation."

"Oh," she murmured.

"I did not forget the terms of your bargain, if that is what you presumed." Being considered the sacrifice she would make in return for her son's life was hardly something that would slip his mind.

Gabe admitted to himself a fledgling hope that sharing a bed with her might have altered matters between them. He would not make that mistake again. Oh, he would make love to her again, if she wished it. He'd be a fool to deny himself such pleasure. From now on, though, he would not forget that what they shared in bed could never equal her bond with her son.

Gabe manoeuvred the gig on to the London road.

They rode in silence for a couple of hours until Gabe sighted a posting inn in the distance.

"We'll stop here. The horse can rest and refresh herself while we enquire about Edwin or Claude."

They enquired if anyone had seen, in recent days, four young gentlemen in a private carriage with a crest on the side, a crest with a bird.

No one remembered seeing such a vehicle, nor did they recall a young Frenchman travelling alone.

They stopped at every posting inn on the road, asking the same questions, receiving the same answers. Gabe and Emmaline travelled almost as far as Manchester before Gabe turned around, taking a different route back towards Blackburn and checking at different inns. The answers were still the same. No hint of Edwin Tranville or Claude.

With each mile Gabe felt Emmaline's distress grow. He could not help but be affected by her growing despair.

The last inn where they made enquiries was nearly back to Blackburn and the sky was turning dark.

"We should stay the night here," Gabe told her. "Tomorrow we'll try in a different direction."

She nodded, looking exhausted and defeated.

That night they shared a room and a bed and Gabriel made love to her again, not quite as impersonally as he'd vowed. Their passion was fuelled by the tension of the day and by Gabe's need to comfort her against her fear that perhaps they were already too late.

Before they roused from the bed the next morning Gabe made love to her again. As they were preparing to head out, he bought a newspaper and searched its columns for news of a murder having already occurred. No news item was found.

This time Gabe drove the gig east towards the Irish Sea, passing through Preston and Leyland and Chorley, attempting to cover any road Edwin and his friends might have taken.

To no avail.

Two more days passed like this as they headed north, then west. Gabe could not ease Emmaline's despair.

"We will try again tomorrow," Gabriel said to her, as he held her in his arms once again. In spite of all it meant to him, the ultimate loss of her, his own heart ached at the pain she endured on behalf of her son.

She pressed her face against the skin of his chest and stifled a sob. "What if we are too late?" she asked him. "What if we are too late?"

Claude swept the floor near the stable doors, keeping busy while anticipation throbbed through his every vein, the anticipation of seeing Louisa Finch. She came to the stable to ride every morning at this time, and Claude made certain he was the groom available to ride with her.

No, not Louisa Finch. He must not make her important to him. It was the prospect of riding a fine horse like Apollo that appealed to him, he told himself. It was the chance to gallop over fields and hills, the air whipping at his clothing and filling his lungs. The pleasure of it almost drove thoughts of revenge out of his mind.

Almost.

At night he'd left his bed to creep up to the house. Already he'd discovered what doors were left unlocked, allowing him entry. He'd managed to glimpse Tranville, but still did not know where he slept. When he discovered Tranville's bedchamber, Claude's plan was to confront him there, make him divulge the names of the two soldiers who'd killed his father, and plunge the stiletto into Tranville's heart.

By morning, when Tranville's body was discovered, Claude would be far away.

The only part that bothered him was that Louisa would know he'd killed Tranville. She would never understand why he must commit murder. She'd hate him for it.

A sound made him glance up from his work.

Louisa walked towards him.

As she'd done the last three days, she would ask to ride Pomona and he would ride with her.

His pulse quickened at the prospect of her bright, daring eyes, her rose-tinged cheeks, her expressive pink lips.

"Good morning, Claude. Will you ride with me today?" This morning her smile seemed forced; her tone, sad.

What had happened? She always appeared happy when she came to ride, as if she, like he, grasped freedom only on the back of a horse.

"Yes, miss." He doffed his cap and banked his initial enthusiasm. "Do I saddle Pomona for you as before?"

"Yes, indeed." She seemed to be making an effort to sound cheerful.

While he saddled Pomona and Apollo she was uncharacteristically silent.

"What is troubling you, miss?" he could not help but ask.

"Troubling me?" She made a pretence of a smile, but her voice cracked. "Why, nothing." She paused. "An attack of the blue devils, I suppose. It will pass."

He did not know what blue devils were, but something had changed her usual sunny manner.

He helped her onto her horse and his senses flared as before, but he felt as if he'd committed some offence by feeling his excitement so viscerally.

When they rode out of the stable, all of the young gentlemen—Tranville included—were walking towards them. Claude was careful to keep his eyes downcast.

"So this is where you disappear to, Cousin?" George Rappard said.

"I like to ride in the morning," she responded in a tight voice.

None of the young men seemed to give Claude any notice, but he was acutely aware of Tranville, his scarred face looking sallow in the morning light.

"Where is the gamekeeper?" her cousin went on. "We have a notion to go fishing and need poles and tackle."

"I have no idea where he is," she responded. "You should find the poles in his shed."

Claude could volunteer to find the poles and tackle for the young men. Perhaps he would be ordered along to assist them as he'd been ordered to ride with Louisa. This might be his opportunity to lure Tranville away from the others, to confront him and to exact his revenge.

All Claude needed to do was speak up.

And leave Louisa.

She moved her horse forwards, her spine rigid in the saddle. "Good day, Cousin. Gentlemen."

Claude followed her.

When they were out of earshot of the young men, she turned to him. "Let us not gallop today," she said.

"As you wish, miss," he responded.

She continued, her voice as strained as it had been speaking with her cousin. "I thought we might ride to the abbey."

There was an abbey nearby? Claude did not know the English had abbeys.

She went on, "George and his friends will not go there. I—I would not wish to disturb their fishing at the stream."

She led him on a path they had not ridden along before. Claude followed, but the brief sight of Tranville again filled Claude's nostrils with the scent of Badajoz. His father's blood. Tranville's drunken stench. Claude shook his head to dispel the memory.

He hated thoughts of Tranville to intrude during these brief interludes with Louisa. Usually when he rode with her the grass seemed greener, the sky bluer, the wildflowers more fragrant.

But today her mood—and his—was like a black cloud rumbling across the sky. He lowered his head and felt the darkness surround him.

They reached the crest of a hill and below them was the abbey.

"This is it?" Claude looked down on what was nothing more than piles of rubble, marking what must once have been walls. One tower still stood. Although it was open to the sky, it gave a hint to what grandeur once must have existed in this small valley.

"Is it not lovely?" she exclaimed, some of her usual liveliness returning.

To Claude it was a dreadful sight. What must have been a huge, thriving place was now nothing at all.

Louisa started down a path. She looked over at Claude. "Come. Shall we explore?"

When they reached the pile of stones, they dismounted. The horses wandered to a steam nearby to quench their thirst. Claude supposed it must connect to the same stream in which he and Louisa usually watered the horses, the same stream in which Tranville and his friends would fish, but here it was no more than a thin strip of water easily crossed with one giant step.

Claude followed Louisa through an arched entrance. All the walls or their remnants were red sandstone, the same as Rappard Hall.

Louisa stared up at a majestically high wall that must have once contained windows of coloured glass. "This place makes me feel peaceful."

Claude frowned. "It is rubble. What happened to it?"

She glanced around. "Centuries ago, King Henry VIII seized all the abbeys and Cromwell sold the land to important men. That is how Lord Rappard's ancestors came here. It has been their property ever since."

Claude had heard of that English king who abolished the Roman Catholic religion so he could divorce one wife and marry another.

"They allowed it to fall down?"

The magnificent Notre-Dame had been preserved for the people as a Temple of Reason. These buildings had been left to crumble and decay.

"I suspect eventually the family wished for a modern house. In fact, many of the stones from the abbey were used to build Rappard Hall and its buildings."

That explained why some walls had all but disappeared, their presence only marked by those remaining in the ground, like paving stones.

She sat on the sill of what once had been a window and gazed around. "Ghosts gather here at night, spirits of the slain monks. A lady in white has also been seen, wandering through the rooms. It is said she is waiting for her lover to return from the sea. Poor thing," she added sombrely. "She cannot escape this place."

She dropped her head into her hands and burst into tears.

Shocked, Claude rushed to her side and, without thinking, put his arm around her. "Miss? What distresses you? Why do you weep?"

She straightened, but did not move away. He handed her a folded handkerchief from his pocket, glad that it was clean. She wiped her eyes with it. "It is silly of me. I am not usually such a watering pot."

It took him a moment to comprehend the meaning of *watering pot.*

She shook her head. "My life here is happy enough. I do not complain, but my—my cousin and his companions are so unpleasant. They yell and shout and run around. They are draining Lord Rappard's wine stores and waste so much food. They have already broken some porcelain that Lady Rappard held dear." She wiped her eyes again. "It is too awful. They talk like—like ruffians. Even in my presence. And I must keep the young maids away from them… I hate it all so dreadfully!" More tears poured from her eyes.

Something hardened in Claude at the mention of her cousin

and his friends. His comfort turned to an effort to gain information. "Surely they will leave soon, will they not?"

"George whines that they are stuck here for a month until he receives his next quarterly portion."

A month? Claude did not intend a whole month to go by before he performed his sworn duty. Although a month of working in the stable and riding with Louisa all day would be very pleasant.

"Where do they spend their time? Perhaps you can avoid them." Where might he encounter Tranville? he meant.

She waved an exasperated hand. "They intrude everywhere. My only escape is to ride with you."

Claude should have felt gratified that this young and pretty girl, who was perfection in his eyes, liked the time she spent with him and treated him like a friend, not a servant. Instead he felt annoyed that she told him nothing of use.

"Oh, Claude!" She threw herself into his arms and wept against his chest. He had no choice but to hold her. Her clean scent and her soft curves finally drove out his thoughts of vengeance.

When she broke away, her smile turned more genuine. "I feel better. Sometimes all it takes is a good cry. Shall we ride some more?"

He merely nodded, too overwhelmed with the pleasure of having held her in his arms to speak. They walked over to the horses. When he lifted her in the saddle, she smiled down at him and his body responded to her.

He quickly turned away so she would not see. In some discomfort, he mounted Apollo, and he had some time to recover as she led them up the hill on the other side of the valley from whence they had come. Claude looked down on some pretty farm buildings, smaller than those at Rappard Hall.

"This is the farm that borders the Rappard property," she explained. "There is a road at the bottom of the hill. We can follow it back to our stables."

She seemed more relaxed on the way back. Claude, on the other hand, was stirred up in many ways. By her. By seeing Tranville. By his purpose for being at Rappard Hall.

They rode into the stable. In the relative darkness, he helped her dismount and she gave him a quick hug before turning away and hurrying back to her dismal life.

That night in the room Claude shared with the other grooms, he tossed and turned on his cot. It was not their snoring that kept him awake this night, but rather thoughts of Louisa, the first girl who had ever stirred his senses.

How ironic that it was an English girl who so enraptured him. Even if there were *égalité* between them, as there would be in France, he would never court an English girl.

Alors. This was foolish thinking. He sat up in bed and rubbed his face. This was no time for romantic reverie. He had more important considerations.

Claude pulled on a shirt and trousers and carried his shoes out of the room, to put on before leaving the building. When he stepped out into the night, stars sparkled in the sky and the almost-full moon turned the grass to silver.

Lights shone from upper-floor windows at the Hall. As if he were a moth to those flames, he headed directly to the house, choosing a spot where he had a good view of the lighted windows, but could not be seen spying.

He waited, his limbs stiffening from the cool, damp air and from fatigue. His lids grew heavy and he struggled not to doze on his feet.

A silhouette appeared in the window, a man raising a bottle to his mouth and drinking from it. Tranville? Claude held his breath and waited to be sure.

The man disappeared for a moment then carried a candle

to the window. For a brief moment the candle illuminated the man's face.

It was indeed Tranville, jagged scar and all.

And now Claude knew exactly which room was his.

Chapter Fifteen

Gabe awoke in yet another posting inn. He blinked his eyes and struggled to remember exactly where they were.

Clitheroe.

They'd been headed north towards Lancaster to see if Edwin and his friends were bound for the Lake District, but it had soon been clear the route was again wrong. Next Gabe chose for them to go west, deciding to circle back to Blackburn on different roads, ones that were far less travelled. It was no real surprise that the young gentlemen had not been seen by anyone Gabe and Emmaline encountered.

Where the devil had they gone?

It was as if they'd fallen off the edge of the world. Of course, it was entirely possible that Gabe had just missed the certain road, certain inn, or one person who would have remembered seeing them.

He rolled over in the lumpy bed and gazed at Emmaline. God help him, she looked worried and fretful even in sleep. Tendrils of hair had escaped her plait and he fought the urge to brush them away from her face.

His heart twisted. How he had utterly failed her!

His bones ached from countless bumps in the road and he pined to stretch his weary muscles. He might wake her by doing so. The least he could do was allow her to sleep.

What a contrast these last three days had been from their lazy days in Brussels, where being together had been so easy, so full of peace and pleasure. Now each hour in his company merely increased the tension he sensed inside her. When they'd first lain next to each other in this bed, she'd been like cracked crystal. Gabe feared a mere touch would shatter her.

She'd wept in her despair for her son; Gabe had held her so close he could feel her damp lashes on his skin. There had been no words he could speak to console her. No such words existed. He'd merely held her until she'd fallen into exhausted sleep.

How confident she'd been of his ability to find Edwin and stop Claude from murdering him. He remembered her earnest entreaty in London, her surety that he alone could succeed in saving her son. Again. She'd staked her whole future on it.

Well, at least if he failed she would no longer feel obligated to marry him. Perhaps that thought consoled her.

Gabe grimaced. How churlish to even think of it. The pain of her misguided promise to marry him seemed inconsequential in comparison to the pain he sensed inside her.

At his failure.

He'd missed something, Gabe was convinced. Some piece of information that should have told him where to search. Something. Again he went over everything they'd learned, every place they searched, trying to find that missing piece of information.

If only he knew what it was.

No longer able to lie still, Gabe slipped out of the bed and stretched to finally ease his stiff muscles. As quietly as he could, he walked over to the bureau and poured some water from the pitcher into the basin. He dampened a cloth and wiped his skin, letting the bracing morning air dry him. Making lather from a piece of soap, he scraped his razor along his cheek. In the mirror, he glanced back at Emmaline. She raised herself on one elbow, before sitting up and rubbing her eyes.

Their gazes caught in the mirror, a silent communication of hopelessness.

He finished shaving and emptied his soapy water so the basin would be clean for her. As he began to dress, she padded across the room, naked. They'd slept together naked, as they had each of these nights, nights spent in passionate oblivion.

Except this past night. They'd not made love this past night.

If she had wanted it, he would have willingly complied. Anything she wanted he would have done for her. Anything to give her solace. If she gave any sign this morning of needing the scant comfort of his body, he would offer it. All he desired was to ease the pain he sensed inside her, the sheer despair that her son was lost.

And Gabe had done nothing to save him.

But she asked nothing of him. What he saw reflected in the mirror was her anguish.

She turned away again. Even in her despair her movement was graceful, so perfectly womanly his senses were aroused. He drank in her flawless skin, her pleasing curves and narrow waist. He knew from memory how it felt to trace his fingers down the length of her spine, how warm and willing she was to his touch.

It would be difficult to part from her. Again.

Gabe's anger at her had been erased by her misery and his failure to ease it. What did his vanity matter when she was so thoroughly unhappy? He could not detest her for loving her son, for wanting to do anything to save her son's life.

He tried to imagine his own mother feeling that way about him.

Impossible.

His mother had many children and grandchildren to fill any small place in her heart she might have once reserved for him. Emmaline had only Claude.

Or, rather, she so filled her heart with love for Claude that there was no room in it to spare for anyone else. Not even for Gabe.

That was reality, not something for self-pity. Gabe had known about her love for her son from the moment he'd looked into her eyes at Badajoz. He'd made the decision to love her for it then; he could not stop now.

He finished dressing.

Emmaline slipped on her shift and undid the plait in her hair. With long graceful strokes she brushed out the tangles as if trying at the same time to soothe herself.

Gabe put on his boots. "Shall I see if there is a newspaper to be found?"

She flinched as if struck by a rod. "Can it wait a little?"

"Of course." He stood. "I could arrange for breakfast, then. Would you like to eat it in the room here?"

She shook her head. "Will you wait for me? I will dress quickly."

He crossed the room to her and stood behind her. Gently he turned her around and held her against his chest. "Whatever you wish, Emmaline."

She melted into him. "What do we do now? We've searched everywhere."

"Make our way back to London." He held her tightly. "Start all over again."

Futile though it would be.

When they were on the road again Emmaline tried to cheer herself. They'd not found any news of Edwin's murder in the papers, after all, and it was another fine day. She should be grateful for good weather. Their travel would have been slower and more miserable if it had rained.

She ought to be grateful to Gabriel, as well, for his tenacity, his willingness to drive all over the countryside, asking at inn after inn, for not giving up, not losing hope. In her heart, though, she knew all hope was gone.

Somewhere in England, Claude was near Edwin, planning Edwin's murder. Or had already accomplished the deed and was arrested, awaiting hanging. Perhaps if a newspaper carried an account of the murder, she could still reach Claude in time to say goodbye.

Emmaline shook away that horrible thought and forced herself to gaze at the rolling hills of pasture and farmland that they passed. She let the steady pace of their intrepid horse lull her and ward off total despondency.

The land reminded her of Belgium, rolling grassy hills dotted with peacefully grazing sheep. She and Gabriel had once driven out into the Belgian countryside to similar scenes.

"This must be sheep-farming land," she commented, to rid herself of the contrast between her happiness then and her misery now.

Gabriel shifted, as if surprised that she spoke. Their conversation had heretofore been less than perfunctory.

"It is." He paused before adding, "I tended sheep on these very hills."

It was her turn to be surprised. "Here?"

"The hill farm where my uncle is employed is close by." His tone was matter-of-fact. "These pastures are part of it."

"C'est vrai?" She glanced at the land again. "Truly? Is this the uncle you told your brother we would visit?"

"Yes."

He'd said when they started out this morning that they were not far from Blackburn. His plan was to return the horse and gig there and secure passage back to London for the morrow.

She set aside her own worries for a moment. "Gabriel, is this the uncle you told me about in Brussels, the one with whom you spent happy days?"

"It is," he responded, his voice remaining even.

"We should call upon him, should we not? We are so close and you told your brother you would." What did an extra hour or two matter? They would still have time to reach Blackburn. There was no real need to hurry now. Claude was lost.

He looked at her carefully. "Are you certain?"

She nodded. "He is your *family*." Her throat tightened at the word family and she turned away in case tears would burst from her eyes.

They quickly came upon an even narrower road leading up a gentle hill. He turned the gig on to it and, as they reached the crest, the farm and all its buildings could be seen in the valley below. A white-stucco farmhouse, three storeys high, with a shingled roof, was framed by large trees and a flower garden. Fanning out from the house was a series of outbuildings and beyond them half-a-dozen tiny cottages.

On their search for Claude they had passed many prosperous country estates with magnificent mansions and numerous farm buildings nearly as grand. This property was much more modest and, because of that, its appeal was greater. Emmaline could imagine a family running this farm, living happily in such a comfortable place.

As they descended into the valley Emmaline could see that the garden was tangled with weeds and the house was tightly shuttered. A dog crossed the path from one barn to another, followed by scampering chickens, the only signs of life. It made her sad. Why was such a lovely place neglected?

As if reading her thoughts, Gabriel said, "The farm is for sale, and the farmhouse is vacant. There are only enough workers left to tend to the sheep."

"It is for sale? What happens to your uncle if it sells?" Would he be out of a job? Gabriel had told her that unemployment plagued the whole country.

"My uncle ought to have been pensioned off, but he stays on to keep the farm running. I do not know what will happen to him." He paused and added. "I once considered purchasing it."

"You have so much money?" She was surprised. "Why did you not purchase it?"

He looked sad. "I lost my reason to. Besides, I am a soldier, not a farmer."

She did not have a chance to ask him what he meant by losing his reason to purchase the farm. An old man emerged from what looked like a stable. He stopped and gazed at them for a moment, then hurried to greet their carriage.

"Gabe! It is you!" The man laughed with delight. "What a surprise."

Gabriel jumped from the gig and embraced the man. "Uncle."

Emmaline's eyes stung with tears at the reunion. She wanted so much for such a reunion with Claude.

"We were nearby," Gabriel explained. With his arm around his uncle, Gabriel's tall frame dwarfed the wiry, grey-haired man. He walked his uncle over to her. "Emmaline, this is my uncle, Mr William Deane."

"I am enchanted to meet you, Mr Deane," she said.

The man shuffled, looking shy.

Gabriel seemed to struggle for words. "This is...Madame Mableau, Uncle. We are travelling together."

Emmaline's brows rose. This time he did not tell his relation they were betrothed.

His uncle seemed to accept Gabriel's explanation. "Well, I am glad you came to visit. I was about to go to the cottage for tea. Young Johnny is in the stable. He can tend to your horse."

He shouted for the stable boy and Gabriel helped Emmaline from the gig. She was silent while she walked next to Gabriel on the path to a pretty thatched cottage. The dog bounded after them.

The cottage reminded her a little of her house in Brussels. It opened to a sitting room with a kitchen in the back. Stairs led to a second floor, but it was spare of colour and decoration. No lace in sight.

Gabriel's uncle swept off the seat of a chair with his hand. "Sit, miss...*madame*...ma'am."

She smiled at him. "Call me Emmaline. But you and Gabriel must do the sitting to share your news." She removed her hat and gloves and set them on a side table near the door. "Show me the kitchen and I will make the tea."

It felt almost normal to be heating water in a kettle and brewing tea. Uncle Will's kitchen was easy to negotiate, as spare as the other room. Hearing Gabriel's voice talking to his uncle gave her an ease almost like they had once shared together.

She brought the tea pot and cups to the small dining table.

"What news of the sale of the farm?" Gabriel asked.

"No one offering as far as I am told." Gabriel's uncle took the cup from Emmaline's hands. "There was some talk of his lordship acquiring the land, but they say he and her ladyship are off to Brighton, so we won't know until hunting season. His lordship will be back then."

Gabriel turned to Emmaline. "He means the earl whose property borders this one." He sipped his tea.

His uncle laughed. "News in the village is that his son and some friends have come to hide from creditors. His lordship will not like that when he hears of it."

Gabriel's tone changed. "His son is there?"

"That he is," his uncle responded, apparently not noticing Gabriel's heightened interest. "Came about a week ago. Mr Appleton—you remember him, Gabe? The blacksmith—Appleton has it from Connor, he's one of the footmen at the Hall—that they have been emptying the wine cellar and causing havoc."

Gabriel stared at him. "How many of them?"

"How many?" His uncle looked puzzled.

"How many of the son's friends came with him?"

His uncle shook his head. "I don't know. More than two, I think, from what was said."

Gabriel shot to his feet. "I am going there."

Emmaline stood, as well. "Is it—?"

"It must be," he said, reaching for his hat.

"Then I am going with you," she insisted.

His uncle rose with more difficulty. "What the devil is going on?"

Gabriel turned to him. "I cannot explain now, Uncle. We have been searching for someone, and I believe he is among young Rappard's party."

"But—"

Emmaline grabbed her hat and gloves, but did not bother to don them. They left his uncle standing in the doorway as they ran back to the stable. Gabriel reached the stable first and was already hitching the resigned-looking horse back to the gig, aided by a puzzled stable boy.

"Stay here, Emmaline," Gabriel told her, quickly double-checking the harness.

"Non." She climbed on to the gig herself and quickly tied her bonnet and pulled on her gloves. "Claude may be nearby."

He climbed up beside her and drove the gig out at a faster pace than heretofore.

Emmaline held on as they raced down dirt-packed roads. The same scenery she'd admired before whizzed by, a blur, while she prayed that Gabe's intuition was correct, that Edwin Tranville would indeed be there. Alive.

A red-stone mansion came into view and Gabriel drove directly to its door. The sides of their stalwart horse were heaving when Gabriel jumped down and turned to assist her. They rushed to the door and Gabriel pounded on it. He glanced at her and Emmaline saw her own anxiety mirrored in his eyes.

If Edwin was not here… If they were too late…

After what seemed a remarkably long time to wait, the door was opened by a liveried footman.

Gabriel did not wait for the man to speak. "Is Mr Edwin Tranville a guest here?"

The footman looked surprised. "May I tell Mr Tranville who is calling?"

Edwin was here! Emmaline took a breath and attempted to calm herself. They'd come in time.

Gabriel spoke in a calmer voice. "I am Captain Deane from Tranville's old company. I have been looking for him to give him news of some importance."

The footman stepped aside to allow them entry. "Come in."

They entered a hall with polished wooden floors and wainscoted walls. A huge painting of a man wearing armour was on one wall. On the opposite wall hung armaments in a symmetrical design surrounding a shield on which was the family crest. In the centre of the crest was a falcon, its wings outspread.

A crest with a bird on it.

Emmaline exchanged a glance with Gabriel. He nodded. He'd seen it, too.

The footman said, "You may wait in the drawing room. I will see if Mr Tranville is receiving callers."

Gabriel handed him his hat and gloves. "Is there someone who can attend to my horse?"

"I will send someone for your horse." The man placed Gabe's things on the hall table and led them to the drawing room.

The drawing room had a carved marble fireplace with a huge mirror above it. There were several sofas and chairs upon which to sit. Gabriel and Emmaline remained standing.

The footman bowed and left them.

"He is here." Emmaline whispered to Gabriel after the man was gone.

"Thank God." Gabriel paced the floor.

Emmaline stared at the door. Her knees shook and she suddenly felt as if she could not breathe. "I have not seen him since that day."

Gabriel came to her and held her arms in his strong hands. "He cannot hurt you."

She nodded, only partly consoled.

They waited for what seemed like eternity. Each minute marked by the mantel clock made Emmaline's heart pound harder.

Why was it taking so long for Edwin Tranville to appear?

Chapter Sixteen

Footsteps finally approached the drawing-room door.

In a moment Emmaline would face him, the man who had inhabited her nightmares for so many years, the man who had thought it a lark to watch her husband slain, who had tried to rape her and kill Claude.

The man whose life she needed to save.

She forced herself to turn towards the door.

It opened.

The creature who stood there was almost unrecognisable, slightly stooped, abdomen as round as a woman with child. He swept limp straw-coloured hair off his forehead and swayed slightly as he crossed the threshold. Surely she had never encountered this man before.

Except his yellow-tinged face was marked with a jagged scar from the corner of his eye to his chin, the scar she'd cut into him.

Edwin Tranville's gaze passed over her without much interest and riveted on Gabriel. "Lawd. What the devil brings you here, Deane? Last time I had the dubious pleasure, you caused me the loss of my employment."

Gabriel straightened his spine. "I lost you your employment? You were insensible from drink. Sidmouth sacked you for it."

Edwin waved him off and slumped into a chair. "No matter.

It is dashed early in the day for a social call, is it not? I had to be roused from my bed."

Emmaline glanced at the clock. "It approaches noon."

Edwin directed his gaze at her and raised his brows. "If we have been introduced, ma'am, it has totally slipped my mind."

She gasped. His face was burned in her memory, yet he had forgotten hers.

Gabriel came to her side. "Do not be insulting."

Edwin smirked. "Why? Do not tell me she is your wife."

Gabriel's hands curled into fists and Emmaline could feel the anger rising in him. With a sudden movement, he seized Edwin by his coat lapels and hauled him back into a standing position.

"This is not a social call," Gabriel snarled.

Edwin's expression changed to shock and fear.

Gabriel shook him. "Cease your nonsense and listen to me."

Edwin nodded.

"This is the woman you tried to rape and kill in Badajoz."

Emmaline's knees trembled. Gabriel's sudden violence frightened even her.

Edwin tried to pull away. "I never—"

"Do not deny it," Gabriel went on, his voice deep and rumbling. "I was there. Others were there. We saw you." He released Edwin as suddenly as he'd seized him. "She cut your face."

Edwin's hand flew to his scar. He staggered back, hatred flashing through his eyes. Emmaline's fingers twitched and she remembered the feel of the knife as it had sliced through Edwin's skin.

Edwin pointed a finger at Gabriel and laughed. "You are inventing this, Deane. I can tell." He shifted to a sing-song voice. "I have no need of your attempt at humour, which cannot be your purpose for calling. Even I cannot believe you would come all this way—" He stopped himself and peered at Gabriel. "How the devil did you know I was here? I've not written to anyone of my whereabouts."

Gabriel glared at him. "We have been searching the country-side for you."

Emmaline's thoughts raced throughout this exchange. Could it be Edwin truly did not remember what had happened in Bada-joz? Surely he was lying about it.

"Searching for me?" Edwin laughed again. "Whatever for? To tell me I'd done something I never did?"

Emmaline spoke up, surprising herself. "You tried to kill my son. Do you not remember? Do you not remember the blade of my knife cutting into your face to stop you?"

Again his fingers flew to his scar, and his eyes darted as if searching for the memory. "I—I was wounded in the siege."

Gabriel shoved him back into the chair. "You hid from the siege, but when it was over, you were eager to take part in the plunder of the city. I do not know what else you did that day, but I know what you tried to do to this lady and her son."

Edwin wrapped his arms around his abdomen and winced as if in pain. "So what is this about? Did you chase me down to ex-tort money from me or some such thing? Are you in that much need of funds, Deane?"

Gabriel stiffened. "I need nothing from you. If you would cease your babbling, I will tell you why we are here."

Edwin made a show of keeping his mouth closed.

Emmaline dreaded Gabriel's explanation. Could a baron's son have Claude arrested for planning to murder him? It seemed a likely possibility.

Gabriel paced several steps before beginning to speak. "We came here to save your life."

Edwin laughed.

"It is true!" Emmaline cried.

Gabriel leaned down to him. "Believe me. Your life is of no consequence to me, but we have knowledge of someone who wants to kill you for what you did at Badajoz. Our concern is for him, that he not commit such a crime, even against the likes of you."

"This is nonsense." Edwin's trembling hands belied his words. "I did nothing. Nobody wants to kill me."

"But he does," Emmaline cried. "He may be nearby even now. You must allow Gabriel to protect you."

"He may be lying in wait for you," Gabriel said.

Edwin shrank in the chair. "No! There is no one lying in wait for me."

Emmaline felt sick inside. How could they convince him?

Gabriel went on. "Listen to me. You were with two other soldiers, men who killed this woman's husband. You tried to rape her, until her young son attempted to stop you. You tried to kill him and this woman battled with you, cutting your face. Another soldier chased off the others, but I also arrived at this time. You were drunk. You were carried back to your billet—at considerable risk, I might add."

"Landon," Edwin whispered. "But he carried me away from the city walls, not from the city. I'd fallen trying to scale the walls."

Gabriel shook his head. "Your father invented that story. I assure you, I would not wish to set eyes on you again if not to prevent this person from killing you and risking a hanging for it."

Edwin glanced away, and it was clear his mind was turning. After a moment, his eyes narrowed and he pointed to Emmaline. "You are in league with him. If not for money, then to ruin me! Deane has always hated me. Is he paying you to go along with this story?"

Emmaline felt outrage. "We speak the truth."

Edwin's voice went up in pitch. "It is not the truth. I would not do such a common thing." He pointed to Emmaline. "I received this scar because of the siege. I remember that." He glanced away and his voice dropped. "I think I remember that."

Gabriel spoke. "We want you to come with us now. I will take you to a place of safety. Some place where you can be protected. Your father's house, perhaps…"

Edwin rolled his eyes.

Gabriel appeared to ignore him. "When we know you are safe, we'll send word."

"Put my life in your hands?" Edwin's laugh was mocking this time. "No, thank you, indeed. I would not do so even if what you say is true. I will stay right here and not listen to your nonsense. It is a trick."

Gabriel shouted, "It is not a trick!"

"It is the truth," Emmaline repeated. What more could they say to convince him?

Edwin shook his head. "I'm too clever to fall for that. Goes with breeding, you know. You've always resented me for my rank, Deane."

Gabriel responded, "I outrank you. I made Captain well before you."

Edwin gave him a scornful look. "I meant my rank as a *gentleman*. You stink of trade and you always have."

Emmaline watched Gabriel flush with anger. With fists clenched he leaned towards Edwin, but somehow kept his temper.

Gabe spoke in a firm, low voice. "I am trying to save your life."

"Fustian!" Edwin stood, almost losing his balance. "You are starting to bore me. Leave me now or give me the great pleasure of having you tossed out."

They could not leave, could they? Emmaline refused to believe they had come so far, with such difficulty, only to be forced to walk away.

"Then we can do no more than warn you," Gabriel said. "Check your back and take care."

"Please, listen to us," Emmaline implored. A warning was not enough.

But Edwin merely made a dismissive gesture and sauntered to the door.

He paused, holding on to the doorknob, and turned back to them. "Now if you will excuse me. I have an attack of the runs."

Emmaline uttered a cry of frustration as he ambled out.

Claude pulled Apollo back as he and Louisa approached Rappard Hall. It would not do to let anyone see them riding side by side like equals.

Louisa sighed. "I wish we could simply ride away to some distant land."

It had been as perfect a morning as Claude was capable of imagining. Louisa had talked to him as a friend, as if none of England's notions about class separated them.

"You know," she went on, speaking loud enough for him to hear her, "I feel as if I have poured out my heart to you, but you say little about yourself."

"It is not my place," he responded. What could he wish her to know? That he was French? That he detested her country and its emphasis on class and status? That he'd sworn to kill for revenge?

She turned around and he was touched by the melancholy look on her face. "We cannot really be friends, can we?"

"Non." For all those reasons.

What would she think of him if she knew he now had a plan to confront and kill Tranville under the very roof where she slept?

He must carry out this plan soon.

After this halcyon morning spent with Louisa, he realised he should not remain at Rappard Hall many more days. He did not know how much longer he could resist asking even more of Louisa. The attachment between them grew stronger with every hour they shared.

Would she despise him after he killed Tranville?

How could she not? That thought pained him as surely as if it were he who felt the stiletto's sharp point.

Louisa glanced back to the vista below, Rappard Hall and its farm buildings.

"I dread returning," she said.

"Your cousin. His guests. I wish I could make them be civil to you." It offended his manhood that they should say things to her that a respectable young woman should not hear. He had no power, however, as a mere stable worker, to come to her defence.

"I will avoid them." She glanced back at him with a smile. "They cannot be rude to me if I stay out of their way."

As they descended the hill, they could see a small carriage drawn by one horse at the door of Rappard Hall.

Louisa shaded her eyes with her hand. "I wonder who that is. It looks like a man in uniform."

A man walked around the carriage. He wore a British officer's red coat and sash.

Claude's nerves went on alert. What was a British officer doing out here?

Louisa laughed. "I hope he has come to chase my cousin and his friends away."

Claude squinted into the sun. The officer climbed into a small carriage and disappeared behind the carriage's hood. He could see no more than the man's hands holding the ribbons. The carriage started off.

"He is leaving!" Louisa cried in a worried tone. "I should have been there to receive him. One never knows how George will deal with matters of importance."

Claude's brow furrowed. The officer could not be looking for him, could he? *Non,* it was impossible. No one in England knew of him. His mother was the only one who knew his plans and certainly she would reveal them to no one.

Even so, the red-coated officer felt like a bad omen, a sign he must no longer tarry.

As they entered the paddocks behind the stable, Claude gazed at Louisa, memorising this image of her, seated so expertly upon her horse. Her back was straight, her waist narrow, and a peek of brown curls were visible beneath her hat.

She turned to glance at him and smiled once more.

Perhaps that was what he would remember the best. Her lovely lips curved into a smile that lit up her eyes and put dimples in her cheeks. Perhaps on lonely nights he would remember that once a lovely English girl had smiled when she looked upon him.

He averted his gaze, following instead the small carriage that made its way down the path to the road. He scanned the farm, thinking how well tended it was, how kind Mr Sellars and the other grooms had been to him, how thrilled he was to have cared for and ridden such beautiful horses.

He patted Apollo on the neck and the horse bobbed his head in pleasure.

Apollo would be the third horse he'd come to love and the third horse he'd endure losing. His father's horse. His own Coco. Now Apollo.

But even that paled in comparison to losing Louisa.

Gabe turned the gig on to the road back to the hill farm.

"What a stupid man," Emmaline exclaimed. "Vile and stupid and stinking of spirits."

"Indeed." Gabe wondered something else, as well. Edwin looked more ill than drunk.

Emmaline shifted in her seat. "He should not have said those awful things to you about gentlemen. *He* is not a gentleman!"

He turned to her. "He was never a man of good character. If he had been, he would never have done what he did to you and Claude."

"Ha!" She pulled at her gloves. "I did worse to him. Every day in the mirror he must look at what I did to him."

Her anger was much more welcome to Gabe than her despair. Soon the fact that he'd failed her would again plunge her into desolation. Finding Edwin had accomplished nothing, after all.

Except they might discover that Claude was near. If they could find Claude and reason with him, Emmaline's wish might come true at last.

She put her hand on his arm. "Do you think he tells the truth that he does not recall what happened?"

He frowned. "He was very drunk that day, much worse than usual. It is possible he has no memory of it."

"It is unfair." She gazed out at the road ahead. "Claude and I must always remember it."

And I must remember as well, thought Gabe.

She grew silent and he knew her mind was filled with thoughts of her son.

He cleared his throat. "Let us stay the night with my uncle. Tomorrow you must rest. I will go to the nearby villages and enquire about Claude. If he is close, someone will know it. Someone will remember him."

She wrapped her arm through his and leaned against him. "I will go with you."

He glanced at her beautiful face. "We'll see."

Gabe turned his attention to the familiar land around him, land whose seasons had remained the same as the days of his boyhood. The scent of the grass, the baying of distant sheep, the warmth of the sun on his face, brought back memories of peaceful days. This land refreshed one's spirits, restored one's hopes.

Perhaps it would work its magic on her.

"What if we do not find Claude?" she asked, her voice taut with tension. "How can we stop him if Edwin will not let us near?"

"We try to find him first."

"I feel Claude near, Gabriel," she murmured. "I feel the danger."

Gabe felt the danger, too, as well as a sudden unshakeable sense of doom.

In spite of the worry, they spent a bucolic evening at Uncle Will's house. Emmaline cooked the dinner, roasting a chicken and making *frites,* the potatoes Gabe had not tasted since their shared dinners in Brussels. Uncle Will ate with such relish he barely spoke, except to say, over and over, "This is delicious."

After dinner Emmaline insisted Gabe sit with his uncle while she washed dishes. Afterwards, she picked up some of Uncle Will's mending, needing to keep busy, Gabe understood. By the time darkness fell, she sat by the lamp pushing a needle through the cloth and Gabe had nothing left to talk about with his uncle.

They sat in silence for several moments, until his uncle leaned back. "So tell me why you were so fired up to find that fellow at Rappard Hall."

Gabe should have known his uncle would get around to asking. It was very apparent that Gabe and Emmaline had remained troubled since their return.

"I cannot speak of it," Gabe said, glancing towards Emmaline.

He made it Emmaline's decision what, if anything, to say to his uncle. Gabe knew Uncle Will would not press the matter, but he also knew his uncle would worry about what distressed his nephew.

Emmaline returned Gabe's gaze with a resigned expression. "Tell your uncle all of it, Gabriel. I want him to know."

He was surprised at her decision, but he faced his uncle and began the story at Badajoz. It was the only way to make Uncle Will understand Claude's need for revenge. Gabe told his uncle how he and Emmaline had searched England for Edwin, knowing Claude might also be near. They'd hoped warning Edwin would be enough to keep him safe until they could locate Claude and convince him to abandon his dangerous plan. Gabe explained Edwin's reaction to their warning.

Uncle Will listened intently, his hands folded in front of his lips. When Gabe came to the end, his uncle slowly opened his hands and rubbed his face. He gazed off in the distance. "A French fellow... Seems to me I heard of a French fellow—"

Emmaline dropped her mending. "Where?"

He tapped his lips before going on. "Appleton—the blacksmith—seems to me he spoke of a Frenchman. Sellars—do you remember him?" he asked Gabe. "Sellars runs the Rappard stable. He hired a new fellow, Appleton said. A French fellow. Good with horses."

Emmaline rose to her feet. "He is hired to work at the Rappard stables?"

He'd been within easy reach when they'd called upon Edwin at Rappard Hall.

Uncle Will nodded. "Best worker Sellars ever had, he told the smithy."

It was like placing the wolf among the sheep.

Gabe shot to his feet. "It must be Claude!"

Emmaline rushed over to him. "We must go now! It cannot wait until tomorrow. Tomorrow might be too late."

"I will go." Gabe turned to his uncle. "Do you have a fast horse I might ride?"

"There's only one horse fit for riding," his uncle replied. "The riding horses were sold. Stapleton's heir sold all he could. All that's left are work horses."

"Let us saddle him now," Gabe said.

Emmaline grabbed her hat and gloves from a table near the door. "I will go with you. I must!"

He grasped Emmaline's shoulders. "I can go faster if I ride alone."

She clung to him. "You must let me go with you!"

He shook his head. "Time is of the essence. Trust me to do this."

She nodded, but tears filled her eyes as she looked up at him. "I have this terrible feeling—"

He gave her a swift embrace and did not tell her he shared her worst fears.

Chapter Seventeen

Claude entered the house through an open door that led to the still room and the kitchen. A glow from embers in the oven gave the only light, but he'd seen and memorised enough of this level to grope his way to the stairway.

He was in luck. He easily discovered the servants' staircase. As he climbed in the darkness, he kept an image of the house in his mind. He needed to find the right room on the right hallway.

On the second floor, he opened the door to the corridor. To his surprise it was lit by a sconce on the wall, making it easier for him to see, but also easier to be discovered. Heart pounding, he closed his eyes to visualize the house again. He was in the correct wing. Now he must choose the correct door. Opening his eyes, he counted. One. Two. Three.

Would he find his enemy there? From outside he'd watched him readying for bed, saw him extinguish his candle. Had Tranville remained in the room?

The rest of the house seemed quiet and dark, except for the flickering candle in the sconce. Holding his breath, Claude stepped out into the hallway and crept quietly to the third door. From somewhere he heard voices, muffled and distant. Dare he go on?

He'd come too far to stop now.

He reached the door and tried the knob. It turned. He opened the door only wide enough to slip through. Enough moonlight streamed through the curtains to reveal the shape of the bed and other furniture in the room. Gradually more details revealed themselves. The shape of bottles on a table. Clothing thrown over a chair.

The whole room smelled foul.

A loud snore startled him. He expelled an excited breath. Tranville was here.

Claude moved slowly towards the bed, reaching inside his coat to slip the stiletto from its sheath. As he got closer, the stench worsened and he recoiled. It was the stink of Tranville, even stronger than before.

He covered his nose and mouth with his hand until he reached the bedside and placed the point of the stiletto against Tranville's throat.

"Wake up, you villain!" he spoke in a loud whisper.

Tranville woke with a start. The tip of the stiletto pierced his flesh. A drop of blood appeared. "What?"

"Silence or I'll stick this all the way through your throat!" Claude pressed the point against Tranville's skin again for emphasis.

"Who—who are you?" The whites of Tranville's eyes seemed to glow in the dark. "You are French? You are the Frenchman? They said—I did not believe them."

"Be quiet!" Claude growled. "I was once the boy whose mother you tried to violate. In Badajoz. Remember? You laughed when the others killed my father. I want their names. I'll kill you if I do not have their names." He would kill Tranville no matter what.

"I do not know their names. I wasn't there, I tell you. You have the wrong man." Tranville retched and the point pierced him again. More blood trickled from the wound. "Don't kill me!"

Claude moved the point away slightly. "I have the right man. I heard your name. My mother sliced your face."

Tranville's hand touched his cheek. "I'm going to be sick." He turned his head and retched.

"Answer my question!" Claude cut him again.

"I cannot!" A gurgle sounded in Tranville's throat and he spat on to the bed linens.

Claude averted his face in disgust.

The man sat up and clutched at his abdomen. "This is a hoax. I told Deane so. He has gone too far."

Claude whipped the stiletto against Tranville's chest.

Deane had been the name of his mother's English lover.

He put pressure on the stiletto. "Why do you mention Deane?"

Had Deane been the British soldier he and Louisa had seen earlier?

"Come, now. He is your partner, is he not? You are all in this together." He sneered. "You made it too coincidental. Not well done at all. They come today; you come tonight. I'm too clever not to figure this out."

"They?" Had there been another person in the small carriage? He'd been unable to seen anything more than a glimpse of a soldier.

Tranville's expression turned defiant. "The French woman who said she cut my face. Did you not say that was your mother? Have you forgotten your lines in this little farce?"

His mother? Here? With Deane?

Claude pushed the stiletto against Tranville's chest and drew more blood.

"I'm bleeding!" Tranville cried, raising his voice. "No!"

"Quiet!" demanded Claude.

He needed to end this. The risk of discovery was becoming too great. Deane was near. With his *mother.* He must finish this now and make his escape.

Claude gripped the stiletto and pushed the point in further. Tranville cried aloud.

A vision of Louisa flashed through Claude's mind. What if she woke from Tranville's cry? What if she discovered him over Tranville's lifeless body?

He moved the knife away.

Another cry rang out, this time a woman's scream.

Louisa?

The sound came from somewhere in the house. Nearby.

"Help me!" It was Louisa's voice. "Help!"

What was happening to her?

Claude could never ignore such a cry. With a frustrated growl he pulled himself away from Tranville's bed and ran out of the room into the hallway, thinking only of Louisa.

"Someone help me!" she cried.

Shoving the stiletto in its sheath inside his coat, he followed the sound of her voice, turning down another corridor on this same floor. A sliver of light shone under a doorway. He made his way to that door and pressed his ear against it.

"Let me go, Nicholas. Go away," he heard. "Someone will come to help me."

A man laughed. "No one can hear you. Edwin is the only one on this floor and he's probably passed out from drink. Stop acting the tease. You want this as much as I do."

Claude opened the door. On the bed Nicholas Frye straddled Louisa, holding her by the wrists. She struggled to free herself.

Hot with rage, Claude crossed the room and seized Nicholas by the collar, jerking him away. *"Ne pas la toucher!"* Do not touch her!

Nicholas rolled to the floor, but quickly found his feet again. Claude punched him in the stomach. A whoosh of air escaped the man's lungs and he staggered back. Claude charged him, pushing him against a dressing table. It shattered and its bottles and pots broke on the floor, making a great noise and filling the room with the flowery scent of Louisa's perfume.

"Help me!" Nicholas shouted, his voice booming much louder than Louisa's. "George! Harry!"

Claude heard the pounding of feet, but he continued his attack, striking Nicholas with his fists in a frenzy of violence.

He heard Nicholas's friends enter the room and one seized him from behind, pulling him off Nicholas and effectively restraining him.

"Now you will get your just deserts," Nicholas cried.

Claude's cheek exploded with pain as Nicholas's fist struck him and struck him again. Blood poured from his nose while Nicholas pounded on his chest and stomach. Claude tried to kick him, but Nicholas easily dodged away.

"Stop! You are hurting him!" Louisa, her hair tumbling loose over her shoulders, scrambled off the bed and grabbed Nicholas's hair in her fingers, trying to pull him away.

Her cousin George seized her. "Louisa, stay out of it!"

Tranville appeared at the door. "Oh, good," he drawled. "Finish him off. He tried to kill me."

"He attacked you, as well?" Nicholas's face turned ugly.

Claude watched the man's fist aim directly for his eye. Ears ringing with pain, he forced his eyes open to see Louisa straining against her cousin's grasp. Another fist hit him and she cried out.

Tranville leaned against the doorjamb, blood trickling down his neck and staining his white nightshirt.

Nicholas was breathing hard when he abruptly stopped the onslaught. Claude fell to his knees. His head throbbed and his vision dimmed.

He'd failed to kill Tranville. He'd failed to rescue Louisa. He'd failed.

Just like at Badajoz.

In that instant he felt transported back to that flame-engulfed Spanish city. Again he watched red-coated men striking his father and plunging a knife into his father's chest.

Claude shook off the vision. He managed to reach inside his coat for his stiletto. He pulled it out.

Harry shouted, "He has a knife!"

"The one he stabbed me with," Tranville said.

Nicholas knocked the stiletto from Claude's hand. Both Claude and Nicholas lunged for it as it clattered to the floor. Nicholas seized it. With a grin he unsheathed it and stepped towards Claude.

Claude glanced up, the taste of his own blood in his mouth, the pounding of pain ringing in his ears. His eyes riveted on the stiletto and he prepared to die.

Like his father.

Gabe approached Rappard Hall, his horse's sides heaving. Through a window he could see a scuffle, a man being beaten.

"Good God!" he exclaimed aloud. Was he too late?

He dismounted at the front door and ran up to pound on it.

It opened immediately. A wide-eyed elderly footman pointed to the stairway. "They are fighting!"

Gabe bounded up two flights of stairs and spied Edwin standing at one of the doors.

"Lawd!" exclaimed Edwin, jumping aside as Gabe ran past him and burst into the room.

A man turned in surprise. He held a knife and looked as if he was about to plunge it into Claude's chest.

"Oh, no, you don't." In one swift motion Gabe seized the man's wrist and twisted it until the knife fell to the floor.

Two other men rushed at him, but Gabe swung the first man around and used him as a battering ram, shoving them all across the room against a wall. They tumbled to the floor like a set of skittles.

Gabe snatched the knife, a thin, lethal stiletto, and was ready for them when they made it back to their feet.

"Get back!" Gabe ordered, whipping the stiletto under their noses like a sword.

The three men retreated until they stood flat against the wall.

From the corner of his eye Gabe saw a young woman run to Claude and wrap her arms around him. Claude's face looked battered. His nose bled as did a cut above his eye. His clothes were ripped and dishevelled.

Gabe swallowed. He'd almost been too late. He'd almost cost Emmaline her son.

He shook the thought away and aimed the knife at Edwin's friends. The scent of perfume filled the room. Gabe quickly glanced around. This must be the young woman's room, not Edwin's, but Edwin had blood on his shirt. What exactly had happened here?

He asked the young woman, "Miss, are you harmed?"

"No," she responded, still holding on to Claude. "But—but this man received a terrible beating."

Claude looked up at him. "Captain Deane," he said in a raspy and pained voice.

"He is an intruder!" cried the man who'd wielded the stiletto. "He attacked our friend and this lady. What did you expect us to do?"

"Claude did not attack me! He came to my aid." The young woman snatched a robe from the foot of the bed and wrapped it around herself. She pointed to the man who'd wielded the stiletto. "Mr Frye accosted me and Claude stopped him."

Edwin entered the room and leaned against the wall next to the door. He gestured to the blood on his nightshirt. "Come now, Deane. You sent this fellow. He tried to kill me."

"Stubble it, Edwin!" Gabe shouted. "You brought trouble on yourself. Unless you want more of it, shut your damned mouth."

Edwin scoffed. "Who could possibly cause me more trouble than you have?"

Gabe glared at him. "Your father. He's seen proof of what happened in Badajoz."

Edwin's eyes flashed with surprise. "Proof?"

"Proof of what?" Frye asked.

Gabe advanced on him and put the point of the stiletto under his chin. "Keep silent." He turned a steely gaze on the other two men. "And you lot? Who are you and what have you to say?"

One replied. "Ha-Harry Stewel, sir. I only saw this stranger fighting with Nicholas. I did not know Nicholas attacked Miss Finch."

Gabe nodded and pointed the stiletto at the last man. "And you?"

This one straightened his spine. "I am George Rappard. This is my house." He pointed to Claude. "This fellow is an intruder! As are you, sir!"

Gabe ignored his accusation. "Is Miss Finch a guest in your house?" he asked, staring him down.

Rappard looked confused. "Guest? No, she's a cousin. She lives here."

Gabe leaned in close so that mere inches separated his face from Rappard's. "You should be less concerned about intruders and more about protecting your cousin from your friend."

Rappard's eyes widened.

Gabe stepped back again and looked at each man in turn. "You are a disgrace to your names." He turned to Frye. "You and Edwin most of all."

George Rappard, looking disturbed, turned to his cousin. "Did Nicholas really accost you?"

Her eyes shone with tears. "Yes."

Frye's voice rose in protest. "She enticed me. It is all her fault."

Claude struggled to his feet. "You cannot blame her!"

"No. No. No." Rappard waved his hand at Frye. "You've been bothering her the whole visit. I did not credit it until now." He faced Gabe. "I would like to end this with as little fuss as possible. I certainly would not like it to become known to the magistrate. Or my parents." He peered at Gabe sheepishly. "May—may I know who you are, sir?"

"Captain Deane, lately of the Royal Scots." Gabe offered little more explanation. "I have been searching for Edwin. I called upon him here earlier today."

Rappard made a mollifying gesture. "I will not ask why, nor what possessed you to return at this hour. I am only grateful that you did." He took a step towards Miss Finch. "Forgive me, Louisa."

Miss Finch nodded.

The young man sounded sensible and the situation was calming. Perhaps Gabe could get Claude safely back to his mother after all.

"I will be content to leave now," Gabe said. "I'll take Claude with me, but you must assure me that this young lady will be safe under your protection."

"You have my word on it." Rappard turned to Edwin. "I do not know what trouble you caused, Edwin, but I think you should leave." He glared at Frye. "I demand you leave, Nicholas. There is a coach passing though the village tomorrow. You both will be on it. You are no longer welcome here." To Gabe, he said. "You may go anytime."

"We leave now, Claude." Gabe retrieved the stiletto's sheath from the floor and put the knife inside his coat. "No argument."

Claude did not argue. He did not speak at all, but merely limped towards the door, one hand pressing his ribs. He looked Edwin directly in the eye as he passed. Edwin shrank back.

In the hallway, Gabe offered Claude an arm, but Claude pushed him away.

"Wait!" cried Miss Finch. "I will walk you out." She ran to Claude and lent him her shoulder for support. Claude accepted her help.

Gabe shrugged and followed them to the stairs.

The servants were clustered at the bottom of the stairway in the hall.

"Miss Louisa," the elderly footman asked, "what happened?"

"I will explain later," she said as they descended the stairs. "All is well now."

She, Claude and Gabe walked out of the door.

As soon as they were outside, Miss Finch embraced Claude. "How can I ever thank you for saving me!"

He shook his head, but held her in return. "Do not make me so good, Louisa. I am not."

Gabe watched them, his hands on his hips. Obviously more than a chance rescue connected these two.

She pulled away and put both palms to his cheeks, making him look at her. "Do not say more. To me you will always be my hero and my good friend."

Claude looked down on her. "I am afraid for you to stay in this house."

She gave a wan smile. "My cousin is in earnest, I believe. But I will also stay the night in the housekeeper's room and remain with the servants until Nicholas and Edwin leave."

He held her close again. "Goodbye, Louisa."

"Make haste, Claude." Gabe spoke gently.

Claude broke away from her. "I must retrieve my satchel."

"I will get it. Where is it?" Gabe asked.

"Around the back of the house behind the large tree." His gaze did not leave Louisa's.

Gabe found the satchel and led the horse to Claude, who still stood with Louisa. She held on to him as if she could not bear for him to leave.

"You ride." Gabe offered an arm to help Claude mount.

Claude ignored it and mounted on his own, uttering a pained cry as he did so.

His Louisa blew him a kiss as Gabe led the horse away.

When they reached the road, Claude, sounding very defeated and in pain, asked, "Where are you taking me?"

Gabe turned. "To your mother."

Chapter Eighteen

Gabe led the horse well past the Rappard gate before Claude spoke. "Why did you bring my mother to this place? I demand you tell me. Why did you bring her here?"

Of all Claude might have said, these words were not what Gabe expected. He stopped the horse and stepped closer. "Do you wish to make me the villain in this escapade?"

Claude's eyes flashed back at him, filled with resentment and accusation.

Gabe schooled his emotions. "Your mother is in England because of you. She journeyed from Brussels to seek me out for the sole purpose of asking my help to find you and stop you from killing Edwin Tranville."

Claude's spine stiffened, but the action seemed to cause him a spasm of pain. "The honour of my family demanded it."

Gabe kept his gaze steady and his voice firm. "Was it honourable to sneak away, to hide your intentions from your mother? You knew she would not approve. Instead of facing up to her, you lied about your whereabouts and informed her in a letter."

Claude lowered his head.

At least Claude showed some guilt for what he'd done to Emmaline. Gabe intended to make it even clearer. "Your mother was frantic for you. She was terrified she would lose you."

Claude's voice turned defensive. "She merely presumed I would fail."

Gabe shot back, "No. She feared you would succeed and be caught and hanged for murder."

In the moonlight Claude's eyes now filled with misery. "I did not succeed, did I? I failed to kill Tranville." The young man turned his face away. "I failed again, like before."

"Before?" How many attempts had Claude made?

"In Badajoz."

Ah! Gabe was beginning to understand. Claude's need for vengeance was fuelled by anger at himself. "When you were merely a boy?"

Claude's nod was almost imperceptible. "They killed my father and I could not stop them. Edwin Tranville tried to rape my mother and I could not stop him." He wrapped his arms around his ribcage and took in a laboured breath.

A memory returned. Young Claude flung over his father's body, crying, *"Papa! Papa!"* Gabe felt a wave of pity.

"You were a boy. They were men. Not only men, they were soldiers. You were helpless against them."

Curse that Frenchman. Mableau had dragged his wife and son into war. He had caused the horror in their lives. Perhaps Emmaline and Claude would have found happiness had they stayed in France, had they never seen Badajoz.

Had they never had reason to meet Gabe.

"It does not matter now." Claude sounded like a bitter child. "Because you have prevented me from killing your friend."

So Gabe was back to being the villain? He laughed. "Edwin is no friend of mine. I stopped you from killing him only for your mother's sake."

Gabe held on to the horse's bridle and signalled the animal to start walking again. Claude winced in pain with each step the horse took. It was no wonder. The young man was bruised all over, in body and in spirit.

Gabe took his time before speaking again, because he suspected Claude would not credit anything he had to say.

Still, the young man deserved an explanation. "Your father was a soldier, Claude. Soldiers die in war. Your father died in the ugliest part of war, when men riot and plunder, but it was still war." Emmaline had given this same explanation their first night together in Brussels. "Three thousand of our men were killed in Badajoz that day. I don't condone what came after, but perhaps none of those men would have acted so barbarically had they not endured such hard fighting. You never had a chance to learn how a battle can affect a man. You were injured too quickly—"

Claude interrupted him. "How do you know I was injured quickly?"

Gabe had assumed Emmaline had told Claude. "You charged my square at Waterloo. I saw you fall and dragged you into the square for safety."

"It is true?" Claude gaped down at him. "You carried me to Brussels, to my mother?"

Gabe glanced away, the pain of that parting with her still raw. "It was the least I could do for her."

Claude looked so distressed that Gabe decided to leave him to his thoughts.

They travelled on in silence until Gabe spied the gate of the hill farm ahead of them.

There was one more matter he must address before returning Claude to Emmaline once again.

He slowed their pace. "I want you to tell me what happened tonight. The whole of it."

Claude's head lifted. An obstinate expression was quickly re-placed with a resigned one. "I went to Tranville's room to kill him. I tried to push the knife into his heart, but I could not make myself do it. You may call me a coward if you like."

"Were you afraid to kill him?" Gabe asked.

"I was not afraid!" Claude responded quickly. He paused as if reluctant to go on. Finally he said, "I thought of how it would be for someone to discover him dead. To see all the blood. I did not wish that experience on—on anyone."

Gabe would wager it had been Miss Finch he'd thought of.

Claude went on. "Then I heard Louisa's cry and I tried to rescue her, but the others ran into the room and overpowered me."

It was not lost on Gabe that Claude, a mere groom, addressed her by her given name.

Claude made a strangled sound in his throat. "I failed at saving her as well."

"She seemed to think you saved her," Gabe said, trying to help the young man salvage some measure of self-respect.

Claude shook his head determinedly. "All I did was nearly get myself killed. You were the rescuer. Not me."

They reached the farm gate, and Gabe stopped again. "I need your word that you will no longer attempt to kill Tranville."

Claude peered at him. "I thought you said he was no friend."

Gabe explained again, "He isn't. I wish I'd killed him myself that day in Badajoz. He's caused nothing but trouble for people I do care about."

"Like my mother?" Claude's resentment re-emerged.

Gabe spoke quietly. "You have already put her through enough grief and worry. She does not deserve more. I need your word that you will not cause her further distress."

Again Claude lowered his head. The young man cared about his mother's feelings; that was one thing to his credit.

He raised his head again and gave Gabe a direct look. "I give you my word. I failed to kill Tranville once; I will never try again."

Gabe merely nodded.

He led the horse through the gate towards the farm buildings, large dark shapes against night sky.

"We are here," he announced, but felt no pleasure in it. "I'll take you directly to your mother."

Emmaline heard the horse approach and hurried out the cottage door. The agony of waiting was over, but what now?

Gabe's uncle, having spent the last two hours pacing outside, grabbed a lantern and was already halfway down the path to the stable. She ran after him.

The indistinct outline of a man leading a horse came into view, but she could not see enough until Gabe's uncle reached them. Then the lantern light shone on Gabe's imposing figure and revealed another man on the horse's back.

Her heart raced. Could it be?

She could not make herself move, as Gabe and his uncle led the horse and rider towards her. When they were about ten feet away, she finally saw him.

"Claude! Claude!" She ran to him.

"Maman." His voice sounded old and in pain. Even in the darkness she could see his face was bloody.

"You are hurt!" she cried.

"We'll take him to the cottage," Gabriel told her.

She walked at her son's side, looking up at him, impatient to examine his wounds, to feel her arms around him.

When they reached the cottage, Gabriel offered a hand to help Claude dismount. Claude pushed it away and dismounted on his own. He almost lost his footing.

Gabriel caught him and held him until Emmaline took her son into her arms.

"Claude." Tears sprang to her eyes. *"Mon fils. Mon cher fils."* Her dear son had been returned to her.

Gabriel had brought him to her one more time.

She kissed Claude's cheeks and hugged him until he uttered a pained sound.

He spoke in French. "My ribs are sore."

Alarmed, she released him, but wiped at the blood on his face. "*Mon Dieu!* We must get you inside." She glanced back to Gabriel and asked in English, "What of Edwin Tranville?"

"Unharmed."

"*Dieu merci,*" she murmured as she helped her son through the doorway.

Uncle Will said, "I'll tend to the horse. And I'm set to bunk with the stable lads, so the cottage is yours."

Mr Deane had told Emmaline earlier that he would leave the cottage for the night. She'd appreciated the kindness, and the privacy for herself and her son. There was so much to say to him, so much to explain.

"Come in and sit, Claude," she said in French, leading him to a sofa. "I'll see to your wounds. Are you hungry?"

"No, Maman. Not hungry." His reply was curt.

"You must be thirsty, then. I'll bring you some tea."

Gabriel stepped through the doorway, carrying Claude's satchel. Emmaline's gaze turned to him and she searched for words to express all that filled her heart. None were sufficient.

Instead, she said, "I need some towels and bandages."

"I'll get them for you." He started up the stairs and she followed him.

He glanced at her in surprise, then placed Claude's satchel in the smaller room. "Claude can sleep in here," he said. "You may use the other room."

She nodded. "Where will you be?"

"I'll sleep on the sofa." He walked over to a chest of drawers and removed a stack of towels and two rolls of cotton cloth.

As he handed them to her, she grasped his arm. "Gabriel." She looked directly into his eyes. "*Merci,* Gabriel. *Merci.* For my son.

For everything." The words were not enough, but it was all she could say.

He drew away, inclining his head to the stairs. "He needs you."

As they descended the stairs together, Claude turned and looked daggers at them.

At the bottom of the stairs, Gabriel said, "I will leave you alone."

Her lip trembled. Her son was still so angry. Did he not understand? Gabriel had done everything for him. He'd done everything for her.

Without looking back, Gabriel parted from her and walked out the cottage door.

Emmaline watched him leave before bringing the towels and bandages to Claude.

"I need to get some water." She went into the kitchen and returned with a basin of water.

She knelt in front of Claude and bathed his face. There was a cut above his eye and dried blood beneath his nose. His cheeks were swollen and already bruises were starting to form.

"After I clean you up, I want you to tell me what happened."

Claude nodded wearily.

She demanded nothing of him while she tended his wounds. After she bound his chest with the bandages, she brought him tea.

His hand shook as he lifted the cup to his lips.

His eyes met hers. "Why are you with him, *Maman?*"

His words took her aback. After what Claude put her through, he should be explaining to her, not the other way around.

She sat next to him on the sofa. "You ask me such a question? I am with Gabriel because of you, because of what you came to England to do. How could you, Claude? How could you think to commit such a sin?"

Claude's hands balled into fists. "I wanted to avenge my father. And you."

She put a hand on his knee and made him look at her. "You would have hanged for it. And then you would be gone to me. You must promise me to give up this revenge. You must promise to forget all about killing Edwin Tranville."

He crossed his arms over his chest. "Your captain has made me give my word."

Gabriel saw even to that. "Oh, Claude. I am so glad." She leaned back. "But what happened? How did you get hurt?"

He told her of trying to kill Edwin Tranville, but stopping short of it. He said Edwin's friends had caught him and beat him, until Gabriel arrived and put a stop to it.

She said another prayer of thanks for Gabriel.

Claude's explanation was choppy and disjointed and left her with many questions. Perhaps Gabriel would answer them for her.

She brushed a hand through her son's hair. "I am glad you did not kill."

He turned away.

She added, "I could not bear being left all alone."

"Alone?" His eyes flashed. "What of your English lover? You do not need a French son."

She gripped his hand. "Do not speak of him in such a tone! After all he has done for you—"

Claude lifted his chin. "Spare me the list of how many times he has come to my aid."

She leaned back on the sofa and pressed her fingers against her temple. Claude remained bitter, as caught up in that long-ago time in Badajoz as ever.

Perhaps Claude could never come back to her as he'd been in his boyhood days, before his father was killed in front of him. She covered her mouth, grieving again at what her only child had endured and again feeling the guilt of her part in it.

Claude would never give up his hatred for the nameless men

who had killed his father, or for Edwin Tranville. It was a hatred so strong it encompassed even Gabriel.

She spoke softly to him. "You should know I am going to marry him."

Claude went pale. *"Non."*

She fingered the ring beneath her dress. "He asked me to marry him in Brussels before the battle, but I said no. I will marry him now, however."

He winced in pain. "Why?"

Why? Because she had promised to marry him if he found her son. No, that was not it. Perhaps it was because she was grateful to him for saving Claude's life yet again?

No. It was because she could not imagine spending a day without him near her, to wake in the morning with him not at her side. She could not bear to tumble into bed alone without the comfort of his arms.

Emmaline blinked in awe. She realised suddenly that, even if he were sent to Brazil or Egypt or China, she would still choose to be with him. She belonged with him.

Claude's eyes narrowed. "It is because of me, is it not? You feel you must accept him because he saved my life. You think it is paying him back somehow."

That had once been the bargain she'd made with Gabriel when they began this journey to find Claude. It was no longer the reason.

She loved Gabriel, needed him, knew he would never fail her. She wanted a chance, a lifetime, to show Gabriel that she, too, would never fail him.

I love you, Gabriel, she said to herself, joy filling her heart.

She met Claude's gaze and unconsciously slipped into English. "I want to marry Gabriel. How could I not after all he has done?"

Claude shot to his feet and responded in French. "You even

abandon our language for your captain? I cannot speak to you any longer. I want to go to bed."

His anger made her want to weep. "You are tired," she said, fighting tears and hoping he would see more clearly in the morning. "We are all very tired. There is a bed for you above stairs. You will find your satchel in the room where you are to sleep."

He grasped his ribs and walked painfully to the stairs. "I presume you sleep with him in another room?"

She ached for him. "Not tonight."

He gripped the banister as he climbed the stairs.

"Claude!" she cried.

He stopped, reluctantly turning to her.

"You will not leave me again?" Her voice rose an octave. "You will be here in the morning and not do anything foolish?"

He answered in a low voice. "I will not leave and I will do nothing foolish." He continued up the stairs, but paused again. "I wish you would make me the same promise."

From outside Gabe watched Emmaline minister to her son. He saw her bathe Claude's battered face and cleanse his wounds. Gabe remained in the shadows, near enough to the open window to see her, to hear them talk together. It was not eavesdropping, because he could understand only bits of the French. He simply needed to watch her. Hear her voice.

She and Claude argued. About him, no doubt. Perhaps she'd told him of the bargain she'd made with Gabe. He'd fulfilled his part of it.

Gabe heard her switch to English. "I want to marry Gabriel," she said. "How could I not after all he has done?"

After all he has done.

She intended to keep her part of the bargain. To marry him out of gratitude. Out of obligation.

Now, even more than when she had first proposed it, he knew

he could never hold her to it. Now his love for her had again flourished, but in a way that meant he could not bear hurting her. If he wished to be selfish, he could marry her and for ever separate her from her son.

But Gabe could never be the sacrifice she must make for her son's life. He loved her too much to deprive her of what she held most dear.

Her son.

Through the window he watched her climb the stairs. He waited longer, alone in the darkness, making certain both she and Claude would be asleep before he re-entered the cottage.

When all remained silent, Gabe opened the door and entered as quietly as he could. He pulled off his boots and padded across the room to the sofa. Removing his coat, he rolled it into a pillow for his head. The sofa was too short, so he positioned a chair on which to prop his legs.

And tried to will himself to sleep.

It was no use.

The loneliness kept him awake, a loneliness that seemed to return from the distant time of his boyhood days.

He made a frustrated sound and rose from the sofa. Padding across the room in his bare feet, he stood at the open window. A breeze wafted the curtains and cooled his face.

It almost soothed him.

He parted the curtain and gazed out into the moon-filled view. The outbuildings. The path leading to the stable. The distant hills.

The silence and neglect made the farm a sad place, echoing his own sadness. It pained him to see the farm's deterioration from something beautiful to something neglected and forlorn. If he closed his eyes he could imagine it as it had been. Bustling. Its buildings repaired. The parks and gardens tidy and flourishing.

He turned and surveyed his uncle's sitting room. He thought of Emmaline in his uncle's kitchen or seated in that chair, mending his uncle's shirt. She would look so perfect in the big house, overseeing the meals and running the household. He could imagine her seated across from him at the other end of a long dinner table, sharing the news of the day. He could envision encountering her in one of the rooms, filling a vase with flowers or opening curtains. He could see her in the garden, her face shaded by a wide-brimmed straw hat, looking as fresh and beautiful as the blooms that once had grown in abundance there.

He'd dreamed of living with her on a farm like this one, sharing hard work and happy times.

And peace.

He ran a hand roughly through his hair.

What did a soldier know of peace? A soldier belonged some place where men fought each other over matters other men considered worth their lives.

He turned back to the window for another glance at the moonlight-filled view, then returned to the sofa and the imposing quiet of the cottage. He again forced his eyes closed.

At least he could pretend he would fall asleep. He could pretend he was not leaving something that might have once been beautiful and now would never be.

But all his mind's eye could see was Emmaline.

Emmaline.

He heard a swish of skirts and opened his eyes to see her moving towards him like some angelic apparition. In the dim light from the window, he could see her hair loose upon her shoulders and the skirt of her nightdress flowing around her.

She came closer. "Gabriel? Are you awake?"

He reached for her, and she settled beside him, curling against him on the sofa, her body fitting perfectly against his. Her scent comforted him. Her warmth soothed him.

"Is anything amiss?" he managed.

"No." She touched his face and with her fingers brushed the hair off his forehead. "I needed to be with you."

He found her lips and she returned his kiss with eagerness, opening her mouth and touching her tongue to his. His senses burst into flames as she urged him on top of her, unfastening his trousers. He ran his hand up her bare leg to her waist, raising her nightdress as he did so. Heedless of being still half-clothed, he entered her and felt the enveloping heat of her connecting them as only a man can connect with a woman.

The loneliness he'd felt a moment ago vanished.

In so many shared beds in inns throughout the countryside they'd reacquainted themselves to the pleasures of their lovemaking. Gabe had long stopped trying to convince himself he was merely using her for pleasure. Making love to her was like breathing air. Necessary for life.

She alone could fill the void within him, he realised. She alone completed him.

He touched her, kissed her, savoured her and brought her desire to the same fevered pitch as his own. When he drove her to her peak, he relished the completeness, the connection, the mounting pleasure this lovemaking gave him.

As his seed spilled inside her, joy flooded through him, then softly mellowed into languor, leaving him with one oppressive thought.

This would be the last time he made love to her.

This would be goodbye.

Chapter Nineteen

Emmaline could not coax Gabriel into bed with her in the chamber above. She knew he would never sleep if she remained with him on the sofa, so she reluctantly left him and climbed the stairs alone. A peek into Claude's room showed him motionless. His even breathing suggested he slept. Suddenly very tired herself she went into the other room and crawled into bed.

The next morning sunlight burst through the window like an abundance of cheer. Emmaline sat up and stretched and thought surely this day was full of promise. Claude was safe, with her and Gabriel. Perhaps, here on this quiet farm, Claude could talk to Gabriel and begin to appreciate what a fine a man he was, even if he was English and an army officer.

She hugged herself. How could Claude not learn to value Gabriel? Gabriel was a marvellous man, steadfast and strong, a performer of great feats. Like returning her son to her.

The ring she wore around her neck swung on its chain as she flung off the bedcovers and rose. She dressed hurriedly. The men would need breakfast and it delighted her to be able to cook the meal for them, as Gabriel had once cooked breakfast for her.

She checked in the other room. Claude still slept, the *cher enfant*. Sleep would help heal his wounds, she hoped, both the visible ones and the ones he hid inside.

She skipped down the stairs, but slowed as she reached the last steps.

The sofa was empty and the sitting room tidy. Gabriel had risen already and was not in the room.

His uncle appeared in the kitchen doorway, wiping his hands on a cloth. He froze when he saw her.

"Good morning, Mr Deane," she said brightly. "I hope that you have not eaten. I wanted to cook your breakfast for you."

He placed the cloth back in the kitchen and his forehead furrowed. He inclined his head towards the table. "There is a note for you."

A prickle of trepidation crawled up her spine, but she ignored it and smiled. "Is it from Gabriel?"

He nodded, but his expression was grim.

She breezed over and picked up the letter, an unsealed, folded piece of paper with *Emmaline* written across the outside in a strong, sure hand.

She unfolded it and read:

Dearest Emmaline,

In my uncle's possession is a sum of money sufficient to take you and Claude back to Brussels. I plan to send you a hired carriage tomorrow to carry you both to Hull, where you can get passage to Belgium. Within a very few days you will be back home.

You must know that I never meant to make you marry me. I'm meant for the army, not marriage, and even your gratitude is not reason enough to drag you into a soldier's life. Nothing is. Please forgive me for making you believe I would require that of you, you who have given me such happiness. You deserve an easier life than the one I have chosen.

I also would never separate you from your son and deprive you of the person who has always been first in your heart. It is enough for me to know he has been restored to you.

Return to Brussels and be happy, dearest Emmaline. I will think of you there, strolling in the Parc or toiling in the shop surrounded by white lace. Time and distance will never dim my memories of you.
With undying affection,
Gabriel

"Non!" She held the letter against her chest. Gabriel's ring pressed into her flesh. She looked up at his uncle. "He has gone?"

The old man's face melted into sympathy. "At dawn. Said he'd take the gig back to Blackburn."

"And then?" Her throat twisted in pain.

He glanced down. "He did not say."

He had simply left? She could not believe it to be true.

"He must have said something," she insisted. "What did he tell you?"

His uncle shrugged. "He told me to make certain you took the purse he left with me."

What did she want with money? She wanted Gabriel. She swung away.

His uncle walked over and put a comforting hand on her shoulder. "Now, do not fret, *madame*. There is nothing to do. I think Gabe wanted to spare you. He said you meant to marry him in gratitude for finding your son, but that he wouldn't—"

"Non!" She shook her head. "Not for gratitude."

Was his leaving her fault? She had never told him of her change of heart. She'd been too wrapped up in Claude. She'd never told Gabriel that she wanted to be with him no matter what, no matter where the army sent him.

His uncle nervously took his hand away. "He said the army was no place for a woman."

Had his uncle read her mind? "He is going back to London to find some regiment to join." And she would never know where he was, nor would she ever see him again. It was unbearable.

"I suppose you are right." His uncle rubbed his chin and nodded decisively, as if he'd just that moment been convinced.

She unfolded the letter and read it again. He did not want her to endure the hardships of a soldier's life. He did not want to separate her from her son.

She squeezed her eyes shut.

So unlike Remy. So unlike the husband who she'd been afraid to defy, whose selfishness had irreparably hurt them all. It was so clear now that Gabriel loved her in a way that Remy never could. Gabriel would not think of himself, but of her. And of Claude.

She refolded the paper and put it carefully in the pocket of her dress.

Footsteps sounded on the stairs and she and Gabe's uncle turned towards the sound. Claude paused on the stairs, gripping the banister. His eyes were ringed with dark bruises and the gash above his eye resembled a slash of red paint.

Emmaline took a breath and spoke to her son in French. "I was about to make breakfast." To Gabriel's uncle she said in English, "Mr Deane, may I cook for you as well?"

"I ate." He stepped towards the door. "I'm late in seeing to the sheep." Pausing at the doorway, he bowed. "If you will pardon me." He glanced up at Claude. "Make yourself at home, young fellow."

Claude inclined his head and waited until the older man had walked out of the door.

He continued down the steps. "Where is your captain?" His tone sounded bitter. Sleep had not mellowed him.

Emmaline averted her gaze and wrapped her arms around the ache inside her. "He is gone."

"When will he return?"

She tried to breathe normally. "He will not return."

His voice rose in surprise. "I do not comprehend."

She turned back to him and snapped, "He has left and will not be back." She started towards the kitchen. She could not speak to Claude about this, not when her feelings were so raw. She felt as if someone had scraped all the flesh from her body. "Sit, Claude. I will cook you breakfast."

Gabriel could still feel Emmaline beside him in the gig as he drove the small carriage they'd shared for so many days. He remembered her tension when she sat beside him. Her worry. Her need to lean on him some of the way.

At least now her worries were over. He'd given her back the chance for happiness by restoring her son to her and sending them both back to Brussels. Gabe felt good about that. It had been a worthy deed.

Even if it had sunk him into gloom.

He glanced around him. The green hills dotted with peaceful sheep were a stark contrast. What a peaceful life the scene represented, another stark contrast to the world he best knew. The army. Battle. Death.

That was all a soldier was good for, fighting battles and vanquishing enemies. Much of the life was grim, but there was an excitement to it as well. Fighting a battle, surrounded by the enemy, pitting man against man—there was nothing like it, nothing like the exhilaration of facing men bent on killing you, but cutting them down instead.

He closed his eyes for a minute and remembered the sounds of battle, the smells, the expressions of despairing shock in the eyes of men when his sword fatally struck them. In the throes of fighting, Gabe had experienced the power of life and death, the thrill of survival.

He opened his eyes to the clear blue sky, where white clouds mirrored the sheep grazing on the green hills. The air smelled of life, of grass and wildflowers and horse. The only sounds in his ears were of the breeze rustling the leaves of trees, the rhythmic pace of the horse's hooves, an occasional bleating from the sheep on the hill. The sounds of peace.

His memories of battle sickened him. What was war compared to a day like this?

Gabe shocked himself. What had happened to that boy who had looked upon such a fine day with boredom, pining for the thrill of the army? What had happened to that soldier?

Emmaline.

Meeting Emmaline had changed him. She'd made him yearn again to belong to someone, to want a family, a home.

How cruel Fate could be! To give him Emmaline, then whip her away. He'd done the right thing by leaving her, he told himself again. She belonged with her son, not with him. He would not be the cause of splitting them up.

He'd return to the army, a place where home and family did not exist.

He laughed aloud, startling some birds who must have thought themselves safe in the shrubbery. Their wings flapped as they took to the air. Fleeing, as he was fleeing.

He did not know if he could return to the army. He still was without a commission. There were still few captaincies to be had. He had no more connections to snag one of them than he'd had before Emmaline had walked back into his life.

Gabe flicked the ribbons, quickening the pace of the horse. In two or three hours he'd reach Blackburn. He'd return the horse and carriage and book passage to London. In a few days he could again visit the War Office. If no other commissions had come through in his absence, at least the Royal Scots would still have a place for him in the West Indies. He could easily return to that oppressive heat and damp, those incessant insects and fevers, and the abhorrent duty of stamping out rebellion among slaves who merely wished to be free.

Good God.

Was that what Fate had in store for him? Was that where he belonged?

Only four days after Gabriel had left her, Emmaline and her son stood on the deck of a packet bound for the Continent.

"I swear I will earn the money to pay him back," Claude said, still fuming about the fact that Gabriel's money had paid for their passage. "Every last *penny*." He spat out the English word as if it were rancid meat.

Emmaline stared at the bank of the River Hull, at the English land she was leaving behind. "It was Gabriel's gift to us."

He made a disparaging sound.

These last few days with Claude had been difficult. His anger was still so palpable, she'd feared he would run off again at any moment to go in search of Edwin. She'd had to be so careful not to upset him any more than he was upset already.

When he was back in Brussels perhaps he could begin to leave the past behind and look to his future. Perhaps his future was in France. It might be best if he did visit her parents in France and not lie about it as he had done before.

It was so much easier to think of what Claude should do, where Claude should go, than think of her own future. To Emmaline, her future loomed empty and lonely, even though her aunt would expect her back at the lace shop.

Without Gabriel at her side, everything seemed empty and lonely.

She glanced at Claude. He'd removed his cap and the river breeze tousled his dark curls, so much like her own. When she blinked her eyes, he looked one moment like the boy he'd once been, another moment, like a man.

The boy reminded her of another voyage for which Gabriel had paid, the one that had got them out of Spain and back to France. The memory stabbed at her heart.

"I am glad to be leaving England," Claude said, although his tone seemed to contain some regret. Regret for not killing Edwin?

She had the sense there was more to it than that, but she took a deep breath. "I am glad you are leaving England, as well."

He glanced at her. "What of you, *Maman?* You do not say you are glad to leave."

She returned his gaze, but did not answer.

He frowned. "You are still pining for Captain Deane, even after he abandoned you."

Smaller boats crowded the river. Ahead of them, Emmaline could see the North Sea. When they reached it, she would truly be leaving England—and Gabriel—behind.

Her throat tightened. "Leave me to my feelings, Claude. I cannot speak of them."

His brows knit in an expression of disapproval that reminded her too much of his father.

She took a breath. "He didn't abandon me, Claude. He left because he thought it was best for me."

"He decided what was best for you?" He sniffed in disdain.

Claude's father had also decided what was best for her and she'd feared defying him. After all she and Gabriel had been through, though, she could never fear him, no matter what.

She watched the land slowly slipping past. "Why do you want to make Gabriel a villain, Claude? He has done only good for you."

He rubbed the wood of the boat's railing and murmured, "He asked the same thing."

"The same thing?" Her brows rose.

"About why I made him the villain." He leaned on the railing. "I do not know why, *Maman,*" he answered with defiance. "I have to credit him with saving me and saving Lou—Miss Finch." He paused. "But his red coat reminds me he is a British soldier and then I remember the red coats who killed Papa."

"But Gabriel had no part of that. He took us to safety. Do you not remember?"

He pushed away from the railing. "I remember. I remember all of it." He paused. "Except about him rescuing me at Waterloo. I thought you made up a story about that, but I now believe it was true. Deane has rescued me countless times." His eyes flashed with emotion. "But that is it, do you not see? He succeeded where my father failed. Where I failed. Time and time again. I know it makes little sense, even to me now, after my time at Rappard Hall." His eyes took on a faraway look for a moment, before filling with pain again. "I only know I cannot forgive him."

He stalked away from her.

Emmaline did not move from the deck until the last glimpse of England faded from her sight. Even then, she did not turn towards the Continent, towards Antwerp where the packet would dock, or towards Brussels, a place she had once called home.

Chapter Twenty

Gabe walked back to Stephen's Hotel, not even seeing the book shops, ironmongers, milliners and tea shops on Bond Street. He'd just come from signing his name to papers that set the course of his future; his brain was still mulling over whether or not he'd made the right decision.

No use in that. His signature made matters final.

He shrugged. He had many regrets in his life. If he regretted what he'd done this day, he could merely add it to the list.

Emmaline was not one of his regrets, however. She had not been far from his thoughts when he had put pen to paper today. How different it would have been if Emmaline could have been at his side. Still, he was not sorry he'd left her. He'd done right by her by leaving. What he did regret was that circumstances made it impossible for him to be with her. That would always be number one on his list of regrets.

Gabe lifted his gaze from the pavement and was surprised to see how near he was to the hotel. He quickened his step.

When he reached the entrance, he prayed the hall would be empty. A few of the men who were here before had found commissions, and others had managed to make advantageous marriages, but there were plenty of men left who would chew his ear off. Bored with their inactivity, they would insist upon knowing all the tedium of his life, and he had no wish to have to dodge questions. He wanted to keep his recent activity to himself.

Gabe entered the hotel and removed his shako and gloves. He threw his gloves inside his hat, as he always did. At least the hall looked empty. Glad of that piece of luck, he started across its length to the stairway.

The footman who attended the lobby suddenly appeared. He dashed to the stairway, pausing when he saw Gabe. "Oh, Captain," the man cried, out of breath. "Someone to see you. Waiting in the front parlour." He continued past Gabe up the stairs. "Forgive me. Have to run."

"Who is it?" Gabe cried, but the man merely waved a frantic hand and pounded up the steps.

Gabe tapped on the banister. So much for his wish to escape any company. He turned and made his way to the parlour door.

Perhaps Allan Landon or Jack Vernon had called. That would be tolerable. He'd sent word to them of his return and had already met with them to fill them in on what had happened with Edwin.

And Emmaline.

As he turned the knob of the parlour door, he had the sensation of being pulled back in time. Entering, he dropped his hat on a table and thought of the day Emmaline had surprised him in this very room.

Just as it had that day, the parlour looked empty. Fresh flowers adorned the mantel and the sound of a swishing skirt came from the high-backed chair facing the fireplace.

Gabe froze.

Emmaline stood before him. "*Bon jour,* Gabriel."

"Emmaline?" His voice was no more than a whisper.

He'd never thought to see her beautiful face again, her fair skin and blue eyes and the lips he'd dreamed of kissing when sleep eluded him at night.

He recovered himself. There was only one reason she would return here. "Is it Claude?"

She blinked, as if confused, then met his gaze again. "*Non. Non.* Claude has not run away again. That is not why I am here."

"Why, then?" Whatever it was, he would help her again, he immediately resolved. He knew now that no other choice was possible for him. Let her ask a thousand times. He would always come to her aid.

She glided towards him with that familiar grace. As she neared, the scent of lavender reached him. "I came to speak to you."

He cocked his head, more puzzled than ever. She did not seem as tense as she had been when she had stood in this same place before. Neither did she seem at ease.

She glanced up at him. "A long time ago, I did not speak up when I should have. I had not the courage. It was a terrible mistake I made then. I made another one when we were together last, by not saying what I needed to say soon enough. You were gone before—" Her voice broke.

She was troubled and he felt the pain of that as if it were his own pain. "What do you mean? Tell me. I will help you in any way I can."

She smiled and raised her hand to caress his cheek. "My *cher capitaine.*"

He seized her hand, lifting it in a silent question about the gold band with its glittering sapphire that adorned her finger.

"I used to wear it on a chain beneath my dress, Gabriel," she whispered. "There has never been a day I did not wear your ring."

He dropped her hand, still puzzled.

She lowered her hand and stepped back, but then looked as if she were steeling herself for combat. "I said I would marry you. I came to tell you that is what I want. I want to marry you."

His spirits dipped. This smacked of her self-sacrificing bargain again. "Emmaline, I already freed you of that obligation. I do not know how to make it clearer to you. I do not require you to marry me."

Her eyes widened. "You do not comprehend. I *want* to marry

you, if—if you also desire it. That is what I travelled here to tell you. I do not want to be apart from you. I will follow you to wherever the army sends you. I do not care where it is as long as I can be with you." She gripped his arm. "I came to say this to you. To make sure you know that I say this because I love you. I have loved you since Badajoz when you were so kind to us. I loved you in Brussels, but I was afraid. I am still afraid, but it frightens me more to be without you."

Gabe felt himself go warm all over, but he dampened his burgeoning hopes. "What of Claude? Surely he will not accept you marrying me."

Her eyes filled with sadness. "No, he will not. Claude said to me that he will never see me again as long as I am with you."

Gabe shook his head. "Then, it is no use. I will not be the cause of you losing your son."

Her fingers tightened on his arm. "You are not the cause. Nor am I. It is Claude who chooses it."

He looked down at her, seeing her suffering at her son's declaration. He also saw something else.

Her resolve.

She went on, "You said yourself that Claude is a man now. He must make his decisions and live with them." A ghost of a smile flitted across her face. "Besides, he said he would still write to me, so that is something. As long as I know he is well and seeking his own happiness instead of revenge, I am content. And who can say? Perhaps he will change his mind after a time."

Gabe's hopes glimmered again. Dare he indulge them? "Are you certain, Emmaline? Are you certain you want to marry me?"

"Mais oui," she murmured. "More than anything."

He gathered her in his arms and held her close to him as if he feared loosening his grip would make her flutter away and he would lose her once again. "Emmaline. My love."

Her voice filled with emotion as he held her. "Gabriel, there is so much I cannot give to you. I cannot give you children. I have no dowry, nothing to bring to a marriage, except my promise to devote myself to you—"

"It does not matter," he reassured her. "We can be a family, just you and me. And I certainly do not need your money. I need you."

"Then I will go anywhere with you, Gabriel." Her voice was firm. "Have you found a commission yet? Tell me where we will go next."

He released her and held her at arm's length so he could look into her eyes. He laughed aloud. "I have no commission! Oh, Emmaline. I am not even in the army any more. I sold out completely. Do you mind returning to Lancashire? I have just today purchased the hill farm, the one my uncle manages. We will own the farm. I can take care of my uncle and all the other people whose livelihoods depended on it. We will make it prosper again. Together."

He drew her to him again, this time lowering his lips on to hers for a kiss that burst forth from the joy in his heart. Beneath the kiss she laughed with happiness, before pressing her lips to his as if never to release them.

When they finally took a breath, Gabe twirled her around, laughing again. When he stopped he gazed at her as if to convince himself that she was real and that this was a dream come true.

He remembered his first glimpse of her amidst the horror of Badajoz, when he'd been alone and her family had been violently torn apart. Something had changed in him that day at the mere sight of her. He was changed still.

But now he understood. She was where he belonged, where he would always belong. He knew it deep in his soul.

He belonged with Emmaline.

He embraced her once more.

They were both home at last.

Epilogue

London—November 1817

It was a celebration dinner, but a quiet one. The recent death of Princess Charlotte in childbirth had the whole country in mourning, and London society remained swathed in black. Emmaline and Gabriel had just returned to London for a brief visit.

Even the tragic death of the English princess could not mar the happiness that had built between them over the past two months. After a quiet and private wedding, Gabriel had taken Emmaline for a tour of the Lake District and then to Manchester to meet his parents, brothers, sisters and countless nieces and nephews. It seemed to Emmaline that she was accepted into Gabriel's family as merely one of the crowd, which delighted her. After that visit, she and Gabriel had spent a few weeks at their new home, the hill farm which had been busy with the breeding season and Gabriel's efforts to return it to its former productivity.

Back in London for Gabriel to complete some business related to the farm, Allan and Marian Landon had insisted upon hosting a dinner to celebrate their marriage. Included as guests were Jack and Ariana Vernon.

Both the Landons and Vernons greeted them as old friends,

and Allan opened a bottle of French champagne and poured for everyone.

He offered a toast. "To your happiness!"

"To us all," Gabriel had countered, looking so handsome in his black coat, white linen and cream breeches that he took Emmaline's breath away.

As they all drank, Emmaline glanced around, remembering her anxiety the last time she had been in this room and her wonder at the willingness of these good people to help her find Claude, her surprise that they had all been connected by Badajoz.

"Tell us about your wedding and your trip!" Ariana insisted. The actress looked even more beautiful than usual. Her August performance in David Garrick's *Katharine and Petruchio* had been a great success, but now she was working on a different sort of production. Her second child.

Emmaline allowed Gabriel to describe the wedding and the trip, adding only a few details he'd omitted. Like some of the wonderful things he'd done for her while they travelled.

The Landons' butler, a huge former soldier, appeared at the door. "Beg pardon," he said.

"What is it, Reilly?" Marian asked.

He looked from Marian to her husband. "Lady Tranville is here. She wishes a moment to speak to you."

Lady Tranville? She was married to Edwin Tranville's father. She was also Jack's mother.

"Have her come in." Allan waved a welcoming hand. "She may meet our guests and say hello to her son and daughter-in-law."

Reilly's expression turned firm. "You had best speak with her first."

With anxious looks, Allan and Marian excused themselves; Ariana attempted to dispel the aura of worry that had suddenly filled the room. "Proceed, please! Tell us all about your farm."

A few minutes later, a grim-faced Allan and a red-eyed Marian returned, accompanied by an older woman Emmaline presumed was Lady Tranville. Gabriel and Jack rose to their feet and Jack crossed the room. It was clear Lady Tranville had delivered some sort of dreadful news.

"Hello, Mother." He kissed her on the cheek and put an arm around her. "What has happened? Is it Lord Tranville?"

She shook her head. "Edwin."

Emmaline's heart rose into her throat.

Allan quickly made introductions. "I told Lady Tranville that everyone here would wish to hear this news." He held fast to his wife's hand and looked from one to the other, his gaze resting on Emmaline. "Edwin Tranville is dead."

"Dead!" Gabriel cried.

Emmaline felt afraid to breathe. "How?"

Lady Tranville answered, "From a liver ailment. He has been ill for many weeks." She patted her son's arm and looked sympathetically at Marian, who had been Edwin's cousin. "I did not wish to send a messenger. It is only a short walk." She backed to the door. "But I really need to return to my husband. He is shattered, as you might imagine." She glanced away. "He is sick with regrets."

After she left, Ariana crossed the room to Marian and embraced her. "How hard this must be for you."

Marian's eyes filled with tears. "I did care about him. In spite of all the bad things he did to us and to everyone here." She directed her gaze at Emmaline. "I knew him as a very sad little boy."

Allan guided Marian to a sofa. He sat beside her and she leaned against him.

Jack surveyed them all, as if memorising the scene they presented. "He died of drink. That is what a liver ailment means, does it not?"

They all seemed lost in their own thoughts.

Gabriel glanced away. "He connected us. He and his father. We would not be here, together, if not for what Edwin did to Emmaline." He shook his head and faced Allan and Marian. "Perhaps we should go."

Emmaline immediately stood. Emotions swirled inside her, none of them the sort of sadness one ought to feel at a man's death. She was relieved that Edwin was dead. She was grateful that Claude had not killed him. Most of all she was still angry at all the suffering he'd caused. "Yes, we intrude."

Marian straightened. "No, do not leave. I will recover in a moment. Gabe is right. Edwin did connect us all, in a strange way. I want us to be together."

So they stayed and had a more subdued dinner than originally planned, even though they quickly changed the subject from Edwin and the past to all their plans for the future.

It looked bright for all of them. Jack's reputation and fortune as an artist was growing all the time, as was Ariana's fame in the theatre. Allan and Marian were determined that Allan would win a seat in Parliament, and none of them doubted that he would indeed be successful. And there was Gabriel's hill farm. His plan might be more modest, but it was dearest to her heart.

Later, when Emmaline lay with Gabriel in the bed they shared in Grillon's Hotel, Gabriel mentioned Edwin again. "Hearing of Edwin's death must have affected you. Has it upset you?"

She thought before answering. "I am not unaffected. I do not have any grief for him," she admitted. "But if he died of drink, he killed himself, did he not? That seems a sort of justice. He destroyed himself as he tried to destroy us."

He nodded in understanding.

She nestled beside him. "We are all of us alive and happy. The Landons. The Vernons. You and me. Maybe some day even Claude. We survived and Edwin did not."

Gabriel held her tighter. "One thing I know is he can no longer hurt you or Claude or anyone else. We can look to the future and know he will never appear in it."

She kissed him. "I treasure our future, Gabriel. I feel very lucky."

He returned her kiss and cradled her next to him. Warmed by his bare skin, she soon heard him slipping into sleep. As she also drifted off, Edwin appeared in her dream, fading like a fog when the sun begins to shine. Into the sunlight appeared Gabriel, smiling at her.

Yes, she thought, waking again. She had found happiness. She was very, very lucky.

* * * * *

THE LADY CONFESSES
Carole Mortimer

Having run away from home, Lady Elizabeth Copeland must keep her drab disguise as a lady's companion at all times. Even when she's called upon to nurse the lady's nephew—who happens to be the handsomest man Elizabeth's ever seen…

THE DANGEROUS LORD DARRINGTON
Sarah Mallory

Lord Darrington may be an earl, but his bad reputation precedes him! Now the wicked Lord has found out the dark secret Beth Forrester will do *anything* to protect. How to buy a rake's silence? There is only one way—with her body!

THE UNCONVENTIONAL MAIDEN
June Francis

Headstrong Beth Llewellyn is put under the guardianship of Sir Gawain Raventon after her father's murder. Working with him to solve the mystery of her father's death, Beth begins to think perhaps marriage isn't such a terrible thing after all…

HER BATTLE-SCARRED KNIGHT
Meriel Fuller

It is only Count Giseux de St-Loup's code of chivalry that sees him escorting a sharp-tongued woman on a quest to help her injured brother. The Lady Brianna is fiercely independent and finds his powerful presence disturbing…but strangely enticing!

Mills & Boon®
Historical

*Another exciting novel available
this month:*

THE LADY FORFEITS

Carole Mortimer

Countess under duress!

Lady Diana Copeland has hot-footed it to London to tell her
new guardian, Lord Faulkner, *exactly* what she thinks of his
outrageous marriage demands! Well, with her two flighty
sisters having run off, no one else is going to do it…

Surely this magnificent man with a naughty glint in his eye can't
be the pompous old fool she was expecting? Inhaling deeply,
Diana fights not to get lost in the depths of Lord Faulkner's
intoxicating gaze… Or to make the worst forfeit—by
agreeing to be the Lord's new Countess!

The Copeland Sisters
Flouting convention, flirting with danger…